The Chosen Few

By Michael John Sheehan

The Chosen Few

BRI Press
P.O. Box 1082
Windsor, CA 95492

Cover design by Kyle R. Smith & Catamaran Marketing
Book design by Catamaran Marketing

ISBN: 978-0-9985004-0-9

First Edition: March 2017

10 9 8 7 6 5 4 3 2 1

For information go to:
www.michaeljohnsheehan.com

Read Another Michael John Sheehan Book

A devastating tragedy.
A shattered rookie pitcher.
Do you believe in miracles?

Best friends Pete O'Brien and Danny Grace dream of playing professional baseball. They make a pact to help each other reach "The Show" and one day play for a championship. When tragedy strikes on a rural, wine country road, Danny's world turns into a nightmare of suffocating grief and shattered faith.

Despite being drafted by an expansion team, Danny continues to reel from the crushing loss until an incredible opportunity thrusts the rookie pitcher into the Major League spotlight. During the season, an aging catcher, an eccentric center fielder, a wise old manager, and a beautiful woman emerge to help him heal emotionally and spiritually. Determined to fulfill the vow to his dead friend, Danny's poignant journey climaxes when he comes face-to-face with the universe's ultimate plan for humankind.

Visit michaeljohnsheehan.com to learn more about the author and his works.

CLICK HERE TO VISIT THE WEBSITE

Foreword

Although fictional, this story is based loosely on my experiences from having spent four years of high school and four quarters of college at St. Joseph High School & St. Patrick's College Catholic seminaries in the Los Altos hills above Mountain View, California. Unfortunately, the campus no longer exists: the Archdiocese was forced to tear down the impressive, 65-year-old building following the 1989 Loma Prieta earthquake that caused severe damage to its structure.

My goal in writing this novel was to provide an inside look at the unusual world of the past century where teenage boys studied for the priesthood. While many students felt they had a vocation to serve God, some attended the school only because their parents wanted a priest in the family or to take advantage of a superior (and inexpensive) Catholic education provided by the Sulpician fathers, an order of priests originally from France who taught in seminaries around the world. At a cost to students of only $1,000 per year for nine months of full room and board, the seminary offered an exceptional education at an incredible price.

With its emphasis on scholarly achievement and tight discipline (for the most part), St. Joseph High School was not for everyone. Many boys lasted only a year or two before quitting or being asked to leave by the faculty. Some 14-year-old freshmen barely made it through their first semester due to homesickness, while other boys could not handle the rigorous curriculum or strict standards of behavior. I recall one priest who often humorously asked his students, "So where do you boys plan on going to school next semester?" as a way to remind them that a lax attitude toward studying or breaking the myriad of rules could very well result in their catching a ride home on the next bus, as many discovered.

One question that readers who reviewed the manuscript asked was, "Did students and priests really have those kinds of classroom discussions? My high school was not like that."

Perhaps not the exact debates as written here, but the Sulpician professors routinely encouraged the exchange of ideas and opinions. In addition, many of the Fathers helped students develop critical thinking skills that served them well for the rest of their lives. And with class sizes sometimes of only six to eight students by the 1970s – when the high school enrollment had dwindled to about 120 – the personal attention provided by the priests in less formal settings (some classes were even held in the good Fathers' living quarters) allowed many boys to gain confidence, ask questions, and engage in informative and challenging dialogs they normally might keep to themselves. The discussions on resurrection and celibacy, for example, included in the book are meant to reflect that exceptional reality.

Contrast this to today's academic environment, especially on a number of elite college campuses across the country. Some undergraduates seek "safe spaces," or launch protests against administrations who fail to bow to those students' narrow-minded, politically correct "theology" that avoids diversity of thought. The young men and women even ask for "trigger" warnings that allow them to steer clear of views with which they disagree or find offensive. Although the Sulpician Fathers' primary job was to train boys for the priesthood and provide a solid understanding of Catholic thought and beliefs, many of the priestly professors represented the antithesis of this kind of rigid, "I-only-want-to-hear-my-side-of-the-argument" indoctrination that sadly passes for education in certain academic circles.

I especially want to thank the St. Joseph-St. Patrick's Alumni Association for allowing me to include photos of the vast 1,000 acre campus and its massive monastery-like building, especially the beautiful aerial view of the seminary in its early days before the addition of a college wing. I hope the photos will help provide readers with a better perspective not only of what the campus looked like, but also of the unique place that I – and thousands of other boys over the decades – at one time called home. Even today, I hold clear, lasting memories of a proud and valuable educational institution that served its purpose well, but whose time waned and now has slipped into history.

Finally, I dedicate this book to all the Sulpician priests and seminary students who lived, taught, studied, worked, and played at St. Joe's and St. Pat's over more than half a century, and to the chosen few who reached their goal of ordination to the Catholic priesthood.

Aerial view of the seminary prior to the addition of the college wing

Photo courtesy of St. Joseph-St. Patrick's Alumni Association

The campus as seen from the top of the “Grinder”

Photo courtesy of St. Joseph-St. Patrick’s Alumni Association

CHAPTER 1

"For many are called, but few are chosen." Matthew 22:14

Spring 2000

The huge, pear-shaped wrecking ball slammed with a thunderous bang into the last standing corner of the four-story building, sending broken chunks of dark-gray concrete and taupe stucco crashing to the ground. A yellow bulldozer roared in, scooped up the rubble like some menacing mechanical monster devouring its prey, and dumped the pieces into a waiting truck.

Dr. Jack Hayes watched from near the edge of the ruined boarding school's expansive front lawn where it met the parking lot. Although 100 yards from the deafening action, he stood only a few strides from where years ago he'd witnessed the most profound and inexplicable event of his life. Ignoring the chaotic destruction, Jack riveted his gaze on that exact spot and envisioned a single intense moment. He stared hypnotically for almost a minute, as if he expected answers to fly up from the debris or to find long-sought closure hidden in a pile of bricks. None came.

He lowered his head. The warm April rays that penetrated the back of his neck brought no comfort. *Nothing but the same old shadows,* he thought. *Coming here today was a waste of time.*

Jack brushed off the feeling of disappointment. After all, perhaps his distraught mind had played a cruel trick back then, a vivid and desperate symptom of a school boy's passion to believe. One thing Jack did know: not even a two-ton steel ball could knock away the gnawing, nightmarish doubts that had lingered for 22 years, the last time he set foot on the rustic grounds. Questions still burned in his soul. The resolution Jack craved remained as elusive as a black panther in the wild.

He drew in a deep breath. Jack could smell the pungent, welcoming aroma of eucalyptus trees from beyond the slow flowing creek off to the west, the same scent that had greeted him as a high-school freshman at St. Paul's Catholic seminary in 1974. Jack closed his eyes and pictured this "Little City of God" in its glory days, a strange and wonderful place he'd once called home. Jack imagined walking into the elegant Grand Foyer with its subtle fragrance of finished carved wood, standing on the cool, white marble floor, and walking up the main staircase that had withstood the cascade of millions of footsteps over the decades. The aromas and images renewed his resolve.

"I know what I saw," Jack whispered, ignoring his festering uncertainty. "This can't be all there is."

A bittersweet half-smile tugged at his lips when he recalled a favorite phrase of Patrick Keane, his best friend from those days.

Tempus edax rerum – time devours all things, Jack reminisced, his four years of Latin classes somehow surfacing on cue. *Except apparently for stubborn doubts that slowly eat away at you. Patrick would have appreciated the irony.*

The sound of the crane operator yelling down to a co-worker broke Jack's train of thought, drawing him back into the unhappy present. Today, at age 40, the 6 foot tall, 190-pound orthopedic surgeon had come to observe the end of an era, the sad swan song of an abandoned campus that in its heyday had been an acclaimed haven. Expectations of anything more from his visit, he knew, had been asking too much.

Cradled among the beautiful, blue-green foothills about 40 miles south of San Francisco, St. Paul's had stood proudly since 1924. The Archbishop modeled its massive, steel-reinforced structure after a Spanish monastery with red roof tiles, travertine tinted walls, and a large bell tower – a campanile – that jutted 50 feet above the top floor, making it the school's most dominant feature. He then carefully placed his "crown jewel" overlooking the valley floor on a 1,000-acre island of serenity cloaked by pine, oak, maple, and eucalyptus trees. While sparing no expense on the building, the savvy Prelate managed to purchase the isolated site with its breathtaking views for $150,000, a bargain-basement price of $150 per acre.

Part Middle Ages, part twentieth century, and completely rigorous, St. Paul's had earned a reputation across the Bay Area as a place of superior education that produced graduates of good character, thanks to the dedicated priests of the 350-year old Society of Saint Sulpice – called Sulpicians – who taught in Catholic seminaries. The school thrived through the Great Depression and World War II, and even into the late 1960s. The Archbishop lavished such financial generosity on St. Paul's that student tuition plus room and board for a full nine months topped out at $1,000 per year, making it affordable for most Catholic families who wanted to set one or more sons on a priestly path.

By the late seventies, however, the school's usefulness declined until a powerful earthquake undermined its six-decade reign as Northern California's premier institution for training young men to enter the diocesan priesthood.

"That damn earthquake," Jack said out loud.

A raw image seized his mind. *Don't go there again. What's the point?*

Jack glimpsed something stirring from the corner of his eye, off to his left. He turned to see a man wearing a black cassock, white clerical collar, and navy windbreaker standing alone, perhaps a well-thrown football pass away, arms crossed, seemingly deep in thought or prayer. The priest's thick brown hair showed blends of gray, and he sported sunglasses. Jack recognized his former mentor immediately, right down to the comfortable, bright red running shoes, not standard dress for a clergyman but a personal trademark.

Are you kidding me? That's him! Jack started jogging over. "Father Joe!" he called out.

When he reached the spot where the priest stood, Jack smiled and stretched out his right hand.

"Mr. Hayes," Father Joseph Marshall said with warmth in his voice as he removed the sunglasses to shake hands. "My goodness, I can hardly believe my eyes. The Lord certainly does work in mysterious ways. You're looking well."

"You too, Father. It's great to see you." To his surprise, Jack realized he found the priest's presence – and especially the familiar shoes – strangely comforting against the background of the ruined building. "Have you been here long?"

"I'm down from Seattle for a couple of weeks. The Vicar from Sulpician headquarters in Baltimore scheduled meetings locally to discuss the future of our two remaining West Coast seminaries. I've stopped by for the past several days, sometimes with other priests."

"Too bad about all this," Jack said, waving his hand toward the destruction.

"Yes, indeed, just heartbreaking. The entire building needed to come down for safety reasons but it's still painful to watch."

Jack nodded in agreement. Although the distinguished-looking priest appeared fit and healthy, especially for a man in his early sixties, he saw sorrow in Father Joe's blue eyes.

"It's the Law of Entropy at work, Father. From complex to simple, from order to chaos, from light to darkness."

"I was told many of the older Sulpicians back east cried when they heard about the demolition. It hurt them."

The words of a former St. Paul's religion teacher eased into Jack's mind: *"You can take the man out of the seminary, but you can't take the seminary out of the man."*

"I can only imagine. Priests such as Father Quinn and Father Delacroix lived at the school for, what, thirty years or longer? The news must have hit them like a punch to the gut."

"Man is like a breath; His days are like a passing shadow," Father Joe said.

"Isn't that from a Psalm?" Jack asked, straining to remember if he'd first heard it in one of his classes. "Patrick used to say something similar. He just used a lot more words."

"Yes, Psalm 144," the priest said with a chuckle. "Good memory. Our unique and brilliant Mr. Keane could always spice up any conversation. I remember hearing that his probing questions in senior religion often drove Father Volk crazy."

Jack displayed a wide grin. "I believe the exact words Father Volk used to describe Patrick was 'enlightened renegade.' I'm not so sure he meant it as a compliment."

In contrast, Jack had contended back in those days that his extraordinary friend would have been perfect for the role of a blond Adonis, or the honorable Teutonic commander in one of those old desert war movies, with his piercing blue eyes and square jaw.

Students and priests across campus literally looked up to Patrick, who stood one-eighth of an inch beneath 6 feet 3 inches tall, a conspicuous cut above the Holy Grail of heights – 72 inches – that many boys secretly yearn to reach.

"Whenever Patrick skipped a prayer period or some other mandatory event, and I'd confront him, he always expressed surprise that the faculty took exception to his unexcused absences," Father Joe recalled.

Jack pressed his lips together. "That was Patrick. I asked him why he did it, especially when he knew he could get detention. He told me God gave each person free will to choose his or her own path, and his sometimes took him on detours around the chapel or refectory."

Father Joe's eyes twinkled with amusement. "Despite all that, Father Volk admitted to me that Patrick was the most impressive student he'd ever taught. Which I suppose is no surprise to either of us. Although I am a bit surprised seeing you here today. I'm certain it's not because you have fond memories of seminary food."

"No way. I was part of the group who ate cold cereal for dinner for a while after the nuns left and that lousy food service took over. Even bought a plastic dog bowl to pour in bunches of those little boxes they kept on racks in the refectory. But as far as being surprised about standing here today, so am I."

"I'm glad you made it back. It's so good to see you."

"Do you ever hear from any of the guys, Father?" Jack asked in an optimistic tone.

"A few. Maybe you heard that Dan Hannigan made monsignor, and Donald Murray was appointed an auxiliary bishop of San Francisco. Weren't they both in your class?"

Jack nodded. "I'd heard about Dan, but not Don." He pictured a lanky, less than coordinated teenaged kid fumbling for an answer in Greek Civilization class. "What was the Pope thinking?"

"As I said, the Lord works in mysterious ways."

A noisy truck drove by filled with broken pieces of the building, making it impossible to hear for a few seconds. Jack watched Father Joe stand in thoughtful silence, fingertips on his chin, scouring his memory for a list of other former students he'd heard from recently.

"Let's see. I also talk to Chuck Wallis every few months or so. He's a detective with the San Jose Police Department. Chuck married a lovely woman. They have two boys and a daughter. How about you?"

"I keep in contact with Tom Hardin and hear from Jimmy Rhodes once in a while. Did you know Jared Bonelli got married?"

"No, but I heard you did. How has life treated you?"

Jack's face took on a look of unmistakable satisfaction. "I count my blessings every day. Jen and I've been married for eleven years now. We have a ten-year-old boy and seven-year-old girl. I was lucky to find such a great woman. And my medical practice has thrived too. As Father Jenkins used to say in sophomore Latin class, *'Aspirat fortuna.'*"

"Good for you, Jack. I wish your family the best. And I seem to recall an elderly Sulpician mentioning something called 'The Hayes Option' when he needed hip replacement surgery. Was that you?"

"Yes, I developed a device to make the procedure safer and improve patients' quality of life. After all, we both know it's not about how long you live but how well."

Father Joe reached out and gave Jack's shoulder a friendly squeeze.

“A doctor and an inventor. Well done, Jack. I’m happy to hear that fortune – and our Lord – has smiled on you.”

“Thank you, Father. Patrick used to tell me, ‘The Lord provides.’ I just wish he was standing here with us here today sharing in that fortune.” Jack twisted his mouth in a sour expression, considering whether to censor what he wanted to say. He felt his jaw tighten and his face flush with anger. “I often wonder if Father Webb ever realized the tremendous harm he caused and the lives he altered. After all these years, I still wake up some nights in a cold sweat.”

Father Joe looked down at his shoes and shifted his weight. Jack felt his discomfort.

“It’s difficult to know,” the priest said. ”One can only pray and hope.”

“When I quit the seminary after graduation, Father, I vowed never to return. A newspaper story about how the Archbishop had decided to tear the place down and sell the land to a developer changed my mind. I needed to see it one more time.”

Jack didn’t mention the part where something smoldering deep inside had bubbled up, ignited by memories of a distant spring day. Something relentless that pulled him, like the Piper’s flute, back to that staggering afternoon.

“I understand, Jack. It’s part of you. And me too.”

A loud boom drowned out Father Joe’s words. Both men jerked their heads around to see a huge section of wall lying on the ground smothered in a veil of dirt and dust.

“Wow, that sounded like a bomb went off,” Jack said. He tilted his head down and frowned. “I thought that following the cleanup and repairs years ago Saint Paul’s might have some life left in it.”

"Yes, I hoped so too. Modern attitudes and declining enrollment ended that."

The annoying beep-beep-beep warning of a truck backing up filled the air. Jack waited for the sound to stop before speaking.

"I recall reading that the San Jose Diocese moved their administration offices here when Saint Paul's closed. Of course, after seeing what we'd done to this building, I doubt anyone would have rented you Sulps another space to house a seminary or anything else."

Father Joe smiled. "Same old Jack, I see. We did leave a bit of a mess, didn't we? I was surprised the bishop managed to use the place as a chancery office for as long as he did. The toll of past injury combined with last October's final insult was too much. Some deep wounds cannot be fixed."

"Amen to that. I suppose it's always some damn thing, Father."

"Ah, one of Mr. Keane's favorite sayings, if I remember correctly... did you get up to see him yet?"

"No, but Patrick has been my best friend for twenty-six years, and I talk with him every day. So I definitely will." Jack paused. "Patrick hated goodbyes. He wouldn't have wanted to see this."

"So why *did* you come?"

Jack contemplated the question, shaking his head slowly. Reading about the planned demolition had brought St. Paul's back into his daily – and, more accurately, almost hourly – thoughts. Despite reservations about returning, Jack knew he had to be here to witness the end and keep a promise.

"In a way, it's like losing an important part of my life. The Sulpician education taught me so much, I made life-long friends, and, well, I suppose I grew up here too. The seminary was so different from anything my friends at home could wrap their heads around. Think about it, Father: some classes my senior year had only six students, which meant the profs kept us on our toes and the discussions were at times exceptional."

"I'm happy to hear you say that, Jack, with all that happened."

"This place and the people will always mean something special to me. Unless you lived here, it's hard to describe the school's effects, both good and bad. I guess it's a little bit like combat buddies who retain powerful bonds more than half a century later."

Jack halted for a few seconds. "Not to sound depressing, but coming here today feels like visiting a dying friend one last time. Or maybe I hoped to find a resolution to…."

He hesitated again. Even now, Jack couldn't force himself to say the words that needed to be said. Painful words about Patrick and the mysterious Father Martin McGrath, secretive words that he'd kept locked away inside since high school.

"I guess I just wanted to be here for its final moment."

The two men watched a violent blow knock down the last piece of fragmented wall. The seminary was gone, its time-honored traditions vanquished in the ruins. Within months, the new property owners planned to replace St. Paul's with a residential development of luxury homes, each built on large lots.

Jack pulled out a pint of Irish whiskey from his coat pocket.

"Join me in a toast, Father?"

"I'd be honored."

Jack opened the bottle and lifted it toward the sky. The beautiful golden spirit glistened in the Sun.

“To Saint Paul’s, and all the priests and students who walked its hallowed halls, especially Patrick.”

“Amen, Jack. To my fellow Sulpicians and all the boys, especially Mr. Keane.”

Jack took a drink and handed the bottle to Father Joe, who pressed it to his lips and downed a long, smooth taste.

“And I can’t forget Father Martin,” Jack blurted out.

“Yes, of course, Father Martin,” Father Joe said in a reflective yet curious tone, like he’d expected Jack to mention the priest’s name. “I need to ask you something: did you ever experience a deeper understanding of his visit or discover anything new over the years?”

Jack knew he didn’t want to try to explain something so personal and profound that, most likely, not even Father Joe would understand. He crossed his arms tightly before answering.

“Not really. I suppose some mysteries are meant to stay that way.”

Jack hoped his words did not betray the haunting doubt that plagued him. Standing in this place, surrounded by devastation, he understood more than ever how the passing years had made him even less confident of what he knew, like a grating pebble that he couldn’t remove from his shoe.

“Almost like a miracle,” Father Joe said. “Wouldn’t you agree?”

“So it seems.”

Jack spotted a fist-sized chunk of concrete and stone lying about 25 yards away across the parking lot. He jogged over, picked it up, and quickly returned.

“A keepsake?” the priest asked.

They both stared at the broken piece.

"It deserved better," Jack said with a sigh.

Father Joe looked past the rubble to a large cemetery cross towering above a distant hill. His eyes grew slightly moist.

"We all deserved better."

CHAPTER 2

Fall 1977

Seventeen-year-old Jack Hayes stood on the St. Paul High School Seminary's main portico, looking out across the front parking area and huge front lawn shaped to represent the Sacred Heart of Jesus Christ. He drew back his strong right arm and fired the football at a moving target. It spiraled 40 yards on a straight line, high above the hard asphalt and over the green grass warmed by the early September sun, finally coming to rest in Jared Bonelli's hands.

"You'd make a great high school quarterback, Hazy," said Patrick Keane, relaxing a few yards away against a textured, stucco-coated column. All three boys had arrived back at school the day before, the first Saturday of the month, to begin their senior year. "Too bad we don't have a team."

Jack laughed. "I'll stick with soccer. At least I can give out as much punishment as I get. I learned from playing Pop Warner that QBs get hammered too much."

"You're right. We can't have a future bishop – if the Church in its infinite wisdom actually ordains you one day – limping around like Chester from *Gunsmoke*. The Vatican might find that a bit, shall we say, tacky."

Jared approached, bounced up the brick steps, and tossed the ball to Jack.

"Nice pass," said the muscular senior. With dark, thick hair, brown eyes, olive complexion, medium height and Roman nose, Jared not only took pride in his fourth-generation, San Francisco family's Italian heritage, he also looked the part. "It's great that Coach Shumaker is letting us play intramural flag football this fall. Too bad we had to wait until senior year."

"I love it," Jack said. "Coach always worried someone would get hurt and miss soccer games. Funny that this could be our best varsity season ever, and now he allows it."

"Could be?" Patrick said with incredulity in his voice. "With Riley, Mateo, and Tony moving up from JVs, we're way stronger than last year. I'm guessing even the big Catholic schools won't look past little old Saint Paul's this year on their game schedules."

"It's at their own risk if they do," Jared said. "And the public schools too."

Jack felt the same way, though more cautious. The soccer program had come a long way, guided by 35-year old Coach Glenn Shumaker, since the class of 1978 arrived on campus three Septembers ago. The eight senior starters expected the team to log its best season ever. Still, Jack didn't want to count his chickens. Perhaps he harbored a bit of an inferiority complex, knowing that their local Catholic high school opponents considered St. Paul's students a "bunch of wimpy priests" who posed no threat on the field, the previous year's stellar 15-7-3 win-loss record notwithstanding. Jack understood changing that perspective would come only through victories. In contrast, while the soccer program was peaking and the players optimistic, enrollment challenges faced by the school had increased with each passing graduation.

"To be blunt, this is Saint Paul's one shot," Patrick warned. "It's now or never."

"You think so?" Jack asked.

"Absolutely. Let's face it, Hazy, our best days often sneak by unnoticed, like a brilliant sunset past a blind man. Creation placed an expiration date on even the brightest star in the heavens. I say grab any speck of magic now, no matter how small, and do something special that goes beyond our time here before the final whistle blows."

"Something earth-shaking?" Jack said.

"Something worth remembering."

While most boys his age gave little thought beyond the present or immediate future, Patrick seemed tuned in to a viewpoint greater than himself. What Jack found most fascinating, however, was his friend's often unorthodox beliefs about Roman Catholicism, even here at a seminary. Patrick seemed so guilt-free, so undaunted, so unaffected by years of strict canon taught by no-nonsense nuns in Catholic elementary schools. Jack couldn't exactly call him a rebel, and never witnessed an incident where Patrick flouted authority with bad intent. Quite the opposite was true. His devoted parents had instilled a love of reading and thirst for knowledge in their only son coupled with an emotional maturity uncommon in boys his age, including respect for those who educated him.

Despite his relaxed, confident manner, Patrick sometimes used words like hand grenades, tossing quips here and there. One *bon mot* was pure Keane original: "bananahead." Jack liked the vivid description so much the word soon became part of his vocabulary. It just fit.

Most students took Patrick's good-natured remarks in stride, like a playful badge of honor. Jack could recall only one classmate who'd held it against him.

Right on cue, Brian Weaver – *that* classmate – walked out the front entrance's big, carved wood double doors.

"So here's where you girls meet on weekends," Brian said in a caustic tone. "I'm surprised you're all not dressed in pink."

A bit shorter than his peers at five foot ten inches, the stocky senior rarely missed an opportunity to criticize or use insult humor. Jack found Brian's attitude so habitually negative that he'd started calling him "Electron" during their sophomore year. After Jared shortened it to Tron, the name stuck.

"Look who's here, Tron and the big chip he carries around on his shoulder," Jared countered. "What's the matter, couldn't you find anyone else around to ruin their morning instead of ours?"

"Ha-ha." Brian looked over at Jack. "Hayes, don't you know that throwing a football in front of the school shows no class. Maybe you haven't heard about the big green patch called an athletic field."

"Who made you Pope?" Jack said. "And speaking of class, I hear you'll be spending time with the juniors for a while catching up before you get to join us in senior Latin. What fun."

A scowl formed on Brian's face. "We all can't be Father Joe's favorites like Keane and you."

"Oh, sure, that's the reason you messed up last year," Jared said. "It had nothing to do with not knowing basic Latin, such as the difference between a declension and a prepositional phrase."

Tron's ears turned red with embarrassment. "Like you're some kind of genius, Bonelli."

"Smarter than you, tough guy," Jared said in rebuttal.

Jack stared at Tron with contempt. *The jerk simply cannot help himself,* he thought. Topping a long list of reasons, Jack disliked Tron because of his apparent close friendship with Father Lawrence "Spider" Webb, the stern Dean of students who ruled St. Paul's with an iron fist. What the short priest lacked in altitude he made up for in girth. Jack had suffered painful encounters with the Dean in the past and knew Father Webb would target him even as a senior if he stepped out of line.

In fact, at the moment, staying out of the Spider's crosshairs – not sports, studies, or preparing for college – worried Jack most. Any slip-ups could cost him everything, including graduating with his class and the opportunity to attend the college seminary next fall. Or, if he decided not to pursue the priesthood, Jack knew he might miss out on being accepted at a top university and even earning a soccer scholarship.

"Enough, you bananaheads; it's time for lunch," Patrick announced. "Come on, Bones, and you too, Brian, let's go see if the new food service's Sunday fare is any better than last year. You coming, Hazy?"

"I'll meet you inside the refectory in about ten."

After Patrick, Jared, and Tron left, Jack packed the football into his gym bag and took a moment to gaze out across St. Paul's manicured grounds. His eyes wandered off to the west, where the restless creek dense with poison oak divided the property in two, separating the main building, gym, and 1950s-era pool facility from the huge athletic field complex. Along with the lush front lawn, the soccer pitch stood out as the head groundskeeper's pride and joy, a deep-green oasis maintained with the help of three ex-convicts. The men, Roy, Elmer, and Bill, were employed and housed by the diocese in special workers' quarters located on campus, having been released from Federal prison after serving their sentences – including time on Alcatraz – years earlier.

Jack thought back to the day he'd arrived at the school as a freshman. He remembered the twinge that welled in his stomach when he'd stood in almost this exact spot and watched his parents' red station wagon roll down the wide, sloping driveway toward home – his home – 100 miles north. That sick, suffocating feeling of being left alone in a strange place, away from his family for the first time and not knowing anyone, plagued Jack for weeks. A short, slight, sweet-natured priest named Father Giovanni had only made the pain worse with a series of tender talks in the chapel on Mary and Jesus, and the important role a mother plays in a boy's life. Jack wondered if the new freshman recruits would endure the same private torture.

Looking back, Jack also wondered how he'd talked himself into enrolling at St. Paul's, especially at such a young age and having attended public schools his entire life. After all, he was close to his parents and grandparents, and got along well with his brother and sister, so why would he want to "go away" to a boarding school run by priests with a reputation for rigorous discipline?

His parish pastor, Father James Ring, had encouraged Jack to consider the priesthood since becoming an altar boy in fourth grade. Despite feeling a nascent vocation to serve God, Jack had been somewhat brainwashed by the strict, gray-haired, impatient priest who hired his favorite acolyte, along with Jack's younger brother, for $1.00 an hour during the summers to work around the church hoeing weeds, washing windows, and picking up trash.

During breaks, Father Ring would sometimes stop by to bring the boys sodas and cookies, examine their progress, and talk about how the crew was doing "God's work," saying they would make fine priests one day. Jack liked the idea, especially the part about standing in front of a congregation to say Mass with all the vestments and ceremony. He also grew to admire the pastor, despite his habit of lightly slapping young catechism students in the back of the head to get their attention. Jack had wondered if that was part of God's work too.

Though not enthusiastic about the plan and thinking Jack too young to leave their home, John and Mary Hayes had supported their oldest son's wishes. Jack's friends, on the other hand, particularly the athletic boys he'd grown up with playing sports since age six, either expressed dismay at his decision or thought he had about as much chance of becoming a priest as they did.

In fact, his plans to serve God almost fell through before they began when even the low annual tuition cost of $1,000 presented an unaffordable obstacle to the family's modest, middle-class income. The local diocese resolved the problem when the bishop stepped in to pick up the tab, wishing to do his utmost to nurture as many vocations as possible.

Jack also could now see that becoming friends with Patrick his very first day in this citadel of God helped him navigate through those difficult early weeks. Walking down the freshman corridor, Patrick had stopped to watch this 5 feet 3 inch, athletic-looking kid with a baby face standing in the hallway outside his open doorway as he pondered the contents of the 12-foot by 10-foot room.

"What do you think?" Jack had asked, staring straight ahead. "My grandmother made those curtains for the window. I'm not sure they work, especially with all the baseball posters."

"I like them," Patrick answered with approval. "Gives the place a feel of home. Much better than the guy next to me who seems to be going for the old monk in a prison cell motif with bare walls and no rugs to warm up the cold floor. Then again, even a famous interior designer couldn't do much working with only a desk, a chair, a metal-framed bed, and an old white sink."

"You're right. I like the curtains too." Jack said, still focused on the window. He turned and extended his right hand toward Patrick. "I'm Jack. Jack Hayes."

"I know," Patrick replied, giving it a firm shake as he looked squarely in Jack's eye. "Your name tag gave you away. By the way, I'm three doors down across the hall. Welcome to the neighborhood, such as it is."

"You too. I guess we're on our own now, and after all this unpacking and moving stuff around, I need a cold one. Care to grab a root beer from the vending machine in the basement? It's on me."

"Yes, thanks. And in case you were wondering, sassafras originally flavored root beer, at least until some guy figured out it was poisonous," Patrick said. "I'm not sure what's in it now. If you're willing to risk it, so am I. After you."

"How do you even know that?" Jack asked as both boys hurried down the steps toward the basement, taking them two at a time. "And why do you talk like an adult? You almost sound like one of the priests here."

"I have a cousin who always answers, 'Momma didn't raise me dumb!' when I ask him the same thing. In his case, I think my aunt did."

"And in your case?"

"Good genes. It pays to have brilliant parents and be an only child who reads a lot. A nun once told me, 'The Lord provides,' and I think she was right. By the way, despite what everyone says about you and your curtains, Jack, I like you." Patrick tried to suppress a laugh but failed.

"Good to hear. Too bad the jury's still out on you."

Later that fall, a kleptomaniac stole Jack's curtains. Although the faculty identified and expelled the mentally disturbed freshman responsible for the strange theft, they never found the window coverings.

The sound of a freshman's high-pitched voice resonating from an open window on the third floor pulled Jack back to the present.

It's been quite a ride, he thought, marveling at how those early days now seemed far away. *I just hope we can make the finale our greatest journey yet.*

*****

Following dinner on a beautiful, early September evening so typical in the South Bay for late summer, Jack, Patrick, and Jared decided to take a quick walk down the front driveway before Prayer Period began at 7:10.

"I suppose you heard by now that we did it," Patrick said with a trace of disbelief in his voice.

Jack flashed a quizzical look.

"Did what?" Jared asked.

"Father Joe told me that our enrollment officially fell below the Mendoza line."

"Really?" Jack said. "We have less than two hundred guys this year?"

"Way less. One fifty-nine to be exact. Only thirty-five freshmen."

"That's a huge drop – why aren't more of us signing up?" Jared said. "Saint Paul's has lost, what, like one hundred students since we arrived. Where is everybody?"

"Maybe it's something we said," Jack joked. "Or in the words of Yogi Berra, 'If people don't want to come to the ballpark, how are you going to stop them?'"

"Vocations are simply getting tougher to come by, guys," Patrick said. "The days of incoming classes with one hundred or even eighty students are gone. Guess the Church is having as much trouble dealing with the Seventies as everyone else."

"Think it could push above two hundred again?" Jack questioned.

Patrick displayed his best "you've got to be kidding" look.

"Father Joe believes the trend will continue. Not everyone *gets* this kind of place. You've heard how the soccer and baseball guys from other schools react when they find out what the seminary is about, like we joined a freak show."

"They probably wandered into one of the jakes and got scared," Jared joked, referring to the shared student restrooms that included old-style toilet stalls made from wood, several urinals, three sets of sinks, and a constant strong disinfectant smell. "I know I'm afraid to go in after Jimmy or Dan use them."

Patrick laughed. "All I'm saying is that we should send the old boy out with a bang."

"What? Do you think the school might close?" Jack asked with genuine concern.

"That's a good question," Patrick said. "Father Joe believes once St. Paul's drops below one hundred students, the Archbishop will make some tough decisions. Give the guy credit – he keeps the high school, college, and the theologate up in Menlo Park open even though the Archdiocese loses more than a million bucks a year."

"Wow, we're expensive," Jared said. "But obviously worth it."

Patrick raised an eyebrow. "You think? It would be smarter only to have a college that feeds the major seminary."

Jared gave a half-hearted shrug. "I suppose that makes more sense than losing a ton of money on a dwindling number of undecided high school kids who may bail out tomorrow."

The three boys reached the bottom of the driveway near where Highway 280 crossed over the seminary property. The deep, rumbling sound of commute traffic clogging the lanes filled the air. Jack picked up a small rock lying near the curb and fired it at an old aluminum soda can someone had tossed out of a car window. The loud ping signaled a direct hit.

"Too bad," he said, brushing dirt from his hands. "I've always thought of Saint Paul's as Disneyland north, kind of a combination fantasyland and great place to live and learn."

Jared scoffed. "Not much of a fantasy if you ask me. We live in seclusion, sheltered from the world, with no girls." He pointed toward the freeway. "I bet thousands of them pass by right here every day and not a one knows we even exist. Does that sound normal to you?"

"Well, I agree we're a little out of the ordinary," Jack admitted. "But I don't feel any different than my friends at home – just smarter and way better looking."

"You must have some hideous, dumb friends back at Junction 8, or wherever you live," Jared said with a grin. "Why ever go home when you can get that here with Dan and Jimmy?"

"Geez, you two are real beauties," Patrick said. "I see nothing to get upset about. The school had a great run and served its purpose well. It produced bishops, priests, and a lot of successful grads."

"Still...," Jack's voice drifted off. A slow smile emerged. "I sure hope they don't decide to shutter the place one night when we're sleeping and take a wrecking ball to it."

"I'll tell you what, guys," Patrick said. "Even though I hate goodbyes, if they ever decide to tear down Saint Paul's, we'll meet here and share a bottle of whiskey, the kind Father Joe keeps in his room. Deal?"

"Deal," Jack and Jared replied in unison.

"For now, let's make this an adventure and see where the road leads us."

Dusk had settled over the campus by the time the boys made their way back toward the main building. As they approached the front steps, Jack looked up and noticed an intense beam of bluish light emanating from the tower's bell room.

"Look, guys," he said. "Up in the tower."

Patrick caught a glimpse before the light blinked out, as if someone had flipped a switch.

"I'd heard the Warden blocked off the belfry years ago so no one could even get into it anymore. That's strange."

"I didn't see anything," Jared said.

"You must be blind," Jack replied. "The beam was so bright people ten miles away could have seen it."

"Could it be that light from the moon or a star came through the belfry?"Jared said.

Jack stared at him with incredulity. "Uh, no. Try opening a science book once in a while."

"Hey!" Patrick placed his index finger in front of his lips. "Whatever it was, it's almost time for Prayer Period to begin. So let's get inside and no more talking!"

*****

Around midnight, Jack awoke from a sound sleep and got up to use the jakes. He'd put in an extra long evening of studying to polish off the pile of homework his professors had assigned and felt mentally exhausted. While walking back to his room barely half alert, he heard a voice whisper behind him.

"Carry on," it murmured softly.

Taken by surprise, Jack whirled. He saw no one.

"Who's there?" he asked. No answer came. Jack stared down the long, silent corridor, straining hard to see through the eerie darkness tempered only by a series of dim blue lights on the ceiling. He waited, sensing that someone or something was near. Jack listened for the slightest sound. Nothing stirred. After about 30 seconds, he relaxed and returned to his room.

The next morning, Jack opened his eyes around 6:30. Rays of sunlight dappled the wall and ceiling. He stretched out in bed, feeling rested and ready for the new day. Jack laughed to himself about the alleged midnight voice, thinking he must have imagined the entire episode.

When he turned his head on the pillow, Jack noticed a pattern on his closet door caused by a stream of light passing through an empty glass soda bottle he'd left on the desk. He studied the blurry pattern for nearly a minute, thinking it looked like a J with two straight lines that resembled the number 11.

Weird, he thought. Jack got out of bed and moved the bottle. The three symbols disappeared from the door. He placed the bottle back in its original spot. No matter how hard he tried, he could not recreate the pattern. Jack dressed and went downstairs to breakfast, still distracted by the curious lights.

"Stop by my room before Latin class," Jack told Patrick as they left the refectory. "I want to talk to you about something."

Back on the senior floor, Patrick knocked once and slid into the room. Jack leaned against two pillows at the foot of his bed, bouncing a tennis ball off the wall and catching it in his well-used baseball glove. A soccer ball, football, sweatpants, and two baseball caps littered the rug-covered, varnished plank floor, while a 34-inch Stan Musial-autographed Louisville Slugger leaned in the corner near the closet. Jared sat in the desk chair working on a Latin assignment. Frustrated, he'd come to Jack's room for last minute help translating a difficult verse into English.

"So what's up, Hazy?" Patrick asked.

Jack tossed the ball and mitt toward the bottom of the bed.

"I had something bizarre happen last night, and also this morning."

"What do you mean?" Jared said, glad for the diversion from the seemingly incoherent Latin text.

Jack explained about possibly hearing a voice, and the symbols caused by the glass.

"Jack and his magic soda bottle," Jared teased. "I suppose it's better than a boring old beanstalk. As for the voice, sounds like you were half-asleep and heard a sound. After all, the pipes and radiators in this old place can be pretty noisy."

"Strange that we saw a light in the tower, and then this stuff happens," Patrick said. "My advice is to concentrate more on keeping the profs happy and less on your closet door. Our plates are going to be plenty full this semester without added distractions. But let's all keep an eye out in case something else peculiar occurs."

CHAPTER 3

Despite Patrick's warning, Jack, like most of the seniors, was excited about being on top of the heap and getting to "run things," at least as much as St. Paul's strict rules and Father Webb would allow. The school that had felt so cold and scary at first now fit Jack like an old pair of jeans or favorite baseball cap. It had become as much a home as his parents' house, only with a truckload of brothers.

Not that he and his classmates would breeze through senior year. In fact, quite the opposite. Patrick was right about that. Upon arriving back at school only days earlier, Jack had sat down at his desk and scanned the single sheet of paper listing his fall semester class schedule, with each 45-minute period separated by a brief break that allowed students to scramble to their next lecture or activity. It read:

7:00 am First Bell

7:15 – 7:45 Breakfast (Refectory)

8:00 – 8:45 4th Year Latin (Father Marshall)

8:50 – 9:35	Classic Poems Fall/Honors (Father Hall) Russian Literature Spring/Honors (Father Townshend)
9:40 – 10:25	Religion/Church History – (Father Volk)
10:30 – 11:15	History of the Civil War Fall (M, W, F) (Father Quinn) Classical Music Appreciation – Spring (M, W, F) (Father Hall) Physical Ed (T, TH) (Mr. Shumaker)
11:30 –	Daily Mass (High School Chapel)
12:15 –	Lunch (Refectory)
1:00 – 1:45	Physics (Mr. Jones)
1:50 – 2:35	Calculus (Father Delacroix)
2:40 – 3:25	Study Period

Not too bad, Jack concluded, knowing that many of his friends at home who attended public schools would think the course load nothing short of insane. Although often swamped with homework, he had grown accustomed to long hours of studying after living the past three years under Sulpician rule, a teaching reign that started in Paris in 1642 and boasted an impressive history of providing seminarians with a well-rounded Catholic education.

With such a packed class schedule, Jack relished the study period at the end of the school day. In addition to getting a jump start on his homework, this welcome "free" time would allow him to suit up early and prepare for the Varsity soccer matches St. Paul's would play two or more afternoons each week from November into early March.

Even though Jack carried a solid "A" average heading into senior year, second period Honors – with its ratio of one Sulpician professor to eight students – concerned him. Most boys saw such a small class size as a blessing and a curse. Reserved for top students, Honors allowed for individual attention and in-depth discussions unheard of in other schools. It also required that each boy ready himself to step into the spotlight at a moment's notice, with no place to hide if he showed up unprepared. When a student did arrive less than primed, some priests showed little mercy in lowering the hammer.

Bucky and Fang back to back. That'll add some bite to the schedule. I just hope we all survive.

The high school seminarian penchant for assigning creative nicknames to nearly every priestly professor, and even classmates, amused Jack. His personal favorites included tags for Father Jerry Volk, who students had affectionately christened "Fang" because he shared the same last name as the popular 1960s bass player in the Paul Revere and the Raiders band; Father Daniel Hall, known as "Bucky" because of two rather prominent front teeth; and Father "Spider" Webb. Other colorful monikers included Father Charles "Pete" Townshend named for the WHO guitarist; St. Paul's president and rector Father Dennis "The Warden" King; Father Pierre "Frenchie" Delacroix; and Father Joe "Smokey" Marshall, who smoked a pipe and also represented the Law as Assistant Dean of Students.

Jack picked up his nickname during the first semester of freshman year, thanks to a big helping hand from Patrick.

"What's wrong with you today?" Jack recalled Jimmy Rhodes asking him one morning before frosh history class.

"I got in trouble last night," Jack had explained. "I needed to use the jakes after lights out. Father Quinn was patrolling the corridor and tells me I can't. He says, 'I don't think you're quite clear on the rule, Mr. Hayes. You cannot be out of your room after 11 pm for any reason. Do it again, and you'll find yourself in detention.' That's crazy. What's a guy supposed to do? When you gotta go, you gotta go."

"Sounds more like you were a little hazy on the rule," Patrick said, who'd been sitting at the desk to Jack's right. "Hayes, hazy. Get it? From now on, I'm calling you Hazy!"

Like many of his schoolmates, Jack also found the 11:30 weekday Mass in the high school chapel at the end of the morning schedule less an obligation than a renewal. Along with the 30-minute Quiet Time before dinner, daily Eucharist offered an interlude for students to recharge their vocations. Accompanied by guitars and at times even drums and electric bass played by students, the St. Paul's community sang uplifting hymns as they joined in festive worship of the Father, Son, and Holy Spirit. Patrick summed up the contrast to the often low-key Sunday Masses in many home parishes as, "the difference in energy and enthusiasm between a four-year-old child and a ninety-year-old man."

Jack particularly looked forward to the inspired, unfettered sermons. More often than not, the Sulpician celebrant delivered a powerful, "tell it like it is" oration, unconstrained by concern that his strong words might offend the devout little old ladies often found sitting in the front pews of local parishes. Or even worse, cause generous donors who filled the Sunday collection baskets to reconsider their support. Moreover, on high Feast days, the high school congregation celebrated services in the ornate chapel on the college side of the campus. These special occasions often featured Gregorian chant, as well as music from a large pipe organ played expertly by Father Delacroix that permeated the towering ceilings and resonated off the colorful array of stained glass windows.

The rest of the daily Monday-through-Thursday schedule remained much as it had since Jack's freshman year:

3:30 – 5:30	Recreation Period
	Intramurals, Varsity & JV Interscholastic Sports
5:30 – 6:00	Quiet Time, Angelus
6:00 – 7:00	Dinner (Refectory)
7:10 – 7:30	Prayer Period
7:30 – 9:00	Study Time
9:00 – 9:20	Class Meetings with Prefect (T, TH)
9:25 – 9:45	Night Prayers (High School Chapel)
11:00	Lights Out

Of course, seniority also meant more responsibility and the assignment of "House Jobs" by the faculty. For example, Patrick had been appointed Key Man. Armed with a large brass ring of keys, his weekday duties required making rounds early each morning and following night prayers to unlock and lock the first-floor classrooms, the main entrance, and a pair of large, double side doors that led out to the gym and pool across from the western wing. Two notable exceptions were the priest's suites – each Sulpician Father had a personal set of keys – and all student rooms, which had no locks on the doors.

"What's your job, Hazy?" Patrick asked.

"Editor of the *Cupertinan*," Jack said, referring to the school's monthly news periodical. "Guess I better finish learning the entire alphabet real fast."

Patrick smiled. "Good. I'll look forward to reading your special investigative report called *'What the Heck Was That?'* about last night's dinner."

Other jobs handled by seniors ranged from distributing the Daily Bulletin – a single sheet that kept students informed of schedule changes and important announcements – to helping out in the library or serving as mailmen who delivered letters and packages to student rooms each morning before Mass.

"Thank goodness that neither of us got stuck being the Regulator," Jack said about the unpopular job that required ringing an obnoxious, earsplitting wake-up bell at 7:00 each morning and at 11:00 each night to mark lights out. "We've got enough to worry about without everyone hating us."

*****

As the warm fall days passed, Jack, Patrick, and their 28 classmates eased into the flow of senior year. The short, four-game, intramural flag football season – during which Jack tossed 14 touchdown passes for his Bears team, but fell in the championship to Riley Moody's Ramblers – soon gave way to Varsity and JV soccer practice. Jack felt upbeat and hoped to shine on the playing field and in the classroom.

Father Webb, however, had a different agenda. Following breakfast on a Saturday morning in late September, Jack wandered into the newly renovated senior lounge to read the newspaper. Located inside the tower – and accessed by a single door off the fourth-floor corridor near the top of the staircase that led down to the foyer – the lounge provided a casual place to relax, boasting two burgundy-colored leather couches, a coffee table, a big, 25-inch Sylvania color TV, end tables with lamps, and a large, solid oak bookcase stocked with hardcovers and paperbacks. The Spider hunted Jack down until he found him sitting alone on a couch.

"Mr. Hayes!"

Jack lowered the sports section of the newspaper, surprised by Father Webb's confrontational tone.

"I've been meaning to talk to you and straighten out a few things." Webb's pulse quickened, and his face took on an intense look. "As a senior, you need to demonstrate more responsible behavior than in the past and stop causing trouble. I hope we're not going to have the kind of problems we saw last year because I won't tolerate it."

Jack bristled inside at the insinuation. He quickly decided any protest would only make the situation worse.

"I learned my lesson, Father. You don't need to worry about me."

"I do worry about you and all our students," Webb claimed. "I'm also aware that some of your classmates, as well as the younger boys, look up to you, so setting a good example is important. You're nearly an adult and need to act like one."

"I'll do my best."

Father Webb glared at Jack, his trademark form of intimidation that the boys had dubbed the "evil eye trick."

"Just know I'll be watching. Do I make myself clear, Mr. Hayes?"

"Yes, Father. Loud and clear."

"Good. Don't forget what I said."

With that, Webb turned and strode sternly out of the lounge.

Jack wanted to scream. *The nerve of that jerk*, he thought, tossing the newspaper onto the coffee table. *I'd like to....* He sat on the couch and fumed for another five minutes before storming down the hall to Patrick's room.

Jack knocked hard, once, and opened the door. Patrick sat reading at his desk.

"I need to take a long walk. Care to join me?"

Patrick could see the anger in Jack's face.

"Sure thing, Hazy. It's not natural to study on a Saturday morning, so thanks for saving me."

Over the years, Jack and Patrick had often taken weekend walks around St. Paul's expansive campus. The boys would make their way down the driveway, cross over to the pristine creek area, skirt the athletic fields, and finish by making a complete tour around the fortress-like main building. Although the archdiocese designed the school as a three-sided structure when it opened, the addition of a four-year college section during the 1950s enclosed the southeast-facing side. The new wing also helped shelter the quiet courtyard that featured cloisters on two flanks and crisscrossing, concrete walkways surrounded by arrays of flowers, trees, palms, and lawns, making it a favorite place for daily prayer and meditation.

"Spider put me on notice," Jack said, as the boys strode along.

"What happened?"

"He burst into the lounge like he was looking for a fight and warned me not to cause more trouble. I'm telling you the guy is sinister."

"Ah, the misguided Twinkie escapade again. Not your finest hour."

The previous spring, Jack had agreed to join several famished classmates in a daring, in-and-out, midnight kitchen raid to grab whatever food they could find. The ill-fated attempt turned into a disaster when a college student serving as night watchman appeared from behind a giant soup kettle and caught the boys with handfuls of the Hostess cakes.

The consequences produced the lowlight of their entire junior year. Jimmy, Dan, and Jack netted four-day suspensions courtesy of Father Webb's bulldog attitude toward enforcing the rules. The harsh, five foot seven inch tall disciplinarian had failed to show any mercy toward the accused looters, leaving Jack to wonder how Tron, the fourth member of their group, had miraculously evaded both detection and punishment.

Father Joe, whose appointment as Assistant Dean a year earlier brought a "good cop, bad cop" balance to the office, argued more as protector than judge on their behalf at a meeting called hastily by Father King. In the end, the council of priests voted for suspension at Dean Webb's strident urging. Regardless, Father Joe managed to reduce the intended sting by phoning the three boys' disappointed parents to assure them not to fret over what he considered "a behavioral aberration."

"It seemed like a good idea at the time," Jack said with a sheepish look.

"Yeah, right, so how'd that work out for you? Worst thing about it, you missed a couple of baseball games, and we lost them both. Lucky that Father Joe stood up for you bananaheads."

"If you recall, Tron pushed the hardest for the raid that sent three of us on an unwanted vacation. And what did he do? The guy hid in the basement stairwell, then kept silent and skated. I wouldn't put it past him to have set up the whole thing so I'd get caught!"

"You're right; it was a joke. And I hope you learned not to let a big bananahead ever talk you into a suicide mission again."

"No way. I told *Der Fuehrer* this morning he didn't need to worry about me."

"The year's still young, Hazy," Patrick said with a laugh. "Don't sell yourself – or me – short."

Jack imagined a worst case scenario. "I guarantee Webb seemed mean enough to kick me to the curb. Look at all the guys he's sent packing over the past couple years, and how he overreacts. Don't you ever feel like he's got it in for us?"

Patrick grinned. "You, for sure. As far as he knows, I'm an angel."

Jack rolled his eyes. "Thanks, pal. I knew I could count on you. I'm telling you all his ill will seems to flow in one direction, right toward me. I don't get it."

"Well, Webb already booted everyone who couldn't cut it academically or was a serial troublemaker. Guess there's no one left to hassle except guys like us."

"Maybe it's because I don't like Tron and Spider does? How anyone can like that bananahead is beyond me."

"Who knows why Webb does what he does? I sure don't."

As they walked down the road between the gym and main building, Jack pointed up to an open window.

"Can you believe the entire second floor is empty this year?"

"Sign of the times," Patrick said.

With the recent decline in vocations, incoming freshman now shared the third floor with sophomores. Juniors still lived on the fourth floor of the west wing, while each senior was assigned a room on the fourth-floor corridor that ran along the front of the building, providing them with a privileged view of the valley below. That left the second floor vacant except for two suites occupied by Father Hall at the front end of the wing, and Father Webb near the rear.

"Webb helped create that ghost town," Jack said. "He must be *sooo* proud, and happy to have a whole corridor practically to himself."

When they reached the back of the complex, Patrick nodded his head toward the abandoned convent and chapel. At one time, about 25 French-Canadian nuns belonging to an Order known as "Little Sisters of the Sacred Heart" had lived there.

"At least the second floor's not quite as empty as the old nuns' quarters," he said. "A lot has changed since we arrived here, and not for the better."

As the late morning Sun climbed in the sky, it lifted the temperature into the low 80s. The boys hurried their pace past the college wing, slowing again once they turned the corner and reached the front parking area. Jack's eyes drifted up to the tower, one of his favorite parts of the seminary campus.

"I've been thinking about that light we saw. Wonder what it's like way up there? Too bad the tower is off-limits."

As the seminary's most recognizable feature, the campanile – now forbidden to nearly everyone because of safety concerns – was seen first by priests, students, parents, and other visitors as they wound their way up the driveway. Located behind, and slightly to the left of, the main entrance area, the tower protruded into the courtyard by nearly all its impressive girth. A large archway cut into the structure at its first floor level led to two heavy wooden doors, providing a busy thoroughfare from the foyer, business offices, periodical room, and faculty lounge out into the courtyard, and across to the dining halls.

Topped by an ornately decorated cupola when first built, the tower lost its stylish, gilded headpiece due to an engineering flaw: St. Paul's had been built directly over the San Andreas Fault, California's major earthquake corridor. During the cupola's 25-year lifetime, numerous small to medium-sized temblors had tested its stability, until the school's rector had the crown removed.

"We should find out what's up there one of these days," Patrick said.

Having completed their loop, Jack gestured toward the school's covered, 20-foot tall portico.

"Let's get into the shade. I'm hot."

The boys walked up the eight brick steps that bordered the rectangular deck of scarlet tiles on three sides. An array of Roman-style pillars and arches made of concrete and stucco rose from the platform to support a walled balcony, which protruded 12 feet beyond the buildings' main structure and covered the landing. Inaccessible to students, the raised terrace sat just below a collection of huge windows that provided light to the school's well-stocked library.

"So what about Webb?" Jack asked as they stood on the large front deck.

Patrick looked him directly in the eye. "Okay, yeah, he's tough. But his job and the job of the other Sulps is to foster vocations, not destroy them."

"Are you sure about that?"

Patrick leaned back and furrowed his brow.

"In my opinion, even if you're not a little paranoid, we can't let him ruin the party. We're not standing on the side of the road and missing out because we're afraid of a guy who doesn't even like us. That's insane. After all, senior year only comes once in a lifetime."

"I'm still worried Webb will try to find any excuse to make trouble."

"In that case, Hazy, always remember what Father Quinn told us as sophomores: 'Be prepared, phenoms.'"

"Right, the old 'hope for the best, expect the worst,'" Jack said. "Just in case, let's make sure Father Joe has our backs."

Chapter 4

Father Joe stood up at the head table where the priests ate and rang a small handheld bell to end dinner. A swarm of boys rose from their chairs as one, shuffled out the refectory's two sets of double doors, and proceeded upstairs to jump into their homework assignments. Many would not come up for air until obligation required that they march down to the chapel for night prayers at 9:20.

Jack and Patrick were not among them. Their eight-man table – with two boys from each grade – along with the one led by Jimmy Rhodes and Tom Hardin, had drawn that week's duty to serve as waiters for the entire refectory. Only when dinner ended, and the waiters finished removing all the dirty plates, platters, and crisscrossed aluminum "piling" trays filled with used utensils from the tables, could they finally sit down to eat.

"That was a workout tonight," Jack said while he relaxed in his wicker-backed chair, enjoying the now quiet dining hall, and watching Patrick finish off a slice of blueberry cheesecake.

"I suppose it's good preparation for parish life," Patrick said between bites. "After all, serving God as a priest also means serving people. What better training than learning to take orders, listen to complaints, solve problems, and handle smart-mouth remarks from our 'customers' without smacking them."

Less than an hour earlier, at precisely 6:00 pm when Quiet Time ended, a crowd of seminarians and priests had stood in silence on the raised tile walkway outside the dining hall with their heads bowed. One student rang a gray bell hung above the doors, while another recited the Angelus prayer – a devotion in memory of the Archangel Gabriel's appearance to Mary that revealed she'd been selected to become the mother of Jesus Christ, the Son of God.

When the doors opened, the hungry herd moved swiftly to their assigned seats without speaking. Each boy stood behind his chair, eyes fixed, watching the evening's reader scale three steps up a large wooden podium to recite a pre-meal Bible passage. Waiting impatiently with empty stomachs, the students appreciated brevity – the shorter the reading, the better. Jack still smiled when he recalled the time one boy had stepped to the lectern and announced in a booming voice, "A reading from the book of John: 'Jesus wept.' This is the Word of the Lord."

As the sound of the collective "Amen" faded, the 16 waiters sprang into action. Directed by the four seniors, the boys bustled back and forth between the kitchen and dining hall, bringing out an initial rush of platters and bowls of food before scurrying back to pick up refills. Throughout the meal, the happy din of lively chatter and laughter resonated off the great hall's high ceilings, tall panel windows, and wood plank floor. The voices mixed with the sounds of knives and forks tapping on heavy, ceramic plates, used silverware clanging against aluminum trays, and the ping of cups, saucers, and glasses. Jack wondered if other boys enjoyed the dinner ritual as much as he did – even the waiting tables part that now kept him sitting here late with nothing to do.

“You ready for tomorrow’s calculus quiz?” he asked.

“Almost.” Patrick finished the last clump of cheesecake and wiped his mouth with a linen napkin. “How about you?”

“Yeah, although I need to review again tonight, just in case.”

“Man, Hazy, you’re such a nervous optimist. You want good things to happen and work harder than anyone to make sure of it. Sometimes you just can’t quite bring yourself to believe they will.”

“Really?”

“Absolutely. For example, you could get a perfect score on ten math tests in a row, but still worry you might not pass the eleventh.”

“I do?”

“It’s what helps make you such a high achiever. You hate the thought of losing or failing. If you’re not ready for the quiz, nobody is.”

Dan, who had stuck around to see if he could commandeer an extra slice of cheesecake to no avail, walked over to the table and interrupted.

“Can you guys believe it? We have to read three whole chapters tonight, AND get ready for a test tomorrow.”

“Wow, first the Spanish Inquisition and now this – when will it end?” Patrick said with a roll of his eyes.

“Don’t worry, Dan. I read the history assignment, and the good guys win,” Jack teased.

“Figures,” Dan said with bite.

"Look at the bright side," Jack said. "At least you don't need to worry about high school being the best time of your life with nothing to look forward to for the next sixty-five years."

Dan walked away muttering under his breath, pushed open the dining room doors, and headed upstairs.

"If Hannigan spent as much time studying as whining, the guy would be at least a 1.9 GPA, maybe even a 2.0 with help from several tutors," Patrick said, causing Jack, who was taking a drink, to spit water onto the tablecloth when he laughed. "Nice, Hazy." Patrick tossed him a clean napkin to wipe up the mess. "So, how would you like to go on an adventure this coming Saturday morning?"

"Where?"

"Right here. It involves climbing." Patrick pointed up with his right index finger. "And breaking the rules."

Jack's eyes widened with interest and apprehension. "What about Webb?"

"Don't go soft on me now. We'll make sure to stay clear."

"Come on, we both know I'm an old rules breaker and have the record to prove it. But is this smart?" Jack thought about the possible consequences if the Dean found out. His mind wrestled with indecision. *Probably not a good idea. I'd sure hate to let Patrick down.* "Ah, geez, what the heck," he finally said. "Count me in. I guess."

"Good." Patrick reached down and picked up a large ring of keys from under his chair. "I've been trying out some of these babies to see what works where, and I think it's time we explored the bell tower."

"We've lived here for three years, and I've never been inside it," Jack said. "Have you?"

"Let's just say I might have wandered in for a glimpse recently, and it deserves a closer look. Especially after what we saw a while back. You up for it?"

"I think so...what's the plan?"

"We need to go in early, around 6 am before anyone's up. No point in risking someone seeing us. And bring your flashlight. We'll need it."

On Friday night, as he lay in bed trying to fall asleep, Jack weighed the risk of a tower adventure against Father Webb's threat. *The guy's a loose canon, and anyone who gets in his way will get crushed.*

On the other hand, Jack also knew that for all its strictness, St. Paul's rule book included some quirky anomalies. First, the school set aside designated smoking areas for its students. Freshman and sophomores were allowed to puff away on one of the two sets of concrete and stucco steps along the building's western wing, while juniors and seniors shared the other. While most schools deterred or prohibited underage smoking, St. Paul's accommodated it.

"That makes as much sense as if they served us vodka cocktails before dinner," Patrick had observed during freshman year. "What's the message they're sending here?"

A second, weekend oddity that students often exploited had mystified Jack since entering St. Paul's. Each Friday, the school assigned a single priest to keep track of students who stayed for the weekend but chose to leave campus. In theory, the boys were supposed to inform the priest in person, and many faculty members offered no compromise in wanting to know where each student was going, and what time they would return.

In reality, however, some priests took a much more relaxed approach to their weekend babysitting job. Students often simply signed their names and intended destinations, such as a local shopping center or movie theater, into a leather-bound register that sat on a table near the front doors and could spend an entire afternoon or early evening on their own with no disciplinarian in sight. The fact that students could not keep cars at the school limited their range. Nevertheless, undeterred nomads either walked, caught rides from college seminarians or hitchhiked.

"I think the lax attitude would surprise a lot of parents," Jack had told Patrick, "especially that their fourteen- and fifteen-year-old sons could run around unsupervised for hours at a time, at least as far as their legs can carry them."

More surprising, no Sulpician Father – even those who had resided at St. Paul's for decades – could ever recall a single reported case where a weekend wanderer had gotten into serious trouble or returned to school in a police car.

"Students who spend the weekend with us have a lot of free time, and we trust them to make the best of it and behave like gentlemen," Father King explained when a parent had asked him about the school's Saturday and Sunday policies. "If not, they don't last here long."

After a long, restless hour fretting about what could happen if Father Webb caught them in the tower, Jack finally fell into a welcome sleep. At 5:30 on Saturday morning, he rose, dressed quickly, and peeked out into the hallway. Seeing no one, Jack headed down toward Patrick's room. Just as he went to knock, Patrick opened the door.

"Coast clear?" he whispered.

"All's quiet," Jack said.

The boys moved in silence until they reached the main staircase. Jack peered over the wooden banister to reassure himself they were alone. Given a thumbs up, Patrick removed the key ring from his large coat pocket and unlocked the tower door.

Once inside, Jack flicked on a flashlight.

"After you," Patrick said.

They started climbing a narrow flight of cement stairs. About 30 feet up, the boys reached a platform with a small, eye-level window that faced northeast on one side, and a door that appeared much like the one they had just entered through on the opposite side.

"What a fantastic view, even better than our floor," Jack said.

"Look, you can see up the peninsula to the lights on the San Mateo Bridge," Patrick added.

"Want to go to the top?"

"First, let's see what's behind this door."

Patrick placed the same key he'd used to enter the tower into the lock. It wouldn't turn.

"Darn," he said aloud. He thought for a minute. "I've been wondering what this one weird little key is for, so let's try it."

Moving his hand down the brass ring, Patrick inserted a short, odd-shaped key that, until that moment, he'd never used. When first given the job as Key Man, Patrick had asked Father Webb what each of the ten metal objects locked and unlocked. The priest didn't seem to know or much care about this tiniest one.

"Then why keep it?" Patrick had asked.

"Because it's always been there, at least for as long as I can remember," Father Webb told him. "It might have been used to lock up a kitchen pantry or a bookcase in the library. At this point, what does it matter? Just leave it alone and do your job."

As he twisted the mysterious key, Patrick heard the lock click. He'd discovered its purpose.

"Got it," Patrick said softly. "Glad I kept it on the ring."

The door creaked open. A cool, dank, dusty smell permeated the air. Jack stepped in, moving the light slowly around the high-ceilinged chamber. Old wooden desks and chairs filled most of the room. Several large, formal portraits of bishops and priests rested on the floor against one wall, while an ornately carved tallboy with two doors and four lower drawers stood in front of another. More than a dozen tied stacks of newspapers and magazines blocked their path to the cabinet.

Patrick signaled that he wanted to take a look inside. He stepped painstakingly through the maze of papers, making sure not to knock any over. Just as his hand reached for a big brass handle to pull open one of the tallboy's doors, Patrick and Jack heard a low groan. They froze. Both boys strained to listen for any sound. Jack's heart raced, and he started to take shallow breaths. After waiting in silence for about ten seconds, they heard faint footsteps that seemed to echo from above the ceiling.

"Let's get out of here," Patrick urged in a whisper.

He didn't need to ask twice. The two explorers scurried from the room, moving with as much stealth as possible, and nimbly retraced their route down the stairs to the fourth floor. Jack opened the door with caution and peeked out into the dimly lit corridor. It was empty. He and Patrick slipped into the adjacent senior lounge. Safely inside, they caught their breath.

"That scared the crap out of me," Jack said, slouching into a couch, as if all his energy had been stolen.

"Worse. I think someone was watching, or at least heard us."

"Watching? Who?"

"I'm not sure. I doubt it was one of the guys or a faculty member. And why would a workman or anyone else be in there at this hour. Kind of sounded like a ghost, to be honest. I'll check things out again tomorrow when the sun's up and more light is coming through the tower windows."

"You're going back?" Jack said in disbelief. "Are you crazy?"

"I hope not. That certainly wouldn't look good on my college applications."

Jack appeared confused. "What? You've applied to outside schools?"

"Of course. You should too. In case things change."

Jack sighed. "You're right. Might as well be prepared." He gave a slight shrug. "I suppose you'll need a partner tomorrow to go with you."

"I knew you'd volunteer."

Jack stood up. "I'm going back to bed. This exploring stuff is hard work. See you at lunch?"

"Sure. How about we head down to St. Joseph's parish for five o'clock Mass later? That way, we can go back in tomorrow while everyone's at chapel."

"Good idea. Less chance of the wrong pair of eyes seeing us."

Sunday morning, while most students who'd stayed at school for the weekend attended Mass, Jack and Patrick ascended the bell tower stairs once again, stopping outside the room. Rays of sunlight streaming in through a small window in the tower wall helped illuminate their passage up and bathed the door, which was cracked open, in brilliant warmth.

"Did you close it yesterday?" Patrick asked.

"I'm not sure; everything happened so fast. Probably not."

Patrick pushed in. He studied the contents. The furniture and portraits sat undisturbed. His eyes scanned the floor.

"Look," he said.

The piles of papers had been moved, creating a narrow lane to the tallboy.

"I don't like this," Jack said. "Someone was here."

"It seems whoever did this wants us to check out what's in that cabinet. We can't disappoint them."

Patrick pulled open the upper doors. The tallboy was empty.

He quietly opened and shut each drawer, finding nothing except dust until he reached the bottom one. Inside rested a large, smooth, brown envelope with an old-style, red button-and-string clasp and the word "Private" printed on the front. Patrick picked up the file, pulled out the papers, and flipped through them for about 30 seconds.

"Oh, man," he said.

"What is it?" Jack asked.

"I'm not sure. Maybe bad news."

"About what?"

Patrick took the flashlight from Jack and scrutinized the walls in slow motion, searching for any holes or large cracks. Finally, he discovered a foot-wide vent near the tallboy, hidden by a stack of magazines.

"Time to leave. Come to my room about fifteen minutes after we get back on the corridor."

In the quiet of his room, Patrick sat at his desk intently studying the papers from the envelope when Jack walked in.

"What did you find?" Jack asked.

"The envelope contained several newspaper articles and also internal memos about a suspected embezzlement by a priest here at Saint Paul's back in the Sixties."

"Was anybody we know mentioned?"

"Looks like the Warden and Spider caught an older Sulp dipping into the kitty, although they didn't file criminal charges against him. One of the memos indicated Webb directed the process to have a priest named Father Martin McGrath banned from teaching. The Society transferred him to a retirement home back East."

"Gee, Spider leading the charge to nail someone – what a surprise," Jack said. "Maybe we could find out more about what happened by asking Father Joe."

"He wasn't here at the time. And how would we explain where we came across this stuff? Let's keep it to ourselves for now and try to find out more before telling anyone. If you need me, I'll be searching the catalogs for old newspaper clips in my favorite sanctuary."

CHAPTER 5

Patrick often found refuge in the school's library that occupied most of the second and third floors at the front of the building and stood as a monument to Catholic higher education. A voracious reader, he enjoyed spending long, tranquil hours in its three, expansive rooms that featured plush blue carpeting, intricate woodwork, large mahogany study tables with polished tops, a dozen elegant, padded chairs, and a collection of old and new volumes – including decades of magazines – that rivaled those found in local colleges and universities. Most of all, Patrick savored the profound quiet that enveloped him each time he stepped in from the second-floor corridor. More than a place to read about ancient cultures or study math, he found the library a peaceful escape to think and meditate, particularly on his vocation.

When Jack once wondered aloud why Patrick wasted time "reading a bunch of old stuff that wouldn't help him get A's," his well-rounded friend smiled and replied, "One, I enjoy it; two, learning isn't just about grades; and three, I believe Hamlet was right when he declared, 'There are more things in heaven and earth, Horatio, than are dreamt of in your philosophy.' I intend to relax in this magical place with my books, discovering them."

But not today. Patrick immediately went to work, scouring the wooden card catalogs and periodical listings for any news related to the alleged scandals. After hours of exhaustive hunting, he came away with only a single mention of the Father McGrath incident. On the other hand, taking a cue from the five-year-old newspaper article included in the envelope – a discovery he had not mentioned to Jack – Patrick also located a pair of short reports about alleged sex abuse by local parish priests.

"How about joining me at the top of the Grinder for sodas and some spectacular stargazing this Thursday night, Johnny?" Patrick asked Jack while they played a board game in the lounge that evening.

Jack had learned over the years that Patrick only called him "Johnny" when something serious was up.

"I suppose it can't wait until Friday?"

"I'm heading home for the weekend. I know you worry about getting caught, but it'll give us a chance to talk outside the building about what we found. Call it *carpe noctem* – seize the night."

Jack nodded his head.

"Good," Patrick said. "You can come with me on my rounds to lock up, and we'll head out from there. And don't worry, I've been going out at least one night a week with no problems."

When the boys finished securing the classroom doors and outside entrances on Thursday following night prayers, they made their way to the athletic fields and up the Grinder. At the top, Patrick unpacked two sodas, one box of cookies, and a pair of powerful 8x50 binoculars from a black canvas satchel.

"It's always good to come prepared," he said. "Help yourself."

Each boy took turns looking through the binoculars while they ate cookies and drank the sodas. Patrick pointed out interesting areas of the sky for Jack to check out.

"This is great," Jack said. "What's so important that we had to come all the way up here?"

"Maybe it's my turn to be paranoid. I feel somehow we're being watched inside. I can't explain it because it's just a sense, a weird intuition."

"What did you find out?"

"The library contained an article in a Catholic publication that confirmed the Father McGrath story, although the Sulpician priest who wrote it questioned the legitimacy of the charges." Patrick stopped and drew a deep breath. "Hazy, I've got some shocking news that I didn't tell you before: the envelope contained a story about local priests accused of molesting boys, guys younger than us. I found follow-up reports in the library."

"What?" Jack said, stunned by the news. Patrick's words felt like daggers. "Not anyone at Saint Paul's, I hope."

"No."

Jack looked puzzled. "Then why was the story in the envelope? And what are we supposed to do? I mean, what even can we do? Didn't this all happen years ago?"

"True. Still, I can feel it. Somehow we've been chosen to uncover something, or maybe right a wrong."

"How exactly?"

"I flat out can't say. It's like a puzzle with a bunch of missing pieces. It's up to us to fill in the blanks."

"I wish we hadn't found that stupid envelope. This whole thing stinks."

"You're right. It's sickening." Patrick shook his head in disgust. "Regardless, I believe we need to find out what happened."

"What do you suggest?"

"For now, keeping our eyes and ears open to see if anything pops up, like in a conversation we overhear, or something we read. It's hard to say. I'm getting signals, and you know what happens when I start feeling it."

Jack thought back to the last time Patrick claimed he received "signals," the same night he warned him not to raid the kitchen for Twinkies. To his regret, Jack had not listened.

"Okay, we'll keep watch and see what happens. Maybe this will all just go away."

"It's always some damn thing, isn't it?" Patrick said. "At least it's a beautiful night."

Having polished off their sodas and the bag of cookies, each took one last look through the binoculars and headed down the hill. They had just crossed the bridge and were approaching the service road near the gym when Patrick grabbed Jack's arm.

"Wait!" Patrick ordered. "Get down."

To his right, Jack saw a shadowy figure approaching slowly along the road. As the specter drew nearer through the darkness and emerged beneath the sad, yellow glare of an outdoor light on the gym wall, he could see it wore a hooded, black cloak, much like the Grim Reaper, and carried a long staff. Jack guessed the ghostly figure stood about 6 feet tall. It paused and turned toward where the boys crouched behind some bushes. Jack's heart raced. He only saw two, slightly bluish glints of light from beneath the hood, the same color as the beam he'd seen coming from the tower. To their surprise, the specter turned away and continued down the road. They watched it disappear into the night.

"What the heck was that?" Jack asked, his eyes wide with alarm.

"Whoever it was, he spotted us," Patrick said.

Jack's face took on a confused look. "Then why didn't ....?"

"I'm not sure. It's like he didn't care we were out here. Let's hope so, or we might be in for it."

"Unless it really was a spook. You've heard the stories about workmen who died in accidents, or old priests who haunt the halls."

"Sheesh, you believe that about as much as I do. This is no time to turn into a bananahead. That guy was real. But who is he?"

The boys entered the building through a side door and quietly climbed the wide stairs to the dark, deserted second floor. Patrick motioned toward the bathroom.

"Got to visit the jakes," he whispered and pushed through the swinging door.

Jack leaned against the corridor wall to wait. Within seconds, he heard footsteps descending from above, and saw a flashlight beam dancing off the wall at the top of the landing between the third and second floor. Unable to get to the bathroom without being seen, Jack took three steps and carefully opened the door to what once had served as the freshman lounge, making sure the old hinges didn't give him away with a squeak. Once inside the empty room, he felt his way around a closet that jutted out a few feet, and tightly hugged its far wall, hiding in the quiet blackness.

The footsteps drew closer in the hallway. Jack heard the lounge door open and held his breath. He felt his heart pound hard again as the flashlight's ray bounce off the window glass.

Just great. First time out on the Grinder at night and I get caught and probably suspended again, or even worse.

Jack was about ready to burst when the sound of the door shutting filled the silent void. He stood frozen, uncertain if the danger had passed. Moments later, he heard the door open again, and Patrick's voice whisper, "Jack! You in here?"

"Yes," Jack replied as quiet as possible. "Is he gone?"

"Down to the first floor. Probably outside by now."

"Thank goodness. Was it Webb or the Warden?"

"No, just the night watchman making his usual rounds. I peeked out the jakes' door and caught a glimpse as he left."

"What? There's a night watchman?" Jack asked.

"Hey, try to keep your voice down. He's one of the ex-cons, a nice old guy named Barney who doesn't see or hear too well anymore. He only works on weeknights and keeps an office in the old convent."

"You know him?"

"A little. Barney got locked out of the building one night, and I helped him out. Being the Key Man has its advantages."

Jack stared at Patrick, his mouth open. "Thanks for letting me sneak around without telling me we could get caught by the new campus police. How about a heads-up next time? I almost passed out thinking Webb or another priest would nail us."

"Sorry, Hazy. We came in later than I normally do, so the watchman's pattern was different. No worries. He won't turn anyone in unless they do something insane, like smoke dope or vandalize the place. As strict as it is here, stargazing and exploring the building aren't criminal offenses unless we get caught by one of the Profs."

"Gee, now I feel so much better."

"Otherwise, I'd say it was a pretty eventful evening," Patrick said, ignoring Jack's jibe. He listened for a few seconds but heard only the soft sweetness of silence. "Let's get to our rooms before anyone else decides to go for a late night stroll."

When they reached the top of the stairs and were about to step onto the junior corridor, Jack and Patrick heard the double doors to the senior floor open around the corner, followed by footsteps. With no time to hide, both boys froze in place. Jack's heart jumped into his throat. *Not again!*

An elderly-looking priest whom neither recognized emerged from the darkness, head bowed, palms pressed together, praying while he walked. Without looking up, he turned to the right and continued down the corridor away from them. Jack and Patrick immediately moved across the hall and slipped through the doors to the senior floor without making a sound. Patrick pressed his finger to his lips, gave a little wave good night without speaking, and each boy went to his room.

The next morning following classes, Patrick signaled Jack to meet him in the courtyard before heading into the chapel for daily Mass.

"Anyone say anything to you about last night?"

"No, not a word," Jack assured.

"Me neither."

"Guess that old guy didn't spot us in the hall, which is amazing. I mean, how could he have not seen us? I thought we were goners."

Patrick nodded his head in agreement. "Lucky for us. By the way, I did a little poking around after breakfast by helping Jared clean up in the priest's private dining room. No one said a word about anything."

"Thank goodness. Looks like we dodged a bullet."

"Maybe, although Webb gave me the stink eye this morning when I walked past him in the refectory. He probably did it on general principle." Patrick laughed at his remark. "After I get back on Sunday night, we need to make plans to go out again real soon."

"No way," Jack protested. "We barely escape Armageddon, and you want to press our luck? Not this time. Count me out."

"Don't worry, this is an inside job, if you catch my drift. And I hold the keys to the city."

"If we get caught...."

"We won't. We'll talk later. Right now, I need to head to the sacristy to help set up for Mass."

"And some of the priests called *me* a bad influence after the suspension," Jack grumbled. "I'm not so sure I'm the one who's the problem. At this rate, I'll be surprised if we make it through this week, much less the school year, without getting our walking papers."

Patrick displayed a wry smile. "Hang in there, Hazy. See you at lunch."

CHAPTER 6

As Jack had worried, the first, intimidating academic challenge of the semester came in the Classic Poetry Honors class. Father Daniel "Bucky" Hall asked each of his eight pupils to write a 12-line poem about the Fall. The top efforts, he explained, would be vetted in class and then submitted for possible publication through a small Catholic Press. On the due date, Father Hall collected the assignments and evaluated them in his suite that evening, checking each line for rhythm, meaning, and style. He handed the sheets back to their authors the next morning in class and told each to prepare to read his work.

"You're up first, Mr. Hayes. Please speak clearly."

Just my luck, Jack thought. Nervous, he stood up by his desk, took a deep breath, and began reciting:

Indian Summer

When Spring reminds of far memories fond, And Summer's lazy sweetness sadly wanes, When Autumn's bounty blankets the brown earth With rich golden hues of last ripened grains

Before Winter's chilling blast cuts the bone And endless night approaches unrestrained, Time reopens a door once tightly closed To still, bright beauty, and wonder regained

Grasp the season bravely, O dauntless soul, Do not consent the soothing warmth to fade, But stand renewed in rousing crimson blaze To keep at bay grim twilight's creeping shade

Jack sat down and looked straight ahead, listening for any sound of snickers.

"Thank you, Mr. Hayes," Father Hall said. "Now, I'm sure he'd like to hear your reactions. Any comments?"

"I kinda liked it," Dan offered. "It would have been even better if someone got shot, or maybe a guy like Dirty Harry could have arrested that shady creep in the crimson blazer standing near TuKeepat Bay."

Several boys laughed out loud, including Jack. Patrick, who sat directly behind Dan, reached out with his pen and playfully thumped him in the back of the head, although a tuft of thick, auburn hair cushioned most of the blow.

"Won't it be fun for you, Mr. Hannigan, watching with a sad, freckled face on the sidelines while your classmates graduate in June," Father Hall said. "Sometimes you really take the cake."

"Sorry, Father," Dan replied, contrite yet unchastened by the censure. "Guess I'm just not very poetic. From what I understood, I thought what Jack wrote captured pretty well the struggle that older people face trying to stay young and fight death to the end."

"You redeemed yourself somewhat. Try to remember that fewer jokes and more contemplation would serve you well." Father Hall looked over at Tom. "Please tell us your thoughts, Mr. Hardin."

"Well, I think Jack's poem contrasts life's seasons with old people's impossible desire to stop the flow of time, and somehow hold onto the spark they used to have. He suggests the door may re-open, at least temporarily. It can't last no matter how hard anyone tries because everything fades. In fact, the poem is a bit dark. Don't you think?"

"Mr. Hayes?"

"Well, I meant it as an inspiration, Father, not something sad. We've all learned from religion classes that death is a part of life. I just thought the idea of an Indian Summer day, like we've had lately, could be compared to an older person trying to stay, what's the word...."

"Alive?" Dan offered.

"...no, more like vibrant, while they can."

"Yeah, before the Grim Reaper takes them out," Dan added. "Nothing like a happy ending."

"Salvation represents a happy ending, Mr. Hannigan," Father Hall said. "As Catholics, we believe in life after death through Christ's resurrection. So the Grim Reaper loses, and we keep twilight at bay, as Jack describes."

"We also pay an earthly price because the older we get, the more we lose," Patrick challenged. "Could be our hearing or ability to walk, people we love, or even plain old dignity. At the same time, we often gain loneliness. That's why faith is so important. Without it, I imagine old age could be depressing and cruel, especially if we're alone at the end."

"So what's your alternative, Mr. Keane?" Father Hall asked. "After all, aging is an inevitable part of accepting God's gift of living."

"Maybe a sweet, short life that leaves an imprint, and where you go out on top, isn't always such a bad thing. No need for an Indian Summer. I think more than a few people would trade away years for a chance to become what they dreamed they could."

"Sounds better than hanging around so long that you don't even know who you are," Brian chimed in.

"Be kind, Mr. Weaver," Father Hall admonished. "Even the most experienced and seasoned among us deserve respect."

One by one, each boy stood to read his work, followed by a short discussion. The final lines of Tom's effort acutely caught Patrick's ear. Tom had likened the season to a departing mother's love. Patrick, whose mother died when he was 12, heard the painful debris in Tom's voice as he read the final stanza:

> ... *You taught me well with loving hands To be caring, brave and clever; Yet one thing you could never teach – How to say goodbye to you forever.*

All the seniors were aware that Tom, who'd arrived at St. Paul's as a junior the prior school year, had grown up in foster care after his young, troubled, unwed mother gave him up for adoption at age three. Yet they knew little else of their lanky, blond classmate's circumstances. Shy and quiet at first, Tom soon fit in well with the "lifers," as Dan liked to call the group who'd stuck it out since freshman year, but kept tight-lipped about most of his unhappy past.

Near the end of class, Father Hall walked out from behind his desk to make an announcement.

"After carefully studying your poems last night, and hearing today's presentations and discussions, I plan to submit Mr. Hardin's and Mr. Hayes' efforts to the publisher. You should all be proud, including Mr. Hannigan, as I believe your poems were worthy labors. Now, before you head out the door, let's have a hand for our top fellow bards."

All eight boys and Father Hall clapped in unison, while Dan also whistled his approval. As they left the classroom, Tom walked over to Jack to shake his hand.

"Way to go, Jack. You deserved it."

"Congrats to you too, Tom."

"I thought you knocked it out of the park, Tom," Patrick said, joining the two boys on their way out the door. "I always expect good things from Hazy, but your poem hit home. Great job."

Inspired to make an imprint, Patrick stirred the pot the very next hour in Father Volk's Church History class. Throughout his years at St. Paul's, Patrick had enjoyed the mandatory religion classes more than any other in the school's curriculum because of the free-wheeling discussions encouraged by the priests who taught them. For example, a freshman year back-and-forth on Church dogma between Patrick and his Sulpician professor had set the stage for later classroom battles, some that left his teachers wondering where a young seminarian had picked up his renegade version of Catholicism.

"The whole idea that we 'have to' do something, like avoid eating meat on Friday, seems pointless," the 14-year-old Patrick had calmly asserted. "I should want to do it, and not be threatened into submission. I doubt God keeps score. What matters is faith that empowers us to surrender our lives to His care, not man-made dogma. It's about what's in your heart. I think He'd prefer we do the right thing out of love rather than blindly follow orders."

Father Volk's class was no exception. As Patrick's knowledge and boldness had grown over the years, he often relished pushing the envelope close to the edge of a precarious cliff – sometimes too close, in Jack's opinion.

"Before we move on to the next chapter, are there any questions about clerical celibacy?" Father Volk asked.

"Yes, Father, although not about celibacy," Patrick spoke up. "I say this with respect: what difference can we make as priests? What difference have you made? Every day, we hear and read news stories about murders, people that lie and cheat, corrupt politicians, and terrible suffering. How can any of us be anything more than a drop in the ocean? After all, no human being can save the universe."

Father Volk stood in silence for a few seconds, taken off guard by Patrick's words.

"Okay, a bit off topic, Mr. Keane. I agree the world has many problems that one priest or a thousand priests will never completely solve. Perhaps we cannot, as you say, 'save the universe.' We can, however, help spread God's Good News. The vast oceans are made up of tiny drops, blending to cover most of the Earth with the water of life. Each of us needs to add our drop to keep it flowing."

"Do you ever worry about offering just one more distraction, Father?" Patrick asked.

"What do you mean?"

"Where people use religion as an escape from reality, something to take their minds off the harshness of living, the same way they do with alcohol and drugs. If a person thought too much about life, I mean really thought about what it means to face the hard, painful, incredibly sad things that happen sooner or later, they'd cry all day, every day."

"A good priest offers his flock guidance, hope and inspiration. He provides a source of comfort during life's inevitable valleys."

“Does it ever seem hopeless and pointless to you, Father?” Tom asked.

“No, I don’t think that way, Mr. Hardin. In fact, all of you, take a look out the windows. Do you see those men?”

Two workers dressed in coveralls stood near the pool facility, repairing a leaking pipe.

“We have reformed sinners who live right here on campus, men who’ve turned their lives around. Some of these workers committed horrific crimes, even murder. At age 16, which is younger than you boys, the man on the left drove the getaway car for a famous gangster. He shot and killed an FBI agent, and spent years in Federal prison on Alcatraz Island. That worker and the other ex-convicts paid their societal debt, and now seek spiritual forgiveness and redemption.”

“He was on the Rock?” asked Jimmy Rhodes, a feisty City kid with brown hair and green eyes who had toured Alcatraz with family members or friends a few times. At five foot seven inches and 150 pounds, Jimmy was shorter and slighter than most of his classmates but made up for it with toughness – both on and off the soccer field – that belied his size. Someone who didn’t go looking for a fight, but who didn’t back away once trouble showed up either. Jack had always liked that about the smaller boy.

“That’s right, Mr. Rhodes, a notorious criminal at one time, someone well known to J. Edgar Hoover at the FBI.”

Father Volk walked out front from behind his desk.

“Eyes front, gentlemen.” He paused to make sure he had his students’ full attention. “Think of the parable of the Prodigal Son. No matter how terrible or hopeless things may seem, God will always welcome His children into His house. As priests, we can shine as examples of God’s unconditional love, and serve as beacons of hope to lead the faithful out of the darkness and toward the light.”

“Father, turn on the TV or read the newspaper and it’s not hard to find so-called role models living hypocritical lifestyles, even in the Church,” Patrick responded. “It makes me wonder.”

“Witnessing widespread bad behavior certainly can lead to doubt and even cynicism. Think about it, Mr. Keane: if your soccer team gets behind 2-0 – and I’m well aware that rarely happens – do you just quit trying your best to overcome the deficit? No, you never give up. Instead, you fight until the end.”

Father Volk walked back behind his desk, picked up a thin day-planner with a black leather cover, and held it high.

“By the way, gentlemen, everyone in this classroom will see what difference I can make when grades come out.”

Uh-oh, Jack thought as he glanced over at Patrick.

“And in case others here harbor your own wonders,” Father Volk added, “I think Mr. Keane made a difference today too.”

“Do you mind then, Father, if I ask another question?” Patrick said, not yet ready to let the dust settle.

“Go ahead.”

“Why not allow priests to marry in today’s Church?”

Better quit while you’re ahead, bud, Jack thought.

“A worthy question, Mr. Keane. Granted, as you’ve learned this week, ordained priests often did marry in the early Latin Church, and even up until the twelfth century despite decrees and canons of Popes and councils. However, in 1139, the Second Lateran Council enacted the first written law prohibiting bishops, priests, and deacons from marrying, and also invalidated the unions of those who had entered matrimony. The reasons were moral, religious, and also economic because it allowed the Church to grow in power by controlling the wealth its priests accumulated through their work."

A pained expression crossed Father Volk's face. "Unfortunately, this obligation resulted in some wives and children being left to fend for themselves. I consider that a sad and regrettable time in Church history that tore apart families." He paused briefly to give his words greater effect. "In 1917, with the Code of Canon Law, Rome finally made being married a formal impediment to ordination."

"And today?" Patrick reiterated.

"Today, the obligation of clerical celibacy and abstinence from sexual intercourse is done for the sake of the Kingdom of Heaven and intended to help priests live in the manner of our Lord Jesus Christ. They can dedicate themselves more completely to their religious work and the service of God and their congregations."

"By not marrying, though, Father, don't priests lack the experience to serve as marriage counselors, or deal expertly with family matters?" Patrick asked. "If you've never lived it, how can you know what you're talking about?"

"In addition to counseling education, many priests gain valuable experience through parish life, as well as their past personal family experiences. But you raise a good point. And since you seem to be most curious today, anything else, Mr. Keane?"

"Just one more question, Father." Patrick hesitated, aware he was about to stir up a hornet's next. "It's a controversial topic – why doesn't the Church allow married Catholics to use contraception?"

Jack cringed at the question, while several boys shifted uncomfortably in their seats. Birth control and the inevitable debate on abortion were not subjects suited for informal and open discussion, even at St. Paul's.

"My, aren't we the gadfly today," Father Volk said. "The Church has condemned the use of contraceptives for millennia, Mr. Keane."

"Why?"

"Their use is in conflict with God's law," the priest replied. "As you studied in Father Quinn's class last year, Pope Paul the Sixth issued a landmark encyclical letter called *Humanae Vitae* about human life in 1968 that accentuated the Church's teaching on birth control. He wrote that it's wrong to use contraception to prevent a new person from being born."

"That same year, an international commission originally established by Pope John the Twenty-third in 1963 voted sixty-eight to four in favor of allowing married Catholic couples to decide what methods they wanted to use," Patrick countered. "The commission concluded that contraception was not a sinful thing."

"And Pope Paul the Sixth rejected their conclusion."

"But, Father …."

"That's enough for today, Mr. Keane." Father Volk's tone left no doubt the matter was closed. He peered down at his watch. "We only have a few minutes left and need to move on now."

Agitated, Patrick opened his mouth to reply. Jack quickly raised his hand and said, "Father, can we review what was discussed earlier about celibacy. I was a little confused about some of the economic reasons for it."

"Yes, Mr. Hayes. Let's review."

Jack peeked over at Patrick. He appeared calm again. Jack thought he even saw the hint of his trademark wry smile.

When class ended, Patrick caught up to Jack outside on the arcade.

"Thanks for having my back, Hazy. It's probably best that the discussion ended when it did."

"You think? I wanted to turn to you and yell 'Stop!'"

Patrick grinned. "I guess I got under his skin today."

"Hey, we both know Fang can become a bit testy at times. I suppose it's all those obligations."

"No doubt. The whole concept seems logical to me. If the Church is against abortion and wants to protect innocent babies, I mean, come on, shouldn't it support contraception, which would lead to fewer abortions?"

"It may make sense from a logical point of view," Jack agreed. "Still, you can't fight city hall."

"Probably not. It just ticks me off to think about all the unwanted pregnancies endured by women in poorer countries because they're afraid to use contraceptives. Their families suffer because they can't afford those kids. Who's for that?"

"When they elect you Pope maybe things will change."

"In that case, Hazy, don't plan on losing the old ways anytime soon," Patrick said shaking his head. "The revolution is a long way off."

CHAPTER 7

Each weekday afternoon in October, starting at 3:30, Coach Shumaker put the eight senior and eight junior soccer players who made the 16-man Varsity roster through a series of rigorous drills and exhausting conditioning. Having named Patrick team captain, the fourth-year coach made clear his high expectations for the upcoming season and each player's fitness level.

"There'll be no hot-house orchids on this team," Coach Shumaker had proclaimed on the first day of practice. "We're going to work harder and smarter than the other schools so that we own the final twenty minutes of every game. I mean completely own it. When the other guys are running out of gas and gasping for breath, I guarantee we'll just be getting warmed up.

"That's why it's important to practice like you play the game," he continued. "Does effort guarantee results? No, but outcome matters, so always remember that whatever extra you do today will show up tomorrow in a match, and help you achieve the results you want."

True to his word, each two-hour session ended with a difficult climb up the 200-yard Grinder. Located behind the baseball diamond's right field wire fence, the notorious rise leveled out on a plateau where the county had built an enclosed concrete reservoir. Not a fan of running the grass-covered hill, Patrick had decided long ago that he much preferred scaling it on clear, moonless nights to sit, stargaze, think, and pray while the rest of the school slept.

Coach Shumaker, clipboard in hand, watched patiently while three stragglers made their way down the last 20 yards of the Grinder and onto the flat area in right-field near where he stood. The rest of the players milled around him, some bent over at the waist with their hands on their knees, others with both arms raised high above their heads, all struggling to catch their breath.

"Pain, torture, and agony," Coach Shumaker barked. "P.T.A. Each of you needs to ask himself, 'What am I prepared to go through to make this team win? How much am I willing to push myself to make my dream and the dream of the guy playing next to me a reality?' Today is a great day to find out." He pointed to the reservoir at the top of the steep slope. "One more time."

Before anyone could let out a groan, Patrick raced toward the challenge, shouting over his shoulder, "Up the Grinder again, guys. Give it your best. If we're going to reach the top, it starts right here, right now."

The line of players moved single file up the hill. About halfway to the top, Dan tripped over a small embedded rock in the worn path and fell to the ground. Just as Jack reached down to help him up, Dan shouted out, "Save yourself, boys, I'm done for." Laughing, several other players stopped to see if their teammate needed assistance. Dan sat up and moved his right ankle back and forth. He felt no pain. Certain the fall had caused no damage, but enjoying the attention, Dan once again cried out in a funny, high-pitched voice, "Shoot me, Jack, I'm useless."

"Get up, bananahead," Jack said with a chuckle. "You're probably lucky Coach isn't holding a rifle with a scope. As Bucky likes to say, you take the cake."

"In that case, make mine chocolate with strawberry filling," Dan replied. "And somehow, I doubt Coach would be that good of a shot from way down there. If he is, I'll just make sure Tron is running behind me for cover."

A few days later, Coach Shumaker announced the school would hold a three-mile race around the grounds, open to all students, including members of St. Paul's cross country team. He also explained that players on both the Varsity and JV soccer teams were required to participate as part of their pre-season conditioning.

"Just great," Dan said. "Like the Grinder isn't bad enough."

The course started and finished on the soccer field. In between, the racers dashed over the bridge and turned south along the service road that ran for about 800 yards behind the school down past the workmen's quarters. After looping back toward the main building, the harriers headed through an apple orchard and up Maryknoll Hill, a soft-sloping incline crowned by a modest, beige colored, stucco building with a distinctive, dark green, Chinese pagoda-style roof. Formerly used to house high school boys who wished to train as priests for missions in foreign lands, the Maryknoll facility closed when enrollment dropped. The Archbishop soon after converted the building into a home for retired priests.

Reaching the top, the runners followed a long, dirt trail out through a vineyard toward Highway 280, descended the hill near the seminary entrance, and took the far western service road back past the old barn, the tennis courts, and the backstop until they hit the finish line at midfield.

For the first mile, Jack, Patrick, Jared, and Riley – who had become good friends with his three senior teammates – cruised along in a group, unconcerned with their time, and thinking they had no chance to compete with the cross country guys. About midway through the race, however, things changed when Jack charged up Maryknoll Hill with ease. At the crest, he unexpectedly found himself in a pack of three lead runners, 50 yards ahead of the nearest challengers.

Where is everybody? Jack thought. Suddenly it dawned on him: he could match the "real runners" stride for stride by maintaining his pace, which at this point still felt comfortable. *Guess all those wind sprints and Grinders do work.*

As the three runners sailed over the hilltop trail and descended toward the western service road, Jack felt a bit stressed, although not the kind of fatigue that would slow him down. With less than 1,000 yards to go, he decided to find out what was left in the tank. Jack picked up his pace to a smooth gallop, inhaling and exhaling deeply through his mouth and nose while the hard asphalt road flew by under his feet. He could feel the pain increase in his legs, and his lungs began to burn.

You can do this. Just keep pushing. Don't even think about slowing down.

By the time he reached the dirt path near the tennis courts, Jack had put 200 yards between himself and the cross country runners. Exhaustion gripped his entire body. With nothing left but determination, he sprinted past the baseball backstop and saw Coach Shumaker standing on the soccer field with a stopwatch, flanked by two boys who held opposite ends of a narrow tape marking the finish line.

Only 50 yards more, 30, 20, 10, ….

Jack lunged across the line. Coach Shumaker clicked the button and looked at the time in amazement.

"Good job, Jack," he said. "You finished the race in fourteen minutes and fifty-five seconds, which averages out to just under five minutes a mile. You also broke the old course record by more than a minute!"

"Wow," was all Jack could say as he gasped for air. "That was tough at the end."

Later that evening at the end of dinner, one of the freshman boys Patrick and Jack tutored in algebra as a way to earn extra credit in physics class walked over to Jack's table.

"I wanted to say thanks for winning me five dollars today, Jack," the Frosh said. "I bet one of my friends that you'd run away with the race. Just like a gazelle."

"You did?" Jack said with total surprise. "I didn't know anyone cared about the darned race. Heck, if I had the slightest idea I had a chance to finish first, I would have bet five bucks too."

*****

At the end of practice the day before St. Paul's first soccer match of the season, Coach Shumaker ordered, "No Grinder today," and sat the entire team down on the grass around him, their backs to the setting Sun.

"Soccer is a game of simple things done well, men. If we hustle, use our speed, control the ball, and keep mistakes to a minimum, we win. It's that simple. From what I've seen over the past few weeks of practice, we can compete with anyone if we play our game. Get a good night's sleep, and see you on the field tomorrow ready to go."

Jack stood in the locker room at 2:45 the next afternoon, studying the Opening Day starting line-up posted on the bulletin board near the main office. Coach Shumaker had already walked down to the field to set up the corner flags and goal nets, so Jack had the entire gym to himself. The line-up read:

Ben Stewart (GK)
Jared Bonelli (Sweeper)

FBs:	Brian Weaver	Patrick Keane	Tony Lombardi
Mids:	Mateo Castro	Dan Hannigan	Jimmy Rhodes
Fwds:	Riley Moody	Jack Hayes	Tom Hardin
Subs:	R.T. O'Neil, Gabriel Perez, Chuck Wallis, Dave Rossi, and Matt King (GK).		

With Riley and Tom flanking him on the wings, Jack liked the balanced attack, which provided rock-solid toughness with speed in the defense, good ball control and excellent passing skills at midfield, and a trio of quick players who could outright fly up front. Jack also knew having a tall, experienced, fearless goalkeeper like Ben, with his powerful right leg capable of booting the ball more than 60 yards downfield, would prove invaluable throughout the season. A reliable group of junior substitutes, led by the versatile R.T. "Artie" O'Neil who played forward or midfield, made him further optimistic about the team's prospects.

Looking good. We've got no holes this year.

Jack also loved the two sets of new uniforms. At home, the Battling Bishops would don white strips with gold numbers and lettering, shorts with double gold stripes down each side, and above the calf gold socks that sported three, white, circular stripes near the top. On the right sleeve near the shoulder, the jerseys bore a black crown of thorns in honor of Christ's sacrifice for all mankind. Jack thought the black and red "Away" uniforms looked even more impressive, especially the two-color jerseys with large red numbers, the black shorts with bold red stripes, and black socks with red tops with a large, red "SPHS" designed into the back.

How St. Paul's paid for these expensive additions had become a topic of conversation among his teammates. Jack heard the rumors. He figured Patrick would know the truth.

"The new strips are great," Jack said. "Do you know how the school could afford them along with the new balls and equipment?"

"I heard Coach paid a visit over the summer to the big rock quarry on the other side of the hill to discuss its illegal runoff into Saint Paul's creek," Patrick said. "Less than a week later, word has it that the quarry made a nice 'donation' to our athletic program."

"Wow, sounds like Coach likes to play hardball."

Whether the Coach's negotiating skills or the Archbishop's coffers provided the new looks, Jack didn't care – he felt the stylish uniforms were well-suited for what the entire school hoped would become one of the top teams in Northern California.

However, the day on which players selected their uniform numbers had created unexpected drama. Seniors chose first, with preference given to those who played on the Varsity the prior year and wanted to keep their same numbers. Brian arrived late to the locker room meeting. By the time he showed up, junior Dave Rossi already had picked number ten. When Brian saw "his" jerseys lying on the bench in front of Dave's locker, he reached down and grabbed them.

"Sorry, Rossi, ten is my number," Brian claimed. "I'm a senior, you're not, and that's that."

Dave stood stunned.

Patrick, who witnessed Brian's bullying, shook his head and grimaced in amusement. "Well, I guess that showed you, Dave."

Patrick walked to the pile of unselected strips, took out the number 14 jersey, and handed them to Dave. "Here's your consolation prize. Thanks for living in Brian's world."

"You're not King around here, Keane," Brian said.

"So true," Patrick said. "Then again, you've always enjoyed a total grasp of the obvious. So it's no surprise you figured that out."

Despite a few rough edges, the first game of the season went according to plan, with St. Paul's cruising to a 5-0 win over visiting Redwood Priory, a small private school with even fewer students than the seminary. Showing a nose for the net, junior Riley Moody led the way with two goals. He also assisted on Jack's pretty, ten-yard head shot that slammed past the outmatched goalkeeper before he could move. Tom chipped in one goal, while Patrick capped off the scoring deluge late in the match when he found the right upper corner of the net with a well-placed free kick from 20 yards out.

"I'll bet you my Mystery that I score a goal in our next game, and you don't, Ginger boy," Jimmy challenged Dan, as all eight senior soccer players relaxed in the lounge that evening.

"You're on, Lucille," Dan said. "I hope they serve chocolate pie or cheesecake for dessert because I'm going to pig out on huge, award-winning slices while you sit there and cry."

Since he first arrived at St. Paul's, Jack had considered it odd that the entire school called dessert "Mystery." When he asked around as a freshmen, no one seemed to know why. Jack guessed that past seminarians started using the term because the nuns who formerly ran the kitchen always cooked up a sweet treat to end the evening meal, such as warm chocolate-chip cookies, berry pie, or lemon tarts. Because the dedicated sisters' kept the daily menu as private as their lives in the convent, no one knew what sugar-laced surprise would show up on their tables.

Jack could guarantee one thing: nothing offered today by the contract food service could beat the Little Sisters' Baked Alaska, an ice cream and sponge cake dish with a browned meringue topping. True, the coveted dessert had shown up only on special occasions. Whenever the *glace au four* – or "ice cream in the oven" – did appear, it routinely received rave reviews from the faculty and students.

"We hardly ever saw the nuns, but I miss them," Jack said. "They did so much."

A cloistered Order, the sisters remained virtually invisible except during meal time. Even then, students caught only brief glimpses of their hands as the women dispensed food from behind a kitchen serving station designed with a solid, adjustable, wooden "window" pulled down to approximately 12-inches above the stainless steel counter. Only the Mother Superior, an imposing, stern-looking woman who wore a traditional black habit with a large crucifix hanging from her waist, ventured out from the expansive kitchen's preparation area to answer questions from students who could muster the nerve to ask.

"I'll never forget two things about the sisters," Patrick said. "One, their Baked Alaska and, two, the Christmas carols."

"And remember how young some of them were when they came out to sing? They helped make this place special."

During past Christmas seasons, their Order had permitted this notable exception to the Little Sisters' seclusion. On a frosty December evening, the nuns emerged from the convent dressed in crisp white habits, lined up on the red tile steps in front of the college chapel, and sang carols in French that resounded throughout the courtyard. Many in the crowd of priests, lay faculty members, and students stood spellbound, as amazed by the youthful appearance of the women as they were appreciative of the beautiful melodies and angelic voices.

“Losing the nuns was the canary in the coal mine,” Patrick warned Jack as they left the lounge. “Sooner than later, the modern world will suck the life right out of the high school seminary system.”

CHAPTER 8

Patrick and Jack waited beneath the sallow glow of the street lamp late on a Monday night, filled with nervous anticipation. They spoke quietly, hoping the distraction would help the time pass. Every 30 seconds or so, Jack peered down the road, straining for any sight of the nightwalker. The earthy smell of the damp ground filled his nose, while the utter stillness made him more anxious by the second.

After about ten minutes, Jack heard the rhythmic "click" of a stick hitting the pavement. As the sound drew nearer, the ghostly figure emerged from the blackness at a measured pace. Jack wanted to run. Instead, he remained motionless until the walker halted a few yards away. Jack heard Patrick draw a deep breath. He followed suit, struggling to prevent his entire body from shaking. The cloaked specter scanned the boys for a few moments but said nothing. Finally, it reached up with one hand and pulled back the large black hood. Jack was relieved to see an elderly man with oversized ears and a shock of snow-white hair.

"Good evening, gentlemen," the man said. "Nice hour for a walk."

"Good evening, sir," Jack and Patrick answered, exhaling a flood of anxiety at the same time.

"Out a little late, though, aren't you? Especially with a big game coming up this Wednesday."

The boys flashed each other surprised looks.

"Wouldn't want to get stuck in detention, would you, Mr. Hayes? Or you, Mr. Keane? The team needs its top players."

"Uh, no, uh, no sir," Jack stammered. "Neither of us wants that. Do we know you?"

"I'm Father Martin McGrath," the priest said. "Please call me Father Martin. We haven't met formally. My suite is next to the bell tower on the top floor. I've seen you both coming and going."

Holy crap, Jack thought, startled by the introduction. *He's the guy who stole money and Webb sent away.*

Patrick eyed the old man with caution. "Really?" he said in a low voice that dripped with worry. Patrick decided to roll the dice. "And I'm guessing you helped clear a path for us in the tower storage room."

A faint smile crept over Father Martin's face. "Sound carries pretty well in the old building, so I hear things, including rumors about rodents. Your voices ruled that out. And we can't have any of the boys smoking dope or doing dangerous things up there."

"No way," Jack said, still feeling unsteady.

"I thought I'd scared you off," Father Martin continued, "at least until the next morning when I heard noise in the tower again. I'm usually active long before daylight."

"Why don't we ever see you around, Father?" Patrick asked. "Do you teach at the college? Or did you come ba…, I mean, are you new here?"

"You might say I'm new, although we almost met the other night. When I saw you trying to hide in the bushes, I thought it best to keep moving and leave the formalities for another time."

"You scared the heck out of us," Jack said, trying to conceal his apprehension. "You looked like a spook."

"Well, we can't have students thinking a phantom is walking the grounds, so I stay away from the building and use the side roads."

"Do you keep mostly to yourself?" Patrick asked.

Father Martin nodded. "I go up to the bell room quite often to pray and admire the view. So, yes, I pretty much keep to myself, now that I'm retired and my superior assigned me to Saint Paul's. Perhaps I'll tell you more about it some other time."

"I'd love to go to the top of the tower," Jack said. He could feel the tension leave his shoulders and legs as the fear drained away, replaced by an unexpected sense of comfort. "Do you think we could join you next time, Father?"

"That might be arranged. But you don't need my help, do you?"

"We'd sure appreciate it," Patrick said. "Especially if you're in good with Father Joe. Jack and I would feel better with a priest for our guide."

"Well, how about Thursday evening, after lights out, for a tour? I don't believe you have a game on Friday. And if you boys wouldn't mind, I'd like to keep things confidential."

"Great," Patrick and Jack chimed in at the same time.

"By the way, did you boys find anything interesting in the storage room?"

"We found …." Jack started.

Patrick quickly interrupted. "Why do you ask, Father?"

"You both seem keen on exploring the place, so I hoped your detective work proved worth the risk."

Patrick studied Father McGrath's face. Despite the old priest's white hair and deep wrinkles, Patrick saw a spark in his eyes, as if he knew a sensational secret that no one else had yet discovered. He suspected Father Martin knew about the file and decided to put all their cards on the table.

"We actually found something quite interesting," Patrick said.

"May I ask what?"

"An old envelope that contained papers."

"I hope it made for informative reading."

"It did," Patrick said. "We aren't quite sure what to do next."

"Well, it's time to continue my walk now. Very nice chatting with you." Father Martin covered his head again with the large hood. "Until Thursday, gentlemen. Have a good night, and carry on."

"Good night, Father. See you Thursday," Jack said.

They watched the old priest make his way down the side road and slowly disappear into the darkness.

"What the hell, Patrick? That's the priest in the articles." Jack felt both baffled and relieved. "I don't get it. Why didn't he ask more questions about the memos?"

"My guess is he already knows everything. Most likely he even placed the envelope in the drawer."

"You mean he wanted us to discover Webb accused him of stealing. Why?"

"This may sound crazy to you. I got the feeling Father's reaching out to us for help."

"How? Like to reopen his case?"

"Or sending a clue to steer us in the right direction, if there is one."

"And what Father said before he left, 'carry on.' That's what the voice whispered the night I heard it in the corridor."

Patrick thought for a few seconds, mystified by Jack's revelation. "I'm not sure what to tell you. Maybe I'm right, or maybe he's just messing with us. We need to keep alert, and watch our backs."

"Alert for what?"

"I'll let you know when I see it. Right now, it's time to get inside."

CHAPTER 9

Jack awoke Tuesday morning to streams of sunlight bathing his room. He looked over at the clock on his desk. It read 7:15 am.

"No!" he shouted and jumped out of bed in a panic. Jack couldn't believe he'd slept right through the morning bell. It seemed impossible. Missing breakfast would result in detention, which also meant skipping soccer practice and riding the bench for the first half of the next game, or perhaps the entire 90 minutes.

As Jack grabbed the pair of pants hanging over the back of his chair, he noticed a gold sheet of paper with big bold black letters that someone had slipped under his door. He picked it up and began to read:

"GO BACK TO SLEEP! The Faculty has canceled all classes to hold a special Free Day. Breakfast will run from 8:30 to 9:30. All students should meet in the first-floor Recreation Hall at 9:45 to begin the day's activities."

Yes! Jack thought, both relieved and surprised. Dressed only in a white T-shirt and briefs, he peeked out his door but saw no one stirring on the corridor. *Guess it's true.*

Unable to go back to sleep, Jack worked on a physics assignment until 8:30 before wandering over to the refectory. Within minutes, Patrick, Jared, Jimmy, Tom, Ben, and Brian joined him at a table.

"Wonder what fun they have installed for us?" Jared said.

"How do you know it will be fun, Bonelli?" Brian asked.

"Unless they plan on throwing everyone off the roof, it's got to be more fun than Latin and Calculus," Jared replied.

"Or putting Tron in charge," Jack added. "In that case, solving derivatives might look pretty good."

It was no secret among the group that Jack had distrusted Tron since freshman year because of a failed prank, with Jack as the intended victim. Brian and two other frosh boys had asked Jack to come into one of their rooms, where minutes earlier another classmate had hidden in the closet. The trio immediately began to bad-mouth their concealed friend, hoping they could trick Jack into joining the attacks, at which point the boy would jump out of the closet and confront him. When Jack refused to say anything nasty or negative, the boy emerged from his hiding place. Frustrated with his failed attempt, Brian called Jack a "wuss," and the two exchanged heated words. The incident left things jagged between them, and, ever since, Jack viewed Tron only as a classmate, not a friend.

Dan drifted into the refectory at about 9:00 am. He plopped into the chair next to Tom, looking blurry-eyed and disheveled.

"Can you believe it? The only problem was waking up again in time to get here."

“Guess this shows how much we rely on bells to run our lives,” Patrick said. “If the electricity ever goes out, this place will be in chaos.”

“We’re like trained seals,” Dan agreed. “The bells tell us when to wake up, eat, go to class, and even pray. And I’ll never forget last April when the bell rang for Quiet Time at five thirty during a baseball game, and they made us quit playing even though we were trailing by only a run in the fifth inning. That was nuts.”

“When I first arrived last year it felt more like boot camp than high school,” Tom said. “Now, I’m used to it.”

“That’s what I call coo-coo,” Dan replied, twirling his right index finger in a circle while pointing it at his head. “I’ll never get used to that obscene wake-up bell that goes on forever. Talk about beyond annoying!”

By 9:45 am, 159 students and 12 faculty members filled the Recreation Hall. Father Joe, dressed in a white polo shirt, blue jeans and red sneakers, called for quiet and addressed the gathering.

“I hope everyone enjoyed the opportunity to sleep in. The purpose of today’s Free Day is to build camaraderie among the four classes while doing some good for the school and having fun. This morning, you’ll receive large garbage bags to take part in a campus-wide cleanup project. We also have gloves for those who want them. Our goal is to pick up at least five hundred pounds of trash, especially up toward the property entrance and down by the creek area. We’ll weigh the bags as you bring them to the front parking lot. A private donor has generously agreed to give Saint Paul’s ten dollars per pound toward the purchase of new athletic equipment, so every scrap helps.”

“I bet that donor runs a rock quarry,” Dan whispered to Jack, who chuckled.

"After lunch, we'll divide all students into two teams and hold a 'Capture the Flag' competition," Father Joe continued. "The faculty will serve as game monitors, and each participant will receive bags of flour to use as ammunition. Remember, gentlemen, the most important rule is to have fun, so let's make this a memorable day."

At 10:00 am, groups of boys and priests grabbed their heavy-duty bags and scattered to every corner of the St. Paul's campus to collect as much debris as possible. By noon, the swarm of eager workers had filled more than 100 bags with 540 pounds of trash.

The refectory resonated with tales of the hunt throughout lunch. The prize for the most eclectic discoveries went to the team of Ben, Tom, and Father Bucky Hall, who found a Chevy steering wheel, a suitcase filled with clothes, several empty oil cans, and a box of horseshoes along the northwest boundary where Highway 280 crossed over the property.

"I could hardly believe it," Tom told everyone sitting at his table. "People toss out everything but the kitchen sink from their cars. It's ridiculous."

The afternoon event began at 1:30 pm. The entire student body assembled in the courtyard, half wearing white T-shirts and half wearing dark colors. Each White Team member picked up baggies of white powder, while the Black Team took baggies filled with blue powder. Next, groups of 20 players from each team hoisted their respective banners – a pair of red, soccer corner flags on five-foot plastic poles borrowed from the gym – and set out for secret locations, hoping the 15-minute head start would allow them to establish well-protected headquarters.

Jack, Dan, and Ben led the White Team squad along the creek to a secluded stand of trees that could only be attacked from one side, giving the defenders a strategic advantage. The boys also hid trios of ambush parties among the brush, hoping to take any invaders by surprise.

Unbeknownst to the faculty, Dan kept a Daisy "Splotchmarker" paintball marker in his closet, hoping it would prove handy one day. The pistol fired encapsulated, oil-based pellets filled with liquid green goo. Having grown up on a ranch, Dan and his younger brothers not only helped their father mark roaming cattle with the paintballs, but they also had taken to running through the nearby orchard shooting at each other. As a result, Dan developed an accurate shot, and the time had finally arrived to put it to good use. Dressed in a red headband and camouflage pants, and packing a satchel filled with paintballs, he climbed one of the trees to a height beyond the range of even a well-thrown baggie and waited, a self-appointed sniper ready to pick off intruders without mercy.

In contrast, the Black Team planted their flag near the top of Maryknoll hill. Surrounded by 30 yards of open ground on all sides, the site provided its guardians with a 360-degree view of any White Team attack.

Once scouts had located their opponents' encampments, both teams drew battle plans. Patrick and Jimmy – who named themselves Black Team Generals – laid out a three-pronged scheme in an attempt to sneak up on the fortified White Team defenders at the creek. Their opposites, led by Jared and two other seniors, waited among the orchard and vines down the hillside. Relying on brute, overwhelming force, they had elected to attempt a "Round Top-type" assault used by the Confederates at the Battle of Gettysburg during the Civil War.

"If we amass a platoon of forty guys for repeated charges up the hill, it'll weaken their defenses enough to where we can overrun them," Jared strategized with his band of attackers. "Let's secure the flag and win the day."

Back at the creek, the three-man, white-shirted squads prepared to launch hit-and-run attacks as their unsuspecting rivals approached.

"Here they come, boys," Dan yelled from his lofty position in the tree. "No prisoners!"

The repeated skirmishes raged for an hour, with boys attacking, retreating, counter-attacking, and running around like wild men, laughing, shouting, and moaning when a baggie hit its mark. When participants' shirts became stained with powder, the faculty monitors led the "wounded" off to an aid station on the front lawn, where cases of soft drinks and candy bars awaited the fallen. This field hospital location also provided a premium viewing area to witness distant assaults on both the hill and creek base camps. As they sat or stood sipping sodas and eating chocolate bars, the boys eliminated from the action continued to cheer on their comrades still in the hunt.

Jared saw a chance to finish the hilltop fight following three failed assaults on the Black Team's flag, A big fan of the board game *Risk*, he knew superior numbers often won out. The attacks had reduced the Black Team defenders to less than ten, while Jared still commanded 15 boys.

"This will be the final rush," Jared told his troops. "Ten of us here will sacrifice ourselves with one-on-one kamikaze-style attacks, leaving five of you to grab the flag and end the battle. Spread out, and pick your target."

In the meantime, Tron and two other boys on the Black Team had hung back down at the creek bed, watching the White Team pick off their teammates one by one. Patrick and Jimmy's plan had failed to produce victory. When a pair of Black Team Generals fell to an ambush, Tron decided playing by the rules would get his side nowhere.

"Time for Plan B, guys," he said. The three boys peeled off their dark shirts, revealing spotless white T's.

"The only way to get through their defenses is to become spies," Tron told his brothers in arms. "Who said cheaters never prosper?"

A lull in the fighting provided the perfect opportunity.

"How we doing here, guys?" Tron asked as the three casually walked into the White Team's encampment, trying not to appear suspicious. "Jared has the situation under control on the hill, so he sent us down here to help."

Just as Tron was about to grab the flag, Dan fired two shots at his chest, turning the white shirt into a green-stained mess. Dan then pumped a round each at the other imposters, hitting one in the stomach and one in the back. Just for fun, he fired off a shot at Father Hall, who stood nearby monitoring the situation. Aiming for the knee area, Dan pulled the trigger as he lost his balance for a second, and the burst hit the priest squarely in the crotch. *"Oh, crap,"* Dan thought.

"Sorry, Padre," he yelled down. "My finger must have slipped." In a much lower voice that no one could hear, Dan added, "It's not as if you need it for anything important."

"Hey!" Tron shouted up. "What are you doing, bozo?"

"Who do you think you're foolin', 'lectron?" Dan said in his best hillbilly accent. "I could see you varmints change shirts 'bout thirty yards down the creek from up yonder here. We don't take kindly to stinkin' spies around these parts."

Jack and the others began to laugh. In response, Tron angrily shoved a White Team sophomore standing nearby to the ground.

"Up yours, you mother …."

"Stop acting like a jerk!" Jack shouted, drowning out Tron's words.

Ben grabbed Tron from behind and spun him around.

"Knock it off, Brian! Now! You want to get detention and miss games? I need my entire defense if we plan on reaching the playoffs this year."

Dan took aim once again and scored a direct hit on Tron's rear end.

"No, up yours, cheater," he called out.

"That's enough, all of you," Father Hall scolded in an usually loud and angry voice. "Show some sportsmanship, Mr. Weaver, or you'll be in detention for a week. As for you, Mr. Hannigan...." He looked down at his pants. "You really do take the cake. Get down from that tree, and give me the gun. NOW!"

As Jack helped the surprised but unscathed sophomore up from the ground, a whistle blew loudly three times in the distance.

"That signals the game is over," Father Hall explained in a much calmer tone, "meaning the White Team has been declared the winner of Capture the Flag."

Jack, Ben, and the others wearing unmarked white T-shirts let out a raucous cheer. Dan climbed down from his tree perch, offered a contrite, "I'm sorry, Father" as he handed the Splotchmarker to Hall, then shook hands with his teammates.

"Well done, guys," Jack said. "And great save, Danny boy. They almost got us."

"Time to head over to the front lawn, gentlemen," Father Hall said. "And by the way, Mr. Hannigan, impressive shooting, although it seems the quality of mercy is not one of your strengths."

By the time the group arrived at the meeting point, a large crowd of students and priests had formed on the grass.

"Good job, men, and well played," Father Joe told the gathering. "Although the Black Team defenders led by Mr. Keane and Mr. Hardin put up a spirited fight, the brilliance of General Bonelli carried the day."

A huge roar went up from the white-clad players while they shook hands and slapped each other on the back.

"I also heard a rumor that Mr. Hannigan helped save the battle for his White Team, so congratulations to him despite his unorthodox methods, and to each of you who joined the fray. I hope everyone had fun, and learned about teamwork and solving problems at the same time. Remember that dinner starts at 6:00 pm. Some of you need to get to practice. The rest are free to do whatever you like until then."

Before Dan and Brian could drift off with the other boys, Father Joe signaled for them to stay behind.

"Father Hall told me what happened," the priest said. "I'm not happy about your behavior. In honor of the day, it ends right here, right now. However, any future indiscretions of this kind will be turned over to Father Webb, who may not deal with you so gently. And Mr. Hannigan, when you next visit home, first stop by my room to pick up your paintball gun and don't ever bring it back on campus. Now both of you, go."

At the end of soccer practice, after the boys had showered and dressed, Patrick asked Coach Shumaker if he could address the team before they headed off to dinner.

"Your captain has something to say, so pay attention," the Coach instructed.

"I'll keep this short: we're a team, so whatever one of us does affects the others," the big center back asserted. "One key strength that allows us to compete with larger schools is our tightness as a group, a unity that puts the team above individual glory or hubris. We cannot afford a me-first attitude from anyone. We all know none of us is perfect. Before you do anything that will hurt this team and everyone on it, listen to your inner voice that speaks to each of us every day. It will help you maintain control."

"Thanks, Patrick," Coach Shumaker said. "And just so we're clear, men, I agree with every word your captain and leader just said. Think before you act. Understand that actions have consequences. And stay away from dumb choices. All of you!"

As the team began leaving the locker room, Dan walked up to Patrick and Jack with a chastened look on his face.

"I hear you, man," Dan said. "I'll think twice next time before doing something stupid like today, even though my history with Jack here on late night excursions to the kitchen might suggest otherwise."

The sound of a bell echoed in the distance, loud enough to penetrate the gym's concrete walls.

"See, a ringing endorsement for my speech," Patrick joked. "We better join the adoring masses in the refectory before they miss us."

That evening, while Jack sat in Patrick's desk chair taking it easy and his friend rested on his bed thumbing through a sports magazine, the discussion of the day's events turned to Dan and Brian.

"You should have seen Bucky's face," Jack said. "What a great shot by Dan."

"He's lucky Hall only yelled at him. From the sounds of it, Brian was the real problem. They both got off easy."

"Why do you stick up for that frickin' bananahead, and always give him a break? Tron doesn't deserve it."

"Because he answered the call, just like us. He's here and has been since the day we arrived. Brian's part of the order, one of our brothers. Unlike a lot of guys who've come and gone, he's stuck it out and lived what we've lived. And we both know how hard Brian competes on the field. Don't you think that's worth a little loyalty?"

"Maybe, but the guy acts like such a first-class fart."

"Ever wonder or ask why, Hazy? I found out some things about Brian's past that aren't pretty. His father was an abusive drunk who abandoned the family when Brian was five, so he grew up dirt poor in a tough Oakland neighborhood. The kind of place where drive-by shootings occurred. His mother and aunt raised him. Brian never had a Dad in his life, not like you and me. He made his way here through Webb, who got to know the family from saying Mass in their parish on weekends and teaching in their elementary school some years back. So, yeah, I do cut Brian some slack. But it's got nothing to do with deserve."

"It doesn't give him the right to take it out on us."

"True. I think it's good that you call Brian on his bad behavior when he gets out of line."

"I'll give him bad behavior," Jack said, shaking his head in exasperation. "I just wish... aw, who cares. The spots on that leopard will never change."

Jack looked down at the floor and thought for a second. "I have to ask, Patrick: what about us? Taking risks sneaking out at night and hanging with Father Martin. Aren't we doing stuff that could hurt the team?"

"You're right, it could. Try to understand that I'm listening to my inner voice, and it's telling me we're doing the right thing."

"I hope so,"

"Now that we've settled that, how about we head down to the kitchen for a Twinkie?"

"How about I toss your magazine out the window and watch it float down four stories into a bush?"

“Ah, just like Shakespeare says, ‘My words fly up, my thoughts remain below: Words without thoughts never to heaven go.’ Enough about Brian and getting in trouble. Time to get to chapel and pray for real.”

Jack shook his head. “Sometimes I have no idea what you’re talking about, and I doubt Shakespeare would either.”

“In that case, you should pray for understanding tonight during night prayers. And I’ll work on clarity.”

Chapter 10

Having worked late into the night of the busy Free Day, Father Joe decided to take a stroll down the long, dark junior corridor before heading to bed. With the help of a small flashlight, he read his divine office, or "Breviary," while he walked. Father Joe loved this tranquil time when the entire school turned silent. Only the sound of his soft-soled footsteps on the hard floor broke the quiet as he prayed the psalms, Scripture readings, and blessings required by the Roman Church.

Turning around at the end of the corridor, Father Joe slowly began to make his way back toward his room. To his surprise, he heard another set of footsteps and stopped to listen. A student entered the corridor from the far stairwell and took several strides before disappearing around the corner and pushing through the swinging doors that led onto the senior floor. Father Joe caught enough of a glimpse to recognize the boy: Brian Weaver.

Awfully late to be up, Father Joe thought. *I'll have to remember to say something to him, and the rest of the seniors. Even fourth-year men need to understand they aren't above the rules.*

Feeling drowsy, Father Joe returned to his suite and went to bed. A few minutes later, the swinging doors opened again, and Patrick, dressed in a warm coat and carrying a pair of binoculars, glided silently down the corridor. He walked several paces past his door and stopped near Brian's room on the opposite side of the hall, listening for any sound. Hearing nothing, Patrick went to his room, stretched out on top of his covers without getting undressed, and fell asleep.

Two nights later, after lights out, Jack and Patrick snuck down to Father Martin's room for their scheduled meeting. Before they could knock, the priest opened the door and signaled for them to enter.

"Have a seat, gentlemen," he said, shutting the door with his left hand while he waved his right toward a pair of overstuffed, brown leather recliners. "I'll be ready in a few minutes."

Jack noticed the carpet felt extra thick under his feet and liked how the amber glow from the floor and desk lamps gave the room a warm, welcoming, comfortable feel. Both boys stared at the large bookshelves that covered the wall behind Father Martin's desk. Stacks of board games that included *Dogfight, Broadside, Hit the Beach, Monopoly, Life,* and *Clue* filled one shelf, while a hockey game where the metal players could be moved up and down the "ice" using levers sat on another. An impressive array of pristine baseball cards preserved in glass displays drew Patrick's interest, especially those of the Yankees and Giants, his favorite teams. Neither boy spoke as they surveyed the collections.

"I'm back," said Father Martin, emerging from his bedroom wearing a jacket. "Shall we go?"

The three quietly left his room and unlocked the access door to the tower. A pair of flashlights guided their journey up the long flight of stairs. When they reached the top, Father Martin stepped up through a square, unobstructed opening into the empty belfry, followed by Jack and Patrick. Three folding wooden chairs sat on the concrete floor.

“What a great view,” Jack said, looking out toward the sea of city lights.

“Not to mention VIP seating,” Patrick added. “Nice perch, Padre.”

“I thought no one could get up here,” Jack said. “We’d heard the entrance was boarded up.”

“You do need to keep your voices down, boys,” Father Martin warned. “With these large portals on each side of the tower, sound carries, and someone down below could hear if you get too loud.”

Patrick nodded. “Wouldn’t want to alarm the powers that be.”

Jack moved to the edge and peered down into the courtyard toward the wall of windows on the school’s west wing. “Look, a few freshman still have their lights on. Let’s slip a note under their doors before first bell that demands they report to the Dean’s office. That ought to teach them to do a better job of hiding the light if they plan to study late.”

Patrick walked over to take a look. “Such amateurs. We can handwrite, ‘Not to worry…beatings don’t begin until after breakfast.’ That ought to help ease their minds.”

“And you’re both professionals when it comes to this sort of thing?” Father Martin asked.

“Not bad, if I do say it myself,” Jack said. “Upperclassmen know you need to use heavy paper to black out the door windows, and also electrical tape to keep the window shades flat, so no light escapes around the edges.”

Father Martin smiled. “Students did the same thing when I taught here years ago, although weekly room inspections required extra creativity on their part to keep from getting caught. In fact, the boys nicknamed me 'The Stalker' because I liked to roam the halls and grounds at night, even in those days."

"Some guys sit in their closets after lights out and study using a flashlight before big tests," Jack said. "Compared to the old days, we've got it pretty good in a lot of ways."

"Did you know that less than fifteen years ago all the boys were still required to wear vestiges of the Medieval Church?" Father Martin asked. "They donned black cassocks on special occasions, and also attended Saturday morning classes because no one was allowed to go home on weekends."

"I heard everyone had to wear ties, dress shirts, and slacks only a couple of years before our class arrived," Jack said. "Now, we get to walk around in jeans and tennis shoes."

"Except for one sacred place," Patrick pointed out. "The faculty still protects the sanctity of the chapel like a bear defending its den."

In fact, chapel rules were simple – no jeans, no jerseys, no shorts, and always act respectfully. Any improperly dressed student who tried to enter for Mass or night prayers could count on being cut out of the herd and sent to his room to change clothes. Or even find himself in detention the next day.

"What happened if you caught a guy studying late back then, Father?" Jack asked.

"Staying up after lights out could mean expulsion, although I tried to show mercy whenever I could."

"It's not exactly applauded even today," Patrick said. "Let's give our current crop of little bananaheads credit for hitting the books. Classes here aren't easy for most guys, at least not like for Jack."

Jack waved his hand, brushing away Patrick's comment.

"If you'd spend less time trying to balance yourself on the back legs of your desk chair, and more time translating Latin or solving math problems, you'd probably be doing better than anyone."

Father Martin raised an eyebrow. "That's how you use your study time, Mr. Keane?"

"A couple of nights ago, Father, I go ask Patrick about a Latin word, and he has his arms spread out wide like this, and his chair's sitting on only two legs. When I returned an hour later, he was in the same position. He'd spent the entire time balancing himself in the chair."

"Hey, it's hard work to keep it steady for that long," Patrick said. "Latin could wait."

"I'd call it a pretty amazing feat," Jack confirmed. "I tried it with my chair. Darn near impossible. The problem is I ended up doing your share of our team's homework. So less acrobatics, and more Cicero or Virgil, would be appreciated."

"Let's sit down, Father," Patrick said. "That was a lot of steps, even for The Stalker."

"First, let me show you both something." Father Martin shined his flashlight beam on the bell room ceiling, revealing a stunning, multi-colored, tile mosaic. "Do you know what this is?"

Patrick and Jack studied the 12-foot by 15-foot depiction carefully.

"It's Saint Paul," Patrick answered. "This shows his conversion on the road to Damascus. What an incredible work of art."

"That's amazing," Jack said. "I'll bet almost no one in the entire school even knows it exists."

"Sadly, you're correct, Jack…but at least you boys do," Father Martin said with a wink. "Always remember that Paul encountered the resurrected Christ, a miraculous event that revealed the truth and changed everything about his life."

The priest removed a small black object from his jacket pocket. He held it high over everyone's heads, pointed it toward the mosaic, clicked a button, and returned it to his pocket.

"One day, this reminder may help bring enlightenment too," Father Martin said.

"No flash?" Jack wondered out loud.

"No, it's a new type of instrument. And now we can sit down and enjoy the view."

The three gazed over the valley below, basking in the crisp night air, and enjoying the sparkling scene in silence.

"Wouldn't it be great to jump out of this tower and fly, like an angel, totally free, soaring above the world?" Jack finally said.

"One problem, Hazy. I think you have to die first to become an angel, right?"

"The key for us all is to learn to soar while we're alive," Father Martin tutored. "Very few people ever do."

"Too bad," Jack said. "This may sound ironic, but being high above everything grounds me to what really matters, and who made all this possible."

Father Martin smiled. "Then there's hope for you yet. Of course, our own Saint Paul had some wonderful things to say about angels that you might want to study sometime."

"Father, I hope you don't mind me asking something personal," Patrick said. "Why were you accused of embezzlement and forced to leave Saint Paul's?"

Father Martin lifted his head and gazed at the mosaic. Both boys detected sadness in his eyes.

"As treasurer, I saw that some poor families couldn't afford to send their sons to the seminary. Not all the dioceses had programs to pay their way, so I shifted funds around without permission to cover their costs. Father Webb served as vice president back then, and we worked together to secure investments. He was an ambitious man who seemed to favor control and power; you might say more politician than priest. Even now, I hear that he expects to be appointed Rector of Saint Paul's when Father King retires at the end of the school year."

"In that case, thank goodness we're graduating," Jack said.

"And then what, Father?"

"When an investment went bad and money got tight, my arrangement with the families came to light. Although no funds were embezzled, Father Webb accused me of financial misconduct. Father King, whom I always found to be a good man, worried the appearance of impropriety could harm the school. He asked that we deal with it internally. Unfortunately, an anonymous source leaked the story to the newspaper. As you can imagine, the Archbishop demanded immediate action. I lost my teaching position and was sent back East in disgrace to a home for elderly priests."

"Sounds like they made you the scapegoat for bad financial decisions," Patrick said. "As we like to say, 'It's always some damn thing.'"

"I don't proclaim complete innocence. I've prayed for forgiveness. Time will tell whether or not those prayers are answered."

"By the Sulpicians allowing you to teach again?" Jack asked.

"That time has passed. Christ's parable of the fig tree teaches that the Lord offers his children second chances, and provides them with renewed purpose. Perhaps mine includes serving as amateur astronomer to help Mr. Keane unmask the heavens."

"I sure would enjoy the company," Patrick said. "Not everyone shares my passion for the night sky."

"I have to tell you, Father, I feel the same way about Dean Webb, how you described him," Jack said. "It's like he's painted a target on my back."

"If you're concerned, why did you come tonight?"

Jack crinkled his forehead and made a funny face.

"Well, 'cuz I didn't want to miss seeing what it's like way up top. Neither of us did."

"You made us an offer we couldn't refuse, Father," Patrick said.

The old priest smiled. "In that case, Jack, do you know Father Webb's motives?"

Jack shook his head slowly. "I really can't say. We figure he got rid of all the obvious problem guys, and we're what's left."

"From my experience, Father Webb always has a reason for what he does. I suggest you think about it."

The three fell silent, listening to the sounds of the night. A soft breeze drifted through the bell room, bringing with it a slight scent that reminded Jack of the air in the storage room with the tallboy.

"Father, I was wondering about something else," he said. "Why was that file in the drawer waiting for us to find it?"

"Why do you boys think it was there?"

"I sense someone placed the file there as a clue," Patrick said. "Perhaps you?"

Father Martin didn't respond.

"A clue to what?" Jack asked.

"To open our eyes to a hidden truth," Patrick said. "To discover something that might otherwise stay concealed."

"You lost me. Discover what?"

"A revelation that will come by looking carefully at the man behind the curtain," Patrick said. "Just like in Oz, things may not always be as they seem, even in these hallowed halls. It's up to us to stay vigilant."

"Well spoken, my boy."

Jack looked closely at Father Martin. The tone of his voice gave away his secret.

"Can you tell us what the envelope will lead to, Father?"

"It's uncertain what you'll discover. That depends on what you choose to see. Many prefer to remain blind to the truth. Unfortunately, boys, far too often you'll run into 'Do as I say, not as I do' hypocrisy in others. Understand that one bad apple can stain others in the same bunch. Seeing and accepting this first hand is often a hard pill to swallow."

"I don't understand. Why don't you go to Father King or Father Joe if a problem exists?"

Father Martin sighed deeply. "Good question, Jack. There's something you boys need to know. My penance – or as I prefer to say, reconciliation – requires that I interact as little as possible with the faculty or students during my stay at Saint Paul's, and keep to myself. To most, I'm not even here, a mere shadow."

"That sounds rough, being alone all the time," Patrick said. "You can count on us to not say a word."

"We won't tell anyone," Jack added.

"Well, gentlemen, I think it's time we head back down. You two need to get some sleep."

"Thank you, Father, for bringing us up here," Patrick said warmly. "If your reconciliation will allow it, Jack and I would like to invite you to join us toward the end of the month to watch a pretty good meteor shower from up on the hill, weather permitting."

"I'm glad you boys could come tonight. I've enjoyed spending this time with you. And yes, I accept your invitation, weather permitting."

When the three reached the door leading out to the fourth-floor corridor, Jack opened it with great care and peered down the empty hall.

"Good to go," he whispered. "See you soon, Father. By the way, even though it's a bit of a climb to the top of the Grinder, we'll make sure you reach it."

"I wouldn't miss it. Good night, boys, and carry on."

*****

When soccer practice ended the next afternoon, Patrick and Jack stayed late to work on penalty kicks, with each taking five attempts while the other played goalkeeper. Neither missed, so the bet of that evening's Mystery remained unclaimed.

"Lucky that Ben plays goalie and not us," Patrick said as they walked off the field alone carrying soccer balls under their arms. "We need to come up with another game that one of us can win."

"For sure," Jack said. "Speaking of games, did you get a load of Father Martin's shelves last night?"

"Yeah, quite the vintage collection."

"More like an unreal collection. He even had a photo of a dog with the words 'Thank you for everything,' on the frame above the picture, and 'I had a wonderful time' below it. The dog looked exactly like Sparky, my family's white pit bull and Dalmatian mix who died four years ago. Don't you think that's bizarre?"

"He also had three of my favorite board games as a kid," Patrick said. "Ones you just don't see around anymore. It's like he knew how to make us feel at home. And you're right, the photo of the Sparky look-alike is beyond strange."

"Why would he have all that stuff?"

Patrick gave Jack a skeptical look. "You're barking up the wrong tree, Hazy. We've spent time with Father Martin and gotten to know him a little. Still, I agree it was surprising to see all those old games and baseball cards."

"But cool at the same time," Jack admitted. "Did you catch that Mickey Mantle rookie card, and the entire Giants team from the 1962 World Series? In mint condition, too."

"Let's ask about the stuff next time we see him. Maybe Father Martin's hobby is collecting memorabilia. After all, we know he's into puzzles and mysteries."

Chapter 11

St. Paul's annual Visiting Day for parents kicked off with Sunday Mass in the large college chapel at 10:30 am, followed by lunch at noon. Patrick's father wanted to see the awesome "senior year" scenery from the window in his son's room, so they took the elevator – usually off limits to students – to the fourth floor.

"The Church may not pay priests much but it certainly provides a million-dollar view," John Keane said.

"Not too bad, especially with the city lights at night. Lunch starts soon. We should head down to the refectory."

Mr. Keane reached over and picked up a small framed photo of his deceased wife that Patrick kept on the desk.

"Son, do you mind if we take your mom with us to lunch? I like to keep her close by."

Patrick grew silent. His intense blue eyes moistened.

"Sorry…I can't, Dad. It still hurts my heart. And the guys…."

John Keane put a loving hand on his son's shoulder. "I understand. We'll spend a few minutes more with her here, just the three of us. She always loved that."

Patrick nodded. He drew in a deep breath. The pain eased as he regained control of his emotions.

"The good news is that they usually go all out in the food department when parents visit."

"Maybe I should stop by more often," Mr. Keane said with a wink. "After we eat, let's take a stroll around the grounds. You're fortunate to live on such a beautiful campus with all the oaks, big leaf maples, and eucalyptus. And who couldn't love the rolling hills? The Archbishop did well when he found this piece of heaven."

"Sounds like a plan, Dad."

By late afternoon, most parents had said goodbye to their sons and left campus. After giving his father an affectionate farewell hug in the parking lot and watching him drive away, Patrick bounded upstairs to the senior corridor, eager to attack a challenging math problem before heading off to dinner. Striding down the hall, he heard what sounded like soft sobs coming from behind a slightly open door. Patrick knocked once and entered. Tom sat on the edge of the wide wooden window sill. He quickly wiped his eyes, but Patrick could see the wet streaks.

"Hey, Tommy. What's wrong, bud?"

Tom didn't look up.

"Nothing. I'm fine."

Patrick thought for a few moments, trying to understand. It struck him. Tom had been watching other students say goodbye to their families from his window.

"Tough day for you, with all the parents on campus?"

Tom took a breath. He finally nodded. "I know, I'm being dumb. It just knocked me for a loop for some reason. Last year, Father Joe took a few of us to a 49ers football game that Sunday, so I wasn't around. This time..." He put a hand to his eyes, trying hard not to let more tears fall. "How can I miss something I never had?"

"It's not dumb at all," Patrick said in a gentle voice. "And if it helps any, I understand what you're feeling. My freshman year, when I saw all the mothers visiting the school and everyone spending the day with their families, it hurt not having my mom around. With my dad here, it made me miss her even more."

"Sounds like you were close with your mom."

"That's right."

Tom lifted his head and looked Patrick in the eye. "I never really knew mine. She was single and had a serious drug problem, so the state placed me in foster care. I ended up shuffled around from one home to the next. Your family loved and wanted you. I felt like a nuisance."

"Do you remember anything about her?"

"Just this song she used to sing, '*You Are My Sunshine.*' Funny that one of the lines says, '*Please don't take my sunshine away.*' But they did."

"Can I ask you a question?" Patrick asked.

"Sure."

"Why did you decide to come to school here in your junior year?"

"Well, I suppose mostly because of a parish priest named Father Jesse. No matter where I ended up, he'd check on me to make sure I was okay. Father Jesse was the one constant I could count on. He'd bring me small toys when I was a kid, take me out for ice cream, that kind of regular stuff. Without him, I'm not sure I'd be anywhere right now." Tom's throat tightened. "So I promised myself I'd take a shot at studying for the priesthood if the opportunity came along."

"Jack, Jared, Dan, all the guys, we're darn happy you're part of our class and the team."

"Thanks. I'm glad I made it here too. Most guys think of Saint Paul's as just a school. To me, it's become home, the first place I've felt grounded, and like I belonged, in a long time."

"Did the foster families treat you okay?"

"They were decent people for the most part and did their best. Now, I wish I could find out what happened to my mom. I even thought about trying to contact her somehow. I'm ready."

"Then that's what you should do. It may not be easy."

"Probably not. Even if it's a pipe dream, I'd like a chance at the kind of connection you have with your dad, and had with your mom."

Patrick realized Tom had seen him walking arm-in-arm with his big, burly father, and their warm parting.

"I'm lucky," Patrick said. "He's a great dad who has always been there for me. And I still have that kind of connection with my mom, just in a different way now. So, what are you going to do?"

"I'll ask Father Joe, and hear what he has to say."

"Good. It's best to talk these things out, kick 'em around a bit, and see what feels right." Patrick paused. "I can tell you this: do not have regrets – and I mean none – with the people you love. It's important to know deep inside that if you lost someone special tomorrow, you could live with it. Make sure you tell them what's in your heart. It's pointless to beat yourself up after it's too late. Say it now."

"Sometimes it's hard to tell others how you feel."

"We all need to get over that," Patrick said. "You doing better now?"

"Yes, thanks. If you don't mind me asking, why are you here?"

"Some of us have been at Saint Paul's so long it's like we've become part of the furniture. I'm still here because Mom's dream was for me to become a priest, and I'd like a career that serves God in some way. I thought I'd try the seminary to see how it suits me. So far it has."

Tom nodded approval. "Thanks again, Patrick, for stopping in. I do feel better. See you at dinner."

Patrick continued down the hall to his room and closed the door. He stood motionless, staring out the window, his eyes fixed on a distant point. Andy Williams' voice flowed softly from the clock-radio on the desk.

"Can't get used to losing you, no matter what I try to do...."

Tom's confession had stirred deep emotions. Patrick thought of his mother, and the final time they were together in the hospital.

"Gonna live my whole life through, loving you."

Five years had passed since her death, but Patrick remembered every moment and word like it was yesterday.

"You've always been my special gift from heaven," Brigit Keane had told her only son. "Whether God chooses you to serve Him as a bishop, a doctor, an athlete, or in another way, you'll be an extraordinary man one

day, and make your father and me proud. I love you, my sweet, sweet angel."

She kissed his cheek. Patrick looked into his mother's tired eyes. An intense emotional pain gripped his entire body.

"I'm going to miss you so much, Mom."

Patrick could barely speak. His throat seized, and his voice choked with tears. He knew this was the last time he'd ever see the woman he loved more than anything in the world. Losing her felt so final, so awful. What if heaven didn't exist and this was the end? Forever. The pain grew unspeakable. Things would never be the same.

Mrs. Keane gently took her young son's hand to help Patrick compose himself.

"You need to promise me one thing – don't lose your faith over this. It's too important." She paused and squeezed his fingers tighter. "I'll miss you more than you could ever know. Until we're together again, stay strong for Dad, and hold your faith close."

Patrick reflected on those words for weeks following his mother's death. He walked around numb and light-headed, almost in a dream state, as if the world no longer existed.

That same surreal feeling started to roll over him.

'Cause no one else could take your place,

Guess that I am just a hopeless case.

Patrick relived how his father had gently lifted his mother from her bed that same evening and held her close as they swayed to the music in their heads for one last dance. Even today, Patrick thought it was the most loving and tragic thing he'd ever witnessed.

Can't get used to losin' you, no matter what I try to do,

Gonna live my whole life through, loving you."

The 6:00 o'clock dinner bell rang. Patrick snapped back to the present, like awakening from a trance. His heart ached. He walked over to the sink, turned on the faucet, and bathed his face in cold water. The pain subsided. He left his room and hurried downstairs toward the refectory.

Jack caught him at the bottom of the brick steps heading out into the courtyard. He immediately sensed a strange heaviness in his friend.

"You okay?" Jack asked.

"Even better. I hope the kitchen serves Baked Alaska tonight for Mystery."

Jack grinned, amused at the improbable suggestion.

"I wish we all had your unwavering optimism. But I wouldn't count on anything from Alaska, baked or not."

"We've got to keep the faith," Patrick said, opening the dining hall door for Jack. "You never know, one day it might pay off."

CHAPTER 12

With the fall Senior Night talent show fast approaching, Jack needed to complete his costume for one of the evening's main skits. At the recommendation of Father Quinn, the show's faculty adviser, Jack decided to look in the well-stocked storage space located off the sacristy, where the school kept the wardrobe and pieces of stage sets used in its annual play. Jack knew school rules prohibited students from entering the room without permission but figured Father Quinn's verbal consent would do the trick.

After physics class ended, Jack headed to the storage room to begin his search. He'd combed about halfway through a large rack of coats, old cassocks, uniforms, and other clothing when a voice interrupted his search.

"What are you doing here, Mr. Hayes?"

Jack turned to see Father Webb standing in the doorway.

"Hi, Father. I'm just checking out costume stuff for the talent show."

"Grab your books and come with me."

"But…."

"Now, Mr. Hayes."

Jack followed Father Webb along the stone tiles of the arcade to an empty classroom. The priest opened the door and pointed to one of the 30 empty desks.

"Take a seat, Mr. Hayes. I'll be back at five thirty. You're in detention until then."

"I have soccer practice," Jack protested.

"I don't care. You know better than to sneak around in the sacristy storeroom. It's off limits."

Jack glared with cold, hard eyes. "I wasn't sneaking around, Father. I needed to find something to wear for Senior Night. You can ask Father Quinn. He told me where to look."

"I will. For the time being, you'll sit here and do homework until I return."

"You're not being reasonable. I didn't do anything wrong."

"You risk overstating your case, Mr. Hayes. You wouldn't want to miss more practices and games, would you? Don't make things worse for yourself."

Jack sighed and sat down, understanding the Dean's threat. He'd lost the argument and didn't want to add to his detention. Jack watched Father Webb leave the room. *What a complete idiot,* he thought. *How did they ever let that guy become a priest? One day I'd love to kick his butt.*

Jack worried that missing practice would cause Coach Shumaker to bench him for the next day's game. Even worse, he grew anxious that some teammates might feel he let them down. Jack brooded for a while. He finally opened one of his books and began reading.

"Might as well make the best of this crap and get something done," Jack said out loud.

More than two hours later, Father Webb entered the study hall just as the bell rang to begin Quiet Time. Jack still sat alone, working on a physics assignment. No one else had received detention that day.

"You're free to leave, Mr. Hayes. In the future, watch where you go and who you associate with because others may drag you down with them."

"How is that fair, Father?" Jack said in a challenging tone. "I hang out with some of the best guys in this school. If anything, they make me better."

"Just don't let this happen again. Now go."

Jack picked up his textbooks and left the hall.

At dinner, Patrick greeted Jack at their table with a slight nod. He waited for the nightly reading to end before speaking.

"The guys heard about what happened with Webb. Totally bogus. Coach was ticked off at first. I saw Father Joe and Father Quinn talking to him in the gym. I think that helped."

"What about pine time?" Jack asked.

"Hard to imagine Coach would sit his top scorer over a bad rap. Word is Coach plans on meeting with Webb."

Jack fidgeted in his chair. "That might only make things worse."

"Maybe for Webb," Patrick said as his voice rose in anger. "Coach can be tough when he wants to be. What Spider did was garbage."

"How he happened to come by the sacristy just at that time was either bad luck or Webb was out hunting again. At least I found a good costume for Senior Night before he took me to jail."

The talent show took place in the first-floor Recreation Hall on a Wednesday evening. Workers had set up a raised stage and 200 chairs to provide extra seating in case staff members and lay teachers also wished to attend. The two-hour event featured the usual fare of student bands, off-beat comedy routines, and other silliness. Dan drew loud applause for his over-the-top impression of the Rolling Stone's Mick Jagger, dressed as a giant pink bunny, singing *Street Fighting Man*. Nevertheless, a skit about the faculty performed by the senior soccer players stole the show.

"We'll see if they can take a joke, or if we get kicked to the curb," Jimmy summed up during final rehearsal. "I hear reform schools are lovely this time of year."

"I thought I wouldn't be doing this kind of dumb stuff by the time I turned seventeen," Jared mused.

"Better try shooting for eighteen," Patrick said. "That way at least you have some wiggle room."

The skit opened with seven "faculty members" – played by Patrick, Jared, Ben, Jack, Tom, Brian, and Jimmy– sitting in a semi-circle discussing what to do about the infamous Twinkie bandits who stole from the kitchen at night. To make the characters instantly recognizable, Patrick "the Warden" wore an orange prison jumpsuit open at the neck; Jared "Fang" held a huge toothbrush; Ben "Bucky" carried a stuffed toy beaver; Jack "Smokey" wore a Smokey the Bear hat, Highway Patrol sunglasses and giant red sneakers; Tom "Pete" pretended to play a bright blue electric guitar with the word "WHO" stenciled in black on the back; Brian "Spider" had eight legs and sat curled in a web; and Jimmy "Frenchie" donned a beret and waved a small white flag. All seven boys wore black clerical shirts and white Roman collars they'd borrowed from several different priests.

Jimmy stood up first and addressed the crowd. "Oh, mon Pere and Perriers, zee Tweenkies are meeesing from zee keetchen! We cannot allow zees kind of beehavior, and surrender eez not an option!" he said in his best French accent while waving his white flag. "If onlee zee scareee Mother Superior and Leettle Seesters were here to handle theeze creeminals. Oh, Mon Dieu!"

"After brushing up on the facts, I say let the kids stay – they all got great teeth, I tell ya," Jared, imitating Fang, enthused. "Have you seen those choppers? They must have fifty or sixty sparklers each. They're so bright, just think of the electricity we can save."

"Well, if that doesn't take the Hostess cake: I'd much prefer to discuss the school's dental plan," Ben as Bucky protested. "We need to put more teeth into it. Our plan simply has no bite, dam it, and it's been a gnawing problem."

"It's all one big Mystery to me," declared Patrick "the Warden" in his best Jimmy Durante voice. "Plus all this talk is making me hungry. What say we raid the kitchen, fellas? Twinkies for everyone. Ha-cha-chachacha."

Pretending to be outraged, Jack jumped up from his chair wearing the Smokey the Bear/police disguise.

"Have mercy!" he shouted like an evangelist. "Let the accused plead insanity because they were crazy about that golden sponge cake with creamy filling. Remember, gentlemen, only you can prevent Wildfires and Child Priors."

"Do you have anything to say, Father Pete?" Patrick "the Warden" asked.

"WHO?" Tom as "Pete" yelled out.

"You!" Patrick said.

"You WHO?" Tom answered.

"Did you want to tell us WHO to blame?"

"Yes, It's My Generation," Tom cried out, raising his guitar high in the air. "And We're Not Going To Take It."

"Forget it," Patrick said, slapping his forehead hard with his hand. "How about you, Father Webb?"

Brian "Spider," who the entire time had been pretending to watch flies circling his head, slowly slid out of his chair onto all fours and crawled to the edge of the stage, his eight legs dangling in all directions.

"I say we can catch more flies with Twinkies than honey," he hissed. "My trap worked perfectly. Let's see them spin their way out of this mess. As we all know, oh what a tangled web we weave when we steal Twinkies by the sleeve."

Throughout the routine, the audience howled and yelled catcalls. At one point, Jack surveyed a row of priests standing near the back of the hall. He was relieved to see Father King, Father Volk, and Father Joe enjoying the show as much as anyone.

Just as "Spider" finished talking, Dan rushed onto the stage from behind the curtain dressed as a big fat Twinkie. He wore a black Lone Ranger–style mask over his eyes and carried two spray cans of whipped cream.

"The boys are innocent I tell you," Dan shouted. "WHO could resist my sweet filling?" He unleashed a spray of whipped cream at Tom, who collapsed on the stage. "And you, crazy legs, stick to this."

He pointed both cans and covered Brian's head in a pile of creamy fluff.

"I'm melting!" Brian screamed as he lowered himself flat on the floor.

One by one Dan overwhelmed each "priest" with the white goo until only Patrick "the Warden" stood untouched.

"Looks like it's just you and me left, Padre," Dan said. "Read my high-calorie ingredients and weep. What have you got to say for yourself?"

"I say it's time for dessert," Patrick answered. "Come on, Fang and Bucky, put your dentures to work and give him the chewing out he deserves."

The boys rushed Dan and tried to knock him to the stage floor. His pumped up costume proved so resilient that both Jared and Ben bounced off him at first, which drew more laughs, until at last Dan finally tipped over and rolled onto his back.

"Just like our show," Patrick said to the crowd, "this half-baked Mystery is done for!"

The stage went dark, and the audience broke into loud applause along with hoots from the rest of the senior class. When the lights came back on, the eight performers stood in a line and grasped hands as they took their bows. Students started chanting, "Twinkie! Twinkie! Twinkie!" Answering the call, Dan jumped down and sprayed the front row with several bursts, then quickly sprang back up and disappeared behind the curtain before anyone could grab him. The skit marked the evening's grand conclusion.

Backstage, the boys wiped away whipped cream while Brian and Dan changed out of their cumbersome costumes.

"If we did ourselves in, it's been nice knowing you boys," Jared said.

"Don't worry, I saw the Warden laughing harder than anyone," Jack assured. "Looks like we pulled it off."

"I think you mean we somehow managed to squeeze by, so to speak," Patrick said with a huge smile. "At least for tonight, the cream literally did rise to the top."

Chapter 13

On a cloudy Saturday morning, the day after St. Paul's soccer team had defeated powerhouse Central Catholic High School by a narrow 2-1 score, Patrick and Jack borrowed a House car and drove four miles to the nearby senior assisted-living center in Mountain View. Patrick had chosen to visit the elderly twice a month for his senior year community service project and asked Jack to tag along.

"I think you're going to like this, Hazy," Patrick said. "My girl Millie is a real pistol. She retired about fifteen years ago from the County Social Services Agency. Millie specialized in adoptions and child protective services, and now she has sort of adopted me as her surrogate grandson. She's a crack-up and always makes me laugh."

They entered through the automatic sliding glass door and headed down the well-lit corridor to the right. A tall, middle-aged black nurse named Agnes greeted them with a big smile at the check-in station.

"She's waiting for you," Agnes said. "Millie always perks up on the days when you visit. Just this morning she was telling everyone her boyfriend was coming to see her. She even asked to wear her new pink nightgown and robe just for you. I swear that woman has more life in her than someone half her age."

"Hi, Millie," Patrick said, stepping through the open doorway to her private room. He walked to the bedside, leaned over and gave the old woman a warm hug. "You're looking exceptionally lovely today. And I've brought you another visitor. This is my good friend, Jack."

"Ah, yes, the one who scores the goals," Millie said, sitting up taller in her bed.

Jack turned to Patrick with a look of surprise.

"You don't think we talk?" Millie said, seeing Jack's expression. "Patrick and I are confidants, aren't we dear?" She took Patrick's hand in her own and smiled as she gazed up at him with loving eyes.

"Nice to meet you, Ma'am. Patrick's told me about you too."

"Call me Millie. By the way, both you boys are way too handsome to become priests. Does everyone over at that seminary clean up as well as you two?"

"We're the cream of the crop, Millie," Patrick said as he gave Jack a wink.

"My kind of crop. If I were 65 years younger, I'd give the Bishop a run for his money as far as keeping you boys on his team. And I can't believe God would deny a couple of sweet young girls a happy marriage just so you can wear black dresses and do all that hokey-pokey stuff with incense and such. Good husbands don't grow on trees. I ought to know. I've had enough of the lousy kind."

"From the photos I've seen, I bet you turned a few heads," Patrick said.

"I had my moments, including a full dance card back in the day," she said wistfully. "That was a long time ago before cruel Mr. Time did his dirty work and put me here."

"Don't sell yourself short, Millie," Patrick replied, touching her wrinkled hand. "Believe me, you've still got what it takes."

She smiled again and placed her other hand gently on top of his. "And the inmates here wonder why I so look forward to these visits. Dummies. I tell them you're president of my fan club. The old crows should all be so lucky." Her eyes twinkled as she looked at Jack. "There's room for you too, sweetie."

"I love offers I can't refuse," Jack said. "Where do I sign up?"

The conversation bounced back and forth, with Millie and Patrick catching each other up on all the news of the past two weeks. About one hour into the visit, a staff member poked her head into the room.

"It's almost time for your walk, Millie. I'll be back in five minutes to get you."

"Thank you, hon. I'll be ready." Millie reached over and picked up her reading glasses off the night stand. "And I want to thank both you boys for coming. It's been a wonderful visit, and a real treat to meet another charming young man. Before you two leave, could you please wait out in the hallway for a few moments, Jack? I need to speak with my dear Patrick alone."

Jack stood in the corridor, surrounded by the distinct sounds of voices laughing, calling out for a nurse, moaning, and conversing quietly as the elderly residents went about their daily routines. He wondered how many of these grandparents and great-grandparents would welcome visitors today, and how many would spend another day alone. His mind drifted to Father Martin and the other older priests living at St. Paul's. Jack reflected on whether they too felt the sting of loneliness. After several minutes, Patrick stepped through the door holding a sealed white envelope.

"What's that?" Jack asked.

"Something Millie and I've been investigating together. If it's successful, we'll find out soon enough."

"Secrets, huh?" Jack uttered. "Is Millie like an 80-year old spy working undercover?"

Patrick chuckled. "You nailed it. Code name 'Prune Juice,' with a guaranteed kick-in-the-pants."

*****

The following Friday after lunch, Jack, Patrick, and Jimmy ran upstairs to grab their textbooks before heading off to physics class. The two waited in the corridor just outside Jack's open door while he changed his shirt, which had acquired a conspicuous blueberry stain during the noon meal.

"I stayed up past midnight studying for today's stupid test," Jimmy whined loudly. "Why do we even need to take science if we're going to be priests? It's almost as ridiculous as Latin class."

At that moment, Father Joe stepped out of the janitor's closet a few yards down the hall, holding a can of cleanser, and walked toward the group. The surprised boys fell silent.

"So, Mr. Rhodes, where do you plan on going to school next semester?" Father Joe asked as he strode by, his black cassock swishing with each step.

A look of confusion and horror gripped Jimmy' face. Patrick appeared amused by the joke.

When Father Joe reached his room, he turned. "Better hurry to class, guys. You don't want to be late for that stupid test."

As they dashed down the main staircase, Jimmy continued to fret over Father Joe's question.

"What did he mean by that?" Jimmy asked defensively.

"Gee, what could he possibly mean?" Patrick said. "He obviously heard you complaining and wanted to yank your chain."

"Either that or you're history," Jack teased. "Don't worry, we'll all help you move your stuff out."

"That's not funny," Jimmy grumbled.

"I thought it was hilarious," Patrick said as the three boys reached the courtyard. "And Father's right about one thing – time to sprint so no one gets handed detention."

*****

Around 8:00 that same evening, Patrick, Jack, Dan, and Jared headed off for a rare night out at a local pizza place. One of the college seminarians had offered to give them a ride to the popular restaurant, and the boys gladly accepted.

"How you guys getting back to school?" the driver asked.

"Father Joe told us to call him when we're ready, and he'd pick us up," Jack said. "If he can't get here for some reason, we'll walk or hitch a ride. Thanks for dropping us off."

"Anytime, fellas. Have a good one."

The hostess seated the four in a booth. About a minute later, a tall girl with striking green eyes and a magazine cover face walked up to their table. She wore a white work blouse and short black skirt that revealed shapely legs.

"How are you guys tonight?" she asked in a warm voice.

"Great," Jared answered with a big smile. "How about you?"

"Busy. I'm Lauren. I'll be your server." She eyed Jared's letterman jacket. "Do you all go to school at Saint Paul's?"

"Yeah," Jared said.

"I graduated from Holy Cross. I'm at the JC now." She stared at the four of them for a minute. "Not sure if you look like priest material to me, but what do I know. So, what can I get you?"

Patrick, Jared, and Dan ordered individual pizzas and drinks.

The waitress turned her attention to Jack. Her eyes sparkled. She brushed back her long, dark hair with a quick flip of her hand. An inviting amount of cleavage peeked out from beneath her blouse.

"How about you, cutie? See anything you like?"

Jack looked down quickly at the menu. He felt the heat rise in his cheeks as his face turned bright red. Jack forgot what he wanted to order. *Say something*, he thought.

"Um, I'll take the cheeseburger with, um, extra pickles, um, and sweet potato fries, I guess. And, you know, a root beer."

Lauren raised one eyebrow. A mischievous smirk played on her full red lips.

"That's a cheeseburger with extra big tasty pickles. Does that sound about right, hon?"

Flustered, all Jack could say was, "Sure."

She winked at Jack and left to place their orders.

"Whoa," Jared said.

"Looks like our Jackie boy here has one hot chili pepper for a fan," Patrick chimed in. "I think she likes you just a little bit there, bud." He spread his palms about three feet apart, indicating a lot.

"She's smokin'," Dan said. "And you handled everything so, uh, well, uh, Jack. You know, uh, smooth."

"Knock it off," Jack scolded, still embarrassed. "She's probably that way with a lot of guys, just looking for a bigger tip."

"It sounded like she's looking for a big tip from you, if you catch my drift," Jared said. The table erupted in laughter.

"Now that I think about it, you're probably right," Jack finally said, trying his best to recover his composure. "Apparently there's nothing like a pickle to keep a girl smiling."

"Only as long as it's extra big," Jared added.

"Now that we've beaten that poor old horse to death, I'd say it's been a learning experience for all of us," Patrick said, wiping tears of laughter from his eyes. "I think she sounds fun. You should get her number."

"Why?" Jack asked. "We're not supposed to date."

Dan looked incredulous. "What? What's wrong with you? The girl is a fox. At least a nine on any scale. Those dumb rules don't apply to women like her."

Jack shook his head in feigned disgust. "Let's talk about something else, guys. She probably has ten boyfriends."

"And possibly some good-looking girlfriends for your three closest pals?" Jared pointed out. "Hello!"

"Right, because they can't wait to date guys from a high school with probably the most virgins per square foot in the entire state of California," Patrick said.

"Speak for yourself," Dan countered.

"Yeah, sure," Jack said, the words dripping with sarcasm. "As if any sane girl would be alone with you."

"I bet I've come closer than any of you casa-NO-ways," Dan said defensively.

"Is this the part where we all throw-up?" Jack asked.

Patrick laughed. "Good one, Hazy."

"No one is buying the bull you're selling, Dan, so give it up," Jared said with a wave of his hand. "And, Jack, all I'm saying is don't forget about your friends if a miracle happens and things work out."

The conversation wandered over the next few minutes, although it always seemed to return to Lauren, or some part of her that either Jared or Dan found irresistible. Jack tuned it out. He watched with interest as a small group of young men wearing black letterman jackets with a giant red "H" stitched on the left front panel from a close-by public high school entered the pizza parlor accompanied by three attractive girls in black, red, and white cheerleader outfits. He thought how much fun it must be for boys and girls his age to meet up after games or go out together on weekend nights, something Jack had never experienced. It looked so normal, so right. A strange feeling filled his stomach, not quite regret, but more like emptiness and that he'd missed out on something important.

Lauren returned with their orders.

"Here you go, fellas," she said, setting the plates and drinks in front of them. "Enjoy." She looked at Jack. "If you want anything else, sweetie, just call me."

Dan stared at Lauren's form-fitting skirt as she walked away.

"Shake what mama gave ya," he said. "Great caboose."

"Pretty much great everything," Patrick agreed. "She is quite the hottie, Jack. You might want to reconsider."

"If you don't get her number, none of us will ever talk to you again," Jared threatened in a playful voice. "Come on, Jack. Do it for all of our classmates who'll never go on a date or take a girl to the prom, losers like Dan here."

"Bite me," Dan said.

"Back on the pickle thing again, I see," Patrick said. "You both really should talk to the school psychiatrist. Too bad we don't have one."

The boys ate, talked, and laughed for the next 45 minutes. Patrick finished his pizza, took a final swallow of soda, and slipped out of the booth.

"Back in a few, boys. I'll give Father Joe a ring to come pick us up. Try not to start a food fight."

After making the call, Patrick found Lauren standing near the door to the kitchen.

"Excuse me, Lauren. Could I talk to you for a second?"

"Sure."

"My friend's a bit shy, but he'd love to get your phone number."

"I thought you Paulies wanted to become priests?"

"Paulies? Is that what we're called?"

"That's what a lot of the kids at Holy Cross called you guys. Better than saints or popes, don't you think?"

"No doubt. And yes, we do plan to become priests, at least at this point. With so many years to go, what's wrong with appreciating beautiful things along the way?"

Lauren smiled. "Not a thing." She tore a piece of paper from her order pad and quickly jotted down the seven-digit number.

"Now tell your very cute friend…."

"Jack," Patrick said.

"Hmmm, I like that. Tell Jack I expect to hear from him. Soon."

"You will. Even if I have to dial the number myself."

Patrick returned to the booth, where his three classmates sat arguing about which pro sports team had the best uniforms. Jared favored the powder blue and lightning bolts of the San Diego Chargers, while Jack liked the 49ers' red and gold, and Dan preferred the Yankees' pinstripes.

"Who do you think, Patrick?" Dan asked.

"Chicago Blackhawks. Best logo in any sport. You gotta love their red home jerseys. End of story."

Patrick grabbed his jacket to leave.

"Ready?" Jack asked him.

"You might ask yourself the same thing, Hazy. Let's go outside and wait for our ride."

The four stood on the sidewalk chatting and laughing. Jack breathed in the sharp, evening air with its distinct smell of fall, a scent he loved. Within minutes, Father Joe drove up near the restaurant's front door.

"Thanks for coming, Father," Patrick said, as the four hopped into the car. "It's a little cold for the thirty-minute stroll home tonight."

"You're welcome. Did you boys have a good time?"

"Jack made a new friend," Dan said. "An actual real girl. We don't expect *you* to believe it, Father, although maybe the Vatican will verify it as a miracle."

"Nothing extraordinary about it, Mr. Hannigan," Father Joe replied. "I'm sure lots of young ladies would find Mr. Hayes, Mr. Keane, Mr. Bonelli, and perhaps even you, appealing."

Patrick, Jack, and Jared laughed.

"In Dan's case, only ones who wear thick glasses," Jared said, "and like to do charity work. At least for as long as he can hide the fact that what they see is all they get."

"Haha," Dan said. "And, Father, I'm surprised that you think Jared would ever give up his love affair with Baby Ruth and Almond Joy for a human girl."

"I'll give you a Baby Ruth," Jared said, shoving Dan in the arm.

"Hey, no fighting in the car, children," Patrick said from the front seat. "And yes, Father, we had a great time. Plus a good-looking waitress about our age took an interest in Jack."

"Our little boy is growing up," Dan teased. "Now if he only had a clue."

"It was nothing, Father," Jack said while he punched Dan playfully in the other arm. "Let's talk about something else."

Back at school, Patrick and Jack headed to the senior lounge to watch TV and talk.

"I'm surprised no one's in here tonight," Jack said.

"Not many guys stayed this weekend. Some might be down in the college gym watching the Friday night movie. Depending on what's showing, they can get a decent crowd." Patrick reached into his pocket and removed a piece of paper. "I have a present for you. Lauren's phone number."

"What? How did you get it?"

"I asked her when I went to call Father Joe, and she wrote it down. She wants you to call her. What are you gonna do?"

"Did you ask about her friends?"

"No, that's your job. First, you need to decide if you want to see her."

"What do you think?"

"You already know what I think, Hazy. I got the number, didn't I?"

Jack thought for a minute.

"We'll, I guess we're not priests yet, and one date couldn't hurt anything. It might be fun. What do I say to her?"

"We'll call tomorrow and try to set it up for next weekend. Don't worry, we'll think of something to impress her. Or at least not scare her off."

"Have you ever gone on a date?" Jack asked.

"My parish held dances in eighth grade, and I've been to weddings that had girls our age. But, no, not an official date."

"In that case I'm for sure asking if she has at least one friend so we can both sweat this out."

"Geez, you make it sound like a math final. Everything will be fine."

"I still say a girl like her has a truckload of guys asking for dates. I'd probably be more like an experiment for her to try to get the 'priest' to fall head over heels."

"Who cares? Just think of how jealous the guys will be," Patrick said with a laugh. "That alone would make it worth the effort. Tell you what, why don't you sleep on it tonight. We'll talk again tomorrow to see whether or not you want to call."

"Deal. At least Lauren will make for sweet dreams."

CHAPTER 14

After a leisurely Saturday morning breakfast, all eight senior soccer players met on the field for extra training. Despite notching two, one-goal victories that week, no one, including Coach Shumaker, was satisfied with the way the team had played.

"Winning isn't enough, boys," Patrick told his teammates as they warmed up. "We need to look good doing it. Dominating games with style is the Saint Paul's way."

Following nearly two hours of passing, shooting, and dribbling drills, the group finished with wind sprints.

"Come on, we have ten more in us, guys," Patrick urged as the players gathered near the midfield line, each trying to catch his breath. "Just think about how good it will feel to walk off the field with three great wins next week. All this extra work will matter a lot if we make the playoffs. Go all out. It's time to show our rivals we mean business."

"What rivals?" Brian asked, exhausted by the running. "Face it, Keane, the Catholic schools don't like us because they think we're a bunch of weenie priests, and we don't like them because they're arrogant jerks who have a bunch of women cheering for them. It's not like they see us as some huge obstacle to winning a title. We're just a tiny bump in the road that they plan to flatten with their steamrollers."

"Why don't you button it, Tron, and run the sprints like everyone else?" Jared said. "No one wants to hear your moaning."

"We can still play those schools tough," Patrick persuaded. "If one of us decides it's not worth the effort, we all lose. You want this too, Brian. It's time to buy in and get busy. Now let's do it together."

Tron shrugged, too tired to continue the argument. "Okay, okay. Ten more and that's it. Don't you ever know when to quit?"

"Never. Ready. Set. Go."

After completing the final sprint, each player grabbed bottles of water and plopped down on the cool grass near a row of cypress trees that offered welcome shade from the sun's surprising November heat.

"Whew, what an incredible practice," Tom said as he stretched out flat on the ground, his red face dripping with sweat. "It sure tested my endurance for punishment."

"Speaking of tests, any of you guys find out what you got on this week's physics exam?" Ben asked after gulping down an entire bottle.

"Ninety-one," Jared offered as he drenched himself with water.

"Too bad, I got a ninety-two," Ben countered.

"Did I say ninety-one? I actually scored a ninety-three," Jared added, perking up.

"Oh, wait. I just remembered Mr. Jones gave me extra credit points to make mine a ninety-four," Ben said. "You should try studying next time, dummy."

"Smarter than you, Keep. Remember, I finished third highest in my eighth-grade class at St. John's parish."

"What? There were only three people in your entire class?" Ben asked.

Patrick laughed. "You lunatics need to be locked up."

"What did you score, Keane?" Brian demanded.

"A ninety-five, boys," Patrick replied, raising his right fist high in the air. "Jones told me it tied Jack and Tom for tops in the class. The rest of you bananaheads need to hit the books, or the Warden will reserve your seats on the express train to public school before the end of the semester."

"Hey, a ninety-one is still solid," Jared protested.

"You just said you got a ninety-three," Ben said.

"Geez, just stop," Jack jumped in. "Can't we talk about something else?"

"Fabulous idea, especially after that scintillating discussion brought to you by our friends with apparently nothing between their ears," Patrick said. "Okay, I have a question for everyone: what would you say guys at this school fear the most?"

"Aside from wind sprints, I'd say getting kicked out," Dan replied without hesitation.

Patrick smiled. "You think so? I'd bet a lot of guys pray that the Sulps will hand them a ticket home. Not that they'd admit it. This place isn't for everyone, and more than a few guys came here only because their mom or dad wanted a priest in the family, almost like a status symbol. The seminary certainly wasn't their first choice."

"What's worse than getting asked to leave?" Brian asked.

"Being called gay."

"Let's ask Jimmy," Dan said with a smirk. "I hear he's an expert."

"The pot calls the kettle black," Jimmy replied. "I know we sometimes kid around about it, Patrick, but you don't think anyone takes it that seriously, do you?"

"Guarantee it," Patrick said. "Aside from you two weirdos, watch how guys react when someone implies they're gay. As a freshman, I saw a couple of seniors who were probably the nicest guys in the school start fighting during a pick-up basketball game in the gym because one called the other a 'sissy-boy.' Plain stupid."

Dan laughed. "I'll have to remember to use that one on Jimmy. Pansy or wuss just doesn't have the same impact."

"Hilarious," Jimmy said, tossing his empty plastic bottle at Dan.

"You joke," Patrick said. "I'm telling you it's like a scarlet letter here."

"Yeah, a big old red 'J' for Jimmy," Dan added.

"Hey, I'm not the one Coach is always telling to stop with the grab-ass, Ginger," Jimmy said. "It's you, Dan Hanni-GAY."

"Real funny, Lucille."

"I've told you before don't call me Lucille. I don't even like Kenny Rogers or that song."

"What song?" Dan asked.

Jack laughed out loud. "Good one, Danny boy. And Jimmy, don't let him get to you. He can't help himself. Just know that you're both making us wish for the dumb conversation about who got the higher grade."

"Speaking of making wishes come true, tell us about your new girlfriend, Jack," Dan said.

"What's this?" Tom asked.

"A good-looking waitress took a big shine to Hazy last night," Patrick said.

"Was she like sixty?" Brian asked.

"Why, does your grandma work as a waitress?" Jared asked.

"Hey, you weren't there, Tron – this sweetie was first-class," Dan said. "And Jack promised to find out if she has some girlfriends for his good buddies."

"WOO-HOO, Jack gonna get him some, and us some too," Jimmy shouted.

"Keep it up, bananaheads," Jack said.

"That's what she said," Dan joked. The entire group laughed.

"Just remember, Jack, that once you taste the forbidden fruit, you can kiss the priesthood good-bye," Ben said. "I met a girl last summer, and she made me realize I didn't want to attend the college seminary, so I've applied to other schools."

"Wow, Keeper hiding secrets from the boys," Dan said, expressing everyone's surprise at Ben's admission. "I'm glad you at least decided to stick around for this year."

"Why not? Saint Paul's offers an excellent education and a super place to play soccer. And since I like knowing different kinds of friends, what better way to promote diversity than hang out with you gay guys?"

"Hey, Jimmy resembles that remark," Dan said. "The Church will need to reset its standards as low as possible if he expects to receive Holy Orders."

"Like more than one of you clowns will make it to ordination," Jack said.

"Or, maybe none of us," Patrick chipped in.

"Come on, Patrick," Jared said. "Someone will make it."

"Possibly. Seeing a vocation through to ordination is a far shore. The rules are tough enough without all the temptations and distractions, including gorgeous waitresses. Let's be realistic: twelve years is a long time to maintain the kind of commitment we'll need."

"You don't think you'll become a priest?" Jared asked.

"All I'm saying is that none of us can see around the corner, or know for sure at this point. A lot could change."

"This can be a pretty great place," Jack said. "What a shame if we all dropped out."

"Not everyone has the same experience as you, Hayes," Brian said. "Some people view things, well, let's just say a whole lot differently. It's not all peaches and cream."

"Your time here is what you make it," Jack fired back. "If life at this school doesn't meet your expectations, do something about it. Whining solves nothing."

"Speaking of life at this school, did anyone else here get a part in the annual play, *Inherit the Wind,* the one about the Scopes Monkey Trial?" Tom asked, doing his best to change the subject.

"Yeah, I got picked to play the role of E.K Hornbeck, the reporter," Dan said. "He's sarcastic and not very religious. That's probably why Father Quinn thought I could handle it. What role did you get, Tom?"

"Henry Drummond, the attorney who defends the high school science guy for teaching evolution. I found out yesterday."

"Wow, that's a big part," Jared said. "I liked the movie with Spencer Tracy."

"The play and movie actually should have been called 'False Reflections of History,'" Patrick pointed out, "because they're not too accurate. But, you're right, Spencer Tracy did a fantastic job."

"When's the play?" Jimmy asked.

"Not until March, so we have plenty of time to learn our lines and rehearse," Tom said. "I hope I don't mess up."

"You'll be great, Tommy, and so will Dan," Jack said. "It's cool that we have star actors on the team. I can't wait to see you two guys perform."

"Well, it's almost noon, and I'm getting hungry," Patrick said, ending the chatter. "Good work this morning, guys. Let's hit the refectory. How about helping me collect the cones and soccer balls, Hazy?"

While Jack and Patrick gathered the equipment, the other boys headed off to shower and eat lunch.

"You didn't sound very optimistic today," Jack said.

"I'm a realist. Four years of college, plus four more at the theologate is a long time. A lot could happen to lead us off-target."

"From what I've been hearing, at least half the class probably will leave after graduation this June."

"Without its priests, the Church is like a classroom without a teacher or an army with no leader. It'll struggle to function and even survive. And so will Saint Paul's."

"Sounds like you think we're the last of a dying breed."

"At least at the high school level. After Vatican Two, when misinterpretations that surrounded the council's intentions took hold, vocations withered by nearly forty percent in less than a decade."

"I'm starting to understand the urgency," Jack said.

"In the Old and New Testaments, God's Word speaks of promise and fulfillment. I believe it's the same for us. The soccer team, June graduation, this school – we need to soar now, like Father Martin said, and see if we can fulfill our promise."

"It feels like now or never."

Patrick nodded his head. "We're standing on a precipice. Whether it's looking over a valley or an abyss is something we can't know yet." Patrick furrowed his eyebrows and tilted his head slightly to the side. "As far as your vocation, though, what would you become if you left the seminary?"

"Well, my grandmother told me she'd love to have a doctor of the soul in the family, although I think she'd be happy with a medical doctor. Probably that. How 'bout you?"

"Maybe a history professor, or even a college athletic director. At this point, I'm still thinking priest."

"Me too. But I heard the college dwindled down to about one hundred twenty students."

Patrick tossed the final soccer ball into the cloth bag and flung it over his shoulder. "One of the auxiliary bishops in San Francisco asked me over for lunch this past summer at his residence. Nice place. He told me too many sissies were becoming priests, and the Church needed more athletic guys, guys like us."

"He said that?"

"His exact words," Patrick said as the two boys walked across the field on their way to the gym.

"Wow. Wouldn't some guys come here for the wrong reasons?"

"Like that doesn't happen now? Look at our class, and how the crowd has thinned over time. It's like Ben said."

"The price sure is right. This place is a steal." Jack calculated the cost per week in his head. "Hey, does that mean we're all breaking the seventh commandment?"

"Sure, about as much as Father Martin did." Patrick looked at Jack with a wry grin. "Speaking of breaking commandments, did you still want to call Lauren?"

Jack hesitated. "You're probably not going to like this, but, no, I don't, especially after what Ben said. Sure, it would be fun to do something normal, like the guys we saw with the cheerleaders last night. If we're in the seminary for the reasons we say, then it doesn't make sense to go on a date. Plus the diocese is paying for my education, so it would feel almost dishonest to go."

Patrick nodded. "Well, I can't argue with that. Tell you what. If you ever change your mind, I'll keep her phone number in my desk drawer. I'll say one thing: if every guy at this school held that attitude, the Archbishop wouldn't have a thing to worry about when it comes to keeping his parishes supplied with priests."

Chapter 15

"I found a note slipped under my door this morning," Patrick told Jack quietly on the bus ride back to St. Paul's following a road game victory. He looked around to make sure no one else could hear him. "The Stalker wants to meet us outside for tonight's meteor shower."

"Great," Jack whispered. "I've been looking forward to seeing him again. I just wish the situation was different so we could spend time in his room."

Around 11:00 that evening, Patrick and Jack met Father Martin near the baseball field's giant backstop. The old priest amazed the boys by handling the slow, flashlight-guided trek up the Grinder's steep slope without any help. When they reached the top, Patrick spread out a blanket on the wet grass and removed three sodas from his jacket pockets.

"Care for a root beer, Father?" he asked.

"No, thank you, son. I don't seem to have a taste for sodas anymore."

Patrick handed a can to Jack, who popped it open.

"As our guest, you get first crack at the binoculars," Patrick said. "It's best to keep them pointed toward the southeast, although all this light pollution will restrict our viewing a bit."

Over the next ten minutes, the three watched several meteors streak across the clear November night sky.

"Wow, that last one was incredible," Jack declared. "Father, do you ever wonder why God left so much debris flying around the Universe, crashing into other things?"

"Perhaps so we could enjoy an awesome show like tonight."

Patrick chuckled. "Good answer, Father. Unscientific. But good."

"We all can't be Galileo or Newton, or even possess the knowledge to build the Voyager space probes that NASA launched recently," Father Martin said. "After all, man is a fragile spiritual being trying desperately to thrive in a harsh physical world. Our human flaws often trip us up. Still, we do our best, and hope."

"Even Patrick?" Jack said playfully with a laugh. Patrick rolled his eyes in mock disgust.

"Yes, I regret that perfection has eluded even Mr. Keane." Father Martin let out a soft sigh. His tone grew solemn. "Always remember that the world is filled with beauty and truth, boys. In his Sermon on the Mount, our Lord Jesus commanded, 'Ask, and it will be given to you; seek, and you will find; knock, and the door will be opened to you.' But not every step on our journey will be the right one, and not every day can be a picnic. Not even for the Lord."

Jack sensed some old, unresolved wound in his voice.

"Blessed are those whose strength is in You, as they pass through the vale of tears," Patrick said. *"Valle lacrimarum."*

"Amen," Father Martin whispered. "Well spoken, Mr. Keane."

Jack surveyed the distant stars. As much as he felt awed by the vast beauty of the night sky, he thought Patrick's uncanny ability to hit the mark with a quotation from Psalms, a line of poetry, or some other words of wisdom at precisely the right moment impressed him even more.

"I just love it up here on the hill at night, all this inspiration laid out in front of us at no charge," Patrick said. "As Emerson wrote, 'All I have seen teaches me to trust the Creator for all I have not seen.'"

"If only we could trust without question," Jack said with the slightest hint of sadness. "Sometimes I wonder."

"What do you wonder, Jack?" Father Martin asked.

"What if this is nothing more than a big cosmic joke on all of us? We're born, we live, we die, and that's it. I mean, come on – if there's no God, and we never learn about the origins and mysteries of the Universe, I think it's one huge ripoff. Do you ever have doubts, Father?"

"I prefer to marvel over God's greatness to have envisioned and set in motion such stunning complexity and power. And even more spectacular, as His beloved children, He has given us the ability and awareness to witness and study the expanse of this creation." He turned toward Patrick, who was lying quietly on the blanket, staring into space. "What are your thoughts, Mr. Keane?"

Patrick sat up. He peered toward the distant stars in silent thought.

"I want to see my Mom again. It would mean the world to me. Faith in resurrection is the only way that can happen."

Father Martin looked pleased. "Saint Paul himself explained that, 'We live by faith, not by sight.'"

"I'm with you, Father," Patrick said. "That's why I love coming out here, to witness this spectacle. It fills me with hope." He paused. "I do have another question, Father."

"Yes, son."

"We miss our loved ones who've passed, but do they miss us? If salvation offers eternal peace and happiness as promised, why would they bother to think about the mess here on Earth? It feels to me more like a one-way street, where we're the unhappy ones doing all the missing."

Father Martin's face beamed with contentment. Just like the old days, the hilltop had transformed into his classroom, a place where students came to learn about the mysteries of their faith.

"Think of heaven as bliss," he explained, "where loved ones wait in joy and anticipation, and without sorrow, for the eventual reunion, like children waiting for Christmas. After all, looking around here tonight, one could argue it almost requires more conviction to believe there is no Creator than that God exists. Even science recognizes the extremely low probability that Earth could have been created by chance without something steering the ship because the odds are so prohibitive. Yet the impossible happened."

"Free will offers us that choice, right, Father?" Patrick said. "We decide if what our inner voice tells us is true, or we can ignore it."

"Belief is a natural part of who we are. Some believe in pure science, while we also choose faith in the Divine. Both camps are seeking eternal truth and enlightenment on a cosmic scale. In my experience, faith is as natural as breathing regardless of whether one finds it in union with God or nature."

Patrick lay back on the cool grass again and gazed up at the blanket of stars. A thousand thoughts swirled through his mind.

"Father, if you don't mind, I have more questions."

"I'm listening."

"Okay. When people die, where does their knowledge go? And their love, joy, humor, and dreams? Does it disperse into the universe to be shared, and become part of something greater than the human mind can imagine?

"And when a child dies, some people say God wanted him back in heaven, which seems like their feeble attempt to make the tragedy easier to understand," Patrick continued. "Doesn't God have enough angels and heavenly beings around Him already?"

Father Martin sat still on the blanket, as quiet as the tranquil night sky.

"Father?" Patrick finally asked, surprised by the silence. "Did I put you to sleep?"

"No, son," he answered in a soft voice. Patrick's words had touched the old priest and pulled deep emotions to the surface. "I heard your wonderful questions about the secrets of life. I wish I could answer them here tonight. All I can tell you is that in time the Lord reveals his plan for each of us."

"I wish I had that kind of certainty," Jack said. "It's not that I doubt God's greatness, it's just I have to ask why all the waiting? Almost 2,000 years have passed since Christ's last mission here. Why not walk the Earth again? Even if hundreds of inhabited planets exist out there, he could have saved them all by now and returned at least to see how we're doing."

"Another enigma, Mr. Hayes. Know that the Lord is within, so looking outside yourself may be like searching for a lost key in the wrong room."

Jack sighed. "If I dwell too long on the Universe's vastness, the whole thing almost gets me down about how insignificant people are, like cogs in a wheel. We're one little planet in the suburbs of a galaxy, like bumpkins in the backwoods. One day the Sun will consume it, and everything will vanish."

"Whoa. Why suddenly so blue?" Patrick asked.

"I'd like you to consider that the Earth will be consumed by the Son, with a happier ending," Father Martin said, hoping Jack would find his words uplifting. "Belief in the resurrection is the heart of who we are, the essence of our Catholic religion, the true way as the Good Shepherd taught us. In John, Chapter Eleven, Jesus said, 'I am the resurrection and the life. The one who believes in me will live, even though they die.'"

Jack suddenly realized what the symbols "J 11" meant that he'd seen on his closet door weeks ago.

"I think about resurrection, Father, and hope heaven's a lot like one of those perfect June days," he responded in a lighter voice.

"How so?"

"Well, although Christmastime runs a close second, early summer's the best time of the year, especially around this area. Bright, crisp mornings, warm, lazy afternoons with a faint breeze, the colors of plants, flowers, and trees in bloom, bees and butterflies everywhere, fields of fresh green grass before the summer heat roasts the blades brown, maybe even a huge, puffy white cloud drifting by without a care. All topped off with a backyard party and the longest light of the year. To me, June is a deep feeling of happiness, like the world renewed, and eternity at its finest."

Patrick stared at the crescent moon. "I like that, Hazy," was all he said.

"Sounds like you've given it some thought, Jack," Father Martin said. "Perhaps you're closer to the mark than you know."

"What do you think, Patrick?" Jack probed.

"I suppose we return to where we came from, one way or the other. We either mix with everything else in the Cosmos or go to an actual heaven and reunite with our Creator and those who made our lives worth living. That's why faith is so important – believing makes the world go round."

"I thought money made the world go round, at least according to the song," Jack said.

"That's only the Jesuits," Patrick joked. "Father Joe told me so."

The three sat in silence for another ten minutes, scanning the sky for streaks of light. Patrick broke the spell.

"As much as I could stay out here all night, it's time to get back," he advised. "After all, we have another game tomorrow."

The stargazers made their way down the hill, over the baseball diamond, and across the bridge, finally stopping in the west parking lot.

"Well, I'll leave you here," Father Martin said. "I'm not quite ready to go inside."

"Thank you for coming with us, Father," Patrick said with genuine warmth. "I hope you enjoyed the show."

"It was a fabulous and informative evening, gentlemen. Good luck tomorrow with your match."

Father Martin started to walk away. He stopped short and turned back to face the boys.

"I have to go away and won't be seeing you, at least for a while." A trace of regret tinged his voice. "I wanted to tell you how much getting to know you both has meant to me."

"Where are you going, Father?" Jack asked. "We'll be sad to see you leave."

"I've been given a different assignment." Father Martin paused and looked deep into Jack's eyes before continuing.

"Just remember, God is great and can do anything. He can make one universe or a thousand. We must always see the world as it is, not as we'd like it to be. We must overcome doubt and disillusionment. Living is about love, hope, and faith. Make them powerful forces in your life. No matter what."

He turned toward Patrick. "I'll be seeing you, son. God bless you always. Good night, and carry on."

"Good night, Father," Jack and Patrick said in unison.

With a slight nod of his head, Father Martin turned away once more and walked – more briskly it seemed to Jack – around the corner toward the front of the building.

"That was odd," Jack whispered as the boys made their way up the brick stairs to the side door. "Why do you think Father said, 'no matter what?' What did he mean?"

"We all go through ups and downs, like a roller coaster. Guess he was saying try to stay prepared for whatever comes along." Patrick placed his right index finger to his lips, signaling for quiet as he slowly pulled the door open. "No more talking. See you tomorrow."

*****

The next afternoon, a cloud-free Tuesday, St. Paul's extended its winning streak with an inspired performance. Led by two goals apiece from Patrick, Jack, and Riley, the Battling Bishops drubbed perennial public school powerhouse and reigning CCS champion Zachary Taylor High in a 6-0 shutout. With eight straight wins, St. Paul's sported a record unmatched by even the largest schools.

"People are beginning to take notice," Coach Shumaker said to his huddled players at the end of Wednesday's practice. "It's easy for outsiders to write off a school this small, but we made headlines in the sports section this morning. That's the good news. The bad news is no independent school has ever received an invitation to the CCS soccer playoffs, so we can't let our foot off the gas. We all understand it's a long-shot, and I don't want to kid anyone. More decisive wins like yesterday represent our best hope to secure a berth. We need to keep turning heads. What do you say, men?"

"I say we get this done," Jack replied, his powerful voice raised in passion.

"Get it done," Jared shouted, clapping his hands together twice. "Get it done."

Seconds later, all 16 players took up the chant, clapping and shouting in unison. "Get it done," clap, clap, "Get it done," clap clap, "Get it done."

"Battle Hymn, boys," Patrick called out, "and let 'em hear it all over campus."

Like a wave, the entire team jogged off the field together led by their captain, swept over the bridge and up toward the gym, singing, "Glory, glory hallelujah, glory, glory hallelujah, glory, glory hallelujah, St. Paul's goes marching on," as they went. Students and priests alike stuck their heads out third- and fourth-floor windows along the western wing, halted conversations in mid-sentence, and even left the comfort of the heated outdoor pool to discover the cause of the commotion.

The team stopped and re-huddled outside the gym entrance. Patrick led a new song, sounding much like a Zulu warrior's war chant, his voice rising and falling in a rhythmic cadence. To the onlookers' amazement, the group responded in tight harmony. The team ended with a raucous, "Win, win, win," and headed inside to take well-deserved showers.

"Bring it on," Jack said to no one in particular. "We're ready."

CHAPTER 16

"Remember, we've scheduled our confessor-penitent conference for this evening, so come by my room after night prayers," Father Joe told Jack as they left the refectory following dinner. "By the way, Coach Shumaker called. He wanted to make sure everyone on the soccer team knew the bus leaves for tomorrow's game at two thirty, so could you head over to the junior floor to tell them?"

"Absolutely. See you tonight at nine forty-five."

Jack stopped by each of the juniors' rooms at the beginning of Study Time to deliver the news. When he arrived at Riley's door, it was open. Riley sat across the width his bed, back against the wall, deep in thought, cradling a stuffed toy soccer ball on his lap.

"What's up, Riles?" Jack asked. "You ready to kick butt tomorrow? Turns out the bus leaves early, so I wanted to make sure you knew and are good to go."

"Sure," Riley replied softly, staring straight ahead.

Jack studied his teammate's face. It looked strange and deflated, like someone who'd just discovered he'd paid a fortune for a fake Rembrandt.

"You sick?"

"No, nothing like that."

Jack walked over and leaned on the edge of the sturdy wood desk. "Well, then what?"

Riley looked directly at Jack. His eyes regained some of their characteristic spark.

"Most of us think we're special, destined to do great things. It comes as a bit of shock to wake up one day and realize we're like everyone else. At least in most ways. Or even worse."

"I dunno. Just being in a place like this makes us kinda unique. " Jack thought for a moment. "This isn't because you're bummed that Artie beat you at penalty kicks today after practice and won your Mystery, is it?"

Riley shook his head. "No way, not at all. I just have a lot of doubts about what I'm doing here. And what others are doing here."

"Join the crowd."

A surprised look crossed Riley's face. "You're kidding? Guys like Patrick and you always seem so sure."

"Not even close. For now, we still believe in our calling. Maybe one of us will even do something that changes the world for the better in a small way, whether as a priest or another career."

"I wish I didn't have so many questions."

"If they're real easy ones, maybe I can help out with a few answers," Jack said with a smile. "Look, Patrick told me something I always try to remember: that life is limited, so it's worth striving to do something that goes beyond your time here. He said we need to ask ourselves, 'Would the world be a better place with or without us?' I guarantee this little world we call home is better off because you chose to go to school here."

"Thanks, Jack. I just wish I was more certain about all this."

"Well, I also believe it's about hanging in there as much as anything. You know, keep moving toward the goal." Jack stood up. "And by the way, Patrick and I both think you're the weirdest guy in the entire school, so that makes you extra special, right?"

"The pot calls the kettle black. Jerk." Riley grinned as he tossed the little soccer ball at Jack, who trapped it on his right thigh, let it fall to his right foot, then blasted the cloth sphere under Riley's bed. He raised his arms and voice together in triumph.

"Jesus Saves, but Hayes scores on the rebound! Bishops win, as usual." He pointed his right index finger at Riley. "Now that was special!"

"And you call ME weird? Sheesh." Riley hopped off the bed and grabbed a small pile of books from the desktop. "I gotta get started on these. Thanks for stopping by, man. See you tomorrow on the bus."

*****

Jack arrived precisely at 9:45 pm for his monthly, face-to-face confessor-penitent meeting with Father Joe. He knocked lightly on the priest's closed door. A robust, "Come in, Mr. Hayes," resounded from inside the suite.

"Hi, Father. Are you ready for me?"

"Good evening." Father Joe sat behind his desk, intently reviewing some papers. He motioned toward a dark-brown leather chair. Jack took a seat and waited.

As with all priest's quarters at the school, Father Joe's suite consisted of a carpeted, 300 square foot living area that doubled as an office – and, at times, a classroom – and a smaller bedroom with private bath. Similar to Father Martin's residence, Jack relished the room's comfortable yet formal ambiance, like that of finely-appointed study, with its stylish oak desk, padded chairs, warm lighting, and built-in bookshelves overflowing with religious volumes, non-fiction historical works, classics, and even a few modern novels. He also particularly liked the rectangular sign in a bright, silver frame that sat on the top shelf behind Father Joe's desk. It read, "If You're Living Like God Doesn't Exist, You'd Better Start Praying He Doesn't." Jack had selected Father Joe for his confessor as a sophomore, so these meetings often turned into friendly chats rather than formal encounters.

After about 30 seconds, the priest rose and moved to a chair across from Jack, carrying the file.

"Your academics look as exceptional as ever. And no reports of any significant behavioral aberrations, which is always good news." Father Joe peeked over his reading glasses. "Anything of specific interest you'd like to discuss?"

"Yes," Jack replied. "Father Oliver is becoming an intolerable grump who needs to be placed in a cage, I mean retirement home."

A disgruntled look mixed with a stern glare swept over Father Joe's face. He removed his glasses.

"I meant would you like to discuss anything about YOU."

"I know, Father," Jack said with a big grin. "I wanted to see if I could bring out that old *skulen* you learned from your Danish mother. It worked."

Father Joe sat back, relaxed and amused. The scowl disappeared from his face.

"Touche, Mr. Hayes."

"Something has been bothering me for a while. I don't think most students at this school, including me, are worthy of becoming priests. When it comes down to it, we're simply not holy enough."

"No one? What exactly do you consider holy?"

Jack half-shrugged. "Okay, I'll grant you a few exceptions, such as Patrick, Hugh Kelly, and maybe Don Mitchell. As a whole, we're just regular guys. Sure, some feel they may have a vocation. From what I've seen, others have no idea why the heck they're here, or they simply like the independence of being away from strict parents. Nothing special or what might be called holy or priestly. It just seems we can never care enough or be good enough."

Father Joe gave an understanding nod. His voice took on a soothing tone.

"Only God is perfect, Jack. As humans, we all fall short. Just as the Bible tells us that Israel is His chosen nation, those who believe in Christ as Savior, and accept His gift of eternal life, are also chosen. It's this faith that makes us holy and sets us apart from the world. It's also why we strive to live according to His Word and teachings, even when we come up short."

"Do you think very many guys here have a chance to become priests?"

"Not everyone, not by a long shot. In fact, history shows most who start out will fall away from this path. On the other hand, God may speak to other boys in ways you don't see or know. They could be much holier than you believe."

"I suppose I can only speak for myself," Jack conceded.

"Don't be so hard on yourself, son. You're doing fine, and, in my opinion, could one day make an excellent priest. Coincidentally, I've noticed you tend to do the same thing on the soccer field and baseball diamond. Give yourself the same kind of breaks you afford others. So, that said, any other concerns I should hear?"

Jack hesitated. "Well…."

"What is it?" Father Joe asked.

He decided to bring it up. "I'm worried about Riley. When I stopped by his room earlier, I got the feeling he's unhappy. I'd hate to lose him as a friend, and Riley's such a big part of the team. It's like he's been withdrawing the past couple of weeks. Patrick told me he's concerned too."

Father Joe leaned forward in his chair. His face wore as serious an expression as Jack could recall seeing.

"Mr. Moody has been going through a rough patch. Family issues and doubts often play a role in these situations. That's all I can say at this time. It speaks well of you boys that you care about his welfare."

"Of course we do. Patrick and I would miss the guy."

"Speaking of, I have a ten fifteen appointment with Mr. Keane. You're sure there's nothing else?"

"No, Father." Jack got up to leave. "Good night. And thanks."

On the way back to his room, Jack passed Patrick in the hall.

"You're next," Jack said. "I brought up Riley."

Patrick nodded. "Good. I will too."

As promised, Patrick spent the first few minutes of his meeting with Father Joe voicing concerns about Riley. Satisfied the priest was fully aware of the situation, Patrick took the discussion in a new direction.

"Something about the kitchen raid from last spring has been bugging me, and I need to ask: did Dean Webb and the faculty need to suspend the guys to teach them a lesson? I mean, do you think their offense warranted four days? In my opinion, Jack was sold out. And by the way, I guarantee he learned a lesson alright, just probably not the one Father Webb and Father King had in mind."

"About loyalty?" Father Joe questioned.

"Yes, about the lack of it. I'm not sure who's more guilty here, the accused, the college snitch, or someone else."

Father Joe drew a deep breath before speaking. "I do agree. The Church needs priests like Jack, intelligent, personable young men with high ideals and good leadership skills. I would hate to see us lose high-quality candidates due to a lack of flexibility or being overly dogmatic, like a machine forcing everyone to obey blindly. I certainly don't favor the old ways of symbolically beating students into conformity. Having said that, even stars like Jack need to follow the rules."

"I've been here long enough to appreciate how the system works, who holds all the power, and who has the final say, right or wrong, especially when it comes to thinking outside the box. Sometimes those in charge can squeeze too hard. For students, it can feel like we're flies caught in a dead spider's web, no pun intended. No one wins."

"I understand your point, son. I'll mention it to Father King. He's a reasonable man who wants what's best for this institution and each student. You may not always see it, but I know it's true."

"Thank you, Father."

"Before you go, Patrick, I have a favor to ask. I believe you've met Henry Smith, a new student this fall in the junior class. He lives too far away to fly home for only a few days over Thanksgiving, and plans to spend the weekend here on campus because he has no place to go."

"He does now," Patrick said. "Dad will love the extra company."

"Good man. Do you want me to tell Henry?"

"I'll handle it. After all, I don't want the guy jumping out a fourth-floor window if he hates the idea."

"Quite the opposite, I'd guess. Have I ever mentioned that you'd make a good priest?"

"Too many times. One day, I might even start believing you."

*****

Jack stood in a first-floor business office located next to the faculty lounge at 9:00 in the evening two days before Thanksgiving, reviewing a draft layout of the monthly *Cupertinan* periodical scheduled for release the next morning. The office, which tonight served as the paper's newsroom and print facility thanks to its modern photocopy equipment, bustled with activity as Jack's staff of five seniors – including his sports writers Jared and Ben – three juniors, and a sophomore went about their tasks like bees in a hive.

"Looks like we're going to have to pull an all-nighter," Jack told the group. "I'll clear it with Father Quinn. Otherwise, we'll never get this issue out in time before everyone heads home tomorrow afternoon for vacation."

Delays in receiving articles and other content from several student writers had pushed back the print date by a week. Regardless, Jack knew it was his responsibility as editor-in-chief to get the job done or face the wrath of Father Quinn, the moderator who oversaw the

16-page periodical's content and production schedule. No excuse, however valid, would get Jack off the hook or appease his mentor if he failed to meet the new deadline.

Since taking over the *Cupertinan's* reins, Jack had managed to form a solid working relationship with the 60-year old, crusty history and religion professor who many boys feared. Father Quinn, it turned out, possessed a sharp sense of humor that surprised Jack, plus the gray-haired moderator supported the students' First Amendment rights to express all types of opinions, within reason. Jack didn't want to ruin what they had built together over one slip-up.

"These sports articles look good," Jack told Ben, putting down the mock-up. He turned to one of the juniors. "Let me know when you finish with the Letter from Home and Puzzle page so we can get them placed."

Jack laughed out loud several times while proofreading the humor pages for grammar and typos. One anonymous student writer known only as FayBull offered a variety of sharp, sarcastic insights into seminary life. And Jack found Dan Hannigan's monthly *Thoughts from a Mindless Entity* opinion column so funny at times that he'd encouraged the fledgling humorist to submit his work to a local newspaper. Dan had refused, saying that it was okay with him if everyone at St. Paul's thought he was crazy, but he didn't want to alarm or alert unsuspecting strangers, especially any local mental health crusaders.

For this issue, Dan offered his take on a proposed change to the daily schedule that had become the talk of the campus. Instead of making the usual pro or con argument, he'd decided to suggest a radical new approach to help alleviate the daily grind. Dan next offered a short comment on sportsmanship. He finished off his column by imitating the "Who do you say that I am?" style in the New Testament to poke fun at Kevin "Dink" Duncan, a well-liked, 26-year-old, youthful-looking deacon who'd been assigned a year-long internship teaching freshman religion at the school prior to taking his vows as a Sulpician priest.

Dan wrote:

Changing Times: Our St. Paul's faculty and student body have been all atwitter about the controversial new proposal to tweak the daily schedule next semester. The way certain people have reacted you'd think the administration intended to board up all the jakes, change our school mascot to a pink Petunia, or teach classes in Greek (well, except for Greek Civilization which would be taught in Klingon because rumor has it the Prof is a fan of Star Trek reruns). As it is my policy to avoid any form of controversy on anything – with the exception of letting you know that the fact I'm wearing green pants and red socks may have colored my judgment – I've written up a new daily schedule that should please everyone (excluding the Archbishop, parents, college admission boards, and those who value books and education):

AM

9:00	Rising (Optional)
9:30	Breakfast in Bed
10:00	Class (Optional)
10:45	Recess

PM

12:00	Lunch
1:00	Recreation (Note: Racing the two, big, Chevrolet Impala House cars around campus is limited to faculty and seniors only)
5:00	Cocktails in the new Father Jack Daniels Hall
6:00	Formal Dinner (For those who can still find the refectory; Smoking jackets required)

7:00 – 9:00	Playtime
9:00 – Midnight	Movies, Mind-numbing TV, or Pillow Fights in the Courtyard

Sports Rap: A few Profs recently expressed concern about a perceived lack of sportsmanship demonstrated by our illustrious athletic teams. No worries! My unscientific and totally fake survey showed that opposing players not only receive the customary handshake and insincere, "Good game," but they usually are allowed to leave with at least 90 percent of their team even if the dirty @&#* win.

In addition, congratulations to JV soccer coach Father Bill who deserves recognition for whatever it was that he did. Another fine example of something, I'm sure.

Deacon Blues? Setting: The new semester. Students sit at their desks waiting for the start of freshman religion class, "Radical Impersonations of a Priest."

Deacon Duncan: My sons, what course do you say that this is?

First Student: Is it, "How to Suppress a Yawn?"

Second Student: Or, "I Never Promised You a Rose Garden?"

Third Student: Or maybe, "No Way Out?"

Deacon Duncan: Children, if you do not know the course name, then who do you say that I am?

First Student: Are you a Freshman?

Second Student: Are you the Inmate Running the Asylum?

Third Student: Are you Mr. Big Stuff, who do you think you are?

Deacon Duncan: No, I am the Dunk, the Deeky Dunk, the big Double Dink.

First Student: Are you the One we've waited for who's brilliant, funny, and an easy grader?

Deacon Duncan: Yes, I've been blessed with all but three of those qualities, so listen to what I say. Hey, hey, hey!

All Students: We need a drink, Dink.

The End

Page by page, Jack and his staff edited copy, inserted artwork – including a fancy cover design created by the artistic sophomore – and finalized the layout. The boys had made enough headway by 2:00 am for Jack to send the four sleepy underclassmen off to bed while his five stalwart classmates continued to work feverishly.

Tired, anxious, and needing a break, Jack stepped out into the cold, eerily silent corridor with its black and white checkered tile flooring, high ceilings, and walls lined with more than 50 framed photos of past graduation classes. He looked up at the Class of 1933 and recognized a familiar face.

Hey, that's Father Ring from home. How did I not see that before now?

Jack wondered if the man who played a key role in his decision to enter the seminary had also struggled through arduous late nights during his tenure at St. Paul's. Perhaps he'd even stood in this same hall staring at a class photo, pondering how he'd ever gotten here. The realization of what others had weathered before him perked Jack up with renewed resolve to get the job done.

Jack turned to go back into the office. A figure standing in the darkness across the foyer caught his eye. Startled, Jack tried to focus his gaze. For a brief second, he thought he saw Father Martin. Just as Jack started to call out, the shadow vanished. He took a few quick steps down the corridor to get a closer look. Only silence surrounded him. Exhausted, Jack guessed he'd seen a reflection in the glass door that led to the college wing.

Man, my mind is playing tricks. Time to put this bulletin to bed.

Just before daylight, the six drained-yet-determined seniors began the printing process. They finished assembling and stapling 200 copies for distribution in time to stagger into the refectory for breakfast at 7:30 on an overcast Wednesday morning.

"Thanks, guys, the hot chocolate and donuts are on me," Jack lightheartedly told his bleary-eyed staffers. "I owe you all big time. We've kept the barbarians at the gate for at least another month."

"Not to worry, Jack," Jared replied. "It's worth losing sleep to see our names in print and hear everyone's reactions to Dan's latest certifiable commentary. And by the way, have a Happy Thanksgiving. You deserve it."

Chapter 17

Christmas season arrived at St. Paul's along with a piercing cold snap. A slight dusting of snow – almost unheard of in the South Bay – covered the rolling hills and treetops, giving the campus a homey, New England feel. A beautifully decorated, 12-foot blue spruce with white lights warmed the Grand Foyer, accompanied by a large, hand-crafted Nativity scene, complete with wooden, painted figures of the Holy Family, a stable, shepherds, wise men, and animals. The maintenance staff also draped fragrant fir garlands with red bows along the marble staircase as a perfect finishing touch.

Not to be outdone, a group of students displayed their Christmas spirit by hanging purple banners with Biblical verses in pink lettering throughout the school to mark the beginning of four weeks of "Advent," or the coming of Christ, in the Church calendar. Many boys also put up small decorations in their rooms, adding to the festive mood.

Looking out his fourth-floor window across the frosted front lawn, Jack half-expected a horse-drawn sleigh filled with men sporting top hats and women in Victorian dress to pull up to the front steps. The scene also made him appreciate the old steam radiator attached to the wall below his window. Despite sometimes making loud hissing and banging sounds during the night, it filled his room with welcome heat, in stark contrast to the cold of the frozen trees and grass.

To enhance the feeling, Jack had placed an 18-inch tall artificial tree with tiny red, green, blue, and gold ornaments on his desktop, along with a stuffed Rudolf the Reindeer whose nose lit up bright red whenever someone squeezed the toy's fluffy right ear. Jack loved this time of year, not only for its warm holiday feeling but because it meant two weeks at home with his family and a break from St. Paul's intense academic regimen.

"As made-up holidays go, Christmas is certainly my favorite," Dan joked as the soccer team stretched before practice on a drizzly afternoon in early December.

"Better not let the Warden hear you talk like that, or he'll kick you straight to Santa's house at the North Pole," Jack warned.

"People create all holidays, Dan, usually to mark a major event in human history," Patrick said. "I'd say the birth of the Savior rates a special day, even if it's a few months off from when it happened."

Before heading home to enjoy the break, however, all 16 Varsity players knew they still had work to do. The four games remaining on their December schedule matched the team against tough opponents, including one defending league champion and a local public school that had evolved into a fierce rivalry over the past few seasons. Regardless, everyone hoped to keep their perfect record intact.

The first game against Los Alamos High School provided a stiffer challenge than expected. Due to their proximity in the affluent Los Altos Hills, the two schools' soccer teams had developed an uncharacteristic dislike for one another. Jack and his teammates didn't need to talk about it – they just knew. The Battling Bishops took the field extra motivated to do whatever it took to win their annual match.

Only minutes before halftime, the physical contest remained a 0-0 standoff. At the exact instant Jack went to take his fourth shot of the afternoon, a muscular defender tried to kick the ball away. He missed. Instead, the blow caught Jack on the outside of his right ankle. The air filled with a popping sound as the fullback's leather boot cracked hard against bone and ligament. Jack got up and continued to play but walked gingerly off the field when the whistle blew ending the half.

"Are you hurt?" the team trainer asked while Jack sat on the ground rubbing the ankle through his sock.

"I'm fine. It just needs a little ice."

Jack's ankle continued to swell throughout the second half. He remained silent about the injury, worried that Coach Shumaker would take him out of the scoreless game. Determined to make a difference despite his pain, Jack sprinted on a breakaway past the same defender who'd kicked him, and drilled the game's lone goal in the 80th minute, extending St. Paul's winning streak to nine games.

Jack finally removed his shoe on the bus ride home. When Coach Shumaker, who was sitting directly across the aisle, saw the golf ball-sized lump on the side of Jack's ankle, he yelled to the trainer at the back of the bus, "Sam, bring an ice bag up here."

"My Lord, when did this happen?" the Coach asked.

"I got kicked pretty hard in the first half."

"The first half? Why didn't you say anything?"

Jack cringed as Sam applied a bag of ice to his swollen, discolored ankle.

"I guess I should have, Coach. I just wanted to make sure we won."

Back at school, Patrick and Tom helped Jack to the infirmary, where the nurse wrapped his ankle and gave him a pair of wood crutches.

"Keep the foot elevated as much as possible, and ice it for twenty minutes at a time," she ordered. "I'll give you a bottle of aspirin for the pain. Stay off it as much as possible."

Over the next ten days, Jack watched three games from the sidelines. St. Paul's edged out a victory in the first one on goals by Riley and Jimmy. Missing Jack's speed and grit, the team suffered its first loss of the year 2-0 in the second match, followed by a hard-fought 3-3 draw against Archbishop Callahan College Preparatory.

"We could have won today if Hardin hadn't made a hash of the final shot," Brian complained that night to several players in the senior lounge following the frustrating tie.

"After me, the Great Flood, right, Brian?" Patrick said, borrowing the declaration of self-absorbed conceit from the debauched King Louis XV of France, although some historians credited it to his most famous mistress, Madame de Pompadou. "I didn't see your name all over the score sheet. Try putting the ball in the back of the net before you criticize anyone else."

"I don't need to you tell me what to do," Brian growled.

"That's real good to know, Tron," Jack cut in. "We were starting to wonder."

"And what are you, some kind of mama's boy, Keane?"

As soon as the words left his mouth, Brian knew he'd crossed a line. He immediately started dancing backward faster than Ginger Rogers in an old black-and-white movie.

"I mean, you know, like a baby or something?"

Despite his bad ankle, Jack aggressively jumped up off the couch. "Shut up, Tron," he said, not waiting for Patrick to respond. "Shut your pie hole before I shut it for you."

"Calm down, Hazy," Patrick said. "It's all right." He turned to Tron. "Brian, one of these days your mouth is going to get you in real trouble, the kind where people end up hurt, or worse. Maybe you should try growing up before that day arrives."

Brian mumbled something under his breath and walked out of the lounge.

"Man, that guy's not happy unless he's complaining," Jack said.

"I have to admit Brian can sound like a pro when it comes to articulating his stupidity," Patrick acknowledged.

"Even Tron knows that Tom had no chance to score with two defenders draped all over him," Jack said. "I hope Santa brings me a baseball bat so I can use it to knock some sense into him."

"He probably wouldn't notice," Patrick said with a chuckle. "Plus you risk damaging your new bat. And if a judge locks you up, even today's Church wouldn't ordain a priest with a criminal past."

Despite the setbacks, the team's record stood at 10-1-1 heading into Christmas vacation. The final day of classes on Friday, December 16th, broke gray and dreary. Not even the cold, wet pavement, which glistened from a light overnight rain, and biting chill could dampen Jack's mood. He'd finished his last test, a draining physics exam, the previous day, and he now looked forward to a morning of carefree classes where little in the way of learning took place. Instead, most Sulpician professors kept the day simple, allowing their charges to discuss how they planned to spend the welcome break, which ended on Epiphany Sunday in early January.

First period Latin transformed into everyone's favorite for the day when Father Joe brought in hot chocolate and pastries. The boys and their mentor spent the next 45 minutes happily trying to translate Christmas phrases into a comatose language, one that remained on life support only in seminaries and the occasional old-style Mass.

"No, Dan, *Stickus ad sockus* does not mean, 'Stick this in your stocking,'" Father Joe joked. "And feel free to take three or even four weeks off before you return. After all, the faculty deserves a nice vacation too."

"No problem, Father. It'll give me more time to hang out in church and light some candles. Maybe even edit a few Papal encyclicals I've been meaning to catch up on."

"I'm sure Rome would appreciate your generous help," Father Joe laughed. "For everyone's sake, let's hope nothing's written in Latin."

That afternoon, most students headed home to celebrate the season with their families. Patrick, Jared, Dan, and a still-gimpy Jack, who at least could walk again without crutches or much pain, decided to stick around for an extra day, so Father Joe put them to work shuttling younger boys to the train and bus stations.

Jared, who loved the freedom of getting behind the wheel whenever he could, jumped at the opportunity to drive the blue 1977 Chevy House car. He even volunteered to drop off boys who lived locally at their front doors. By the time the smiling senior walked into the refectory at 6:30 carrying two tins of Christmas cookies given to him by grateful mothers, dinner was nearly over.

"Nice haul," Jack said. "Remember, it's the season for sharing."

"Help yourselves. I already took a box of chocolate candy up to my room for safe keeping. You'll never find it."

"Thanks, Santa," Dan said as he opened a tin and took out a handful of homemade oatmeal raisin cookies. "Got any gold and frankincense in there?"

"You're mixing myths with fact again," Patrick pointed out with a laugh. "I doubt Santa rode camels with the wise men, although from what I've read as many as a dozen or more Magi showed up from the East. Now I understand why Fang only gave you a B on Wednesday's Church History test."

"I got a B?" Dan replied, his eyes brightening. "Great! I worried it was touch-and-go for even a C+. Now I'm really in a good mood. How'd you find out?"

"He posted our grades in the senior lounge," Patrick explained. "Word is he printed 'Great guesswork' next to your name."

"So it's true what they say. Studying does make a difference," Dan said. "Who knew?"

"Yeah, right, Einstein," Jared said. "More like studying Jack's paper by looking over his shoulder."

"No way. I gave up making sure Jack had the right answers at least two years ago. I earned this one. And unlike you brainiacs who've already reached your mental peak, I can feel myself growing smarter by the day."

"If you say so, Danny boy," Jack said. "At least your holidays will be happy."

*****

As with most school vacations, the welcome time off flew by far too fast. On the first Sunday evening in January, the St. Paul's student body and faculty gathered in the first-floor Recreation Hall for the traditional Epiphany gift exchange. Known as the Twelfth day of Christmas and end of the blessed season in the Catholic Church,

Epiphany not only marked the visit of the wise men who brought gifts to the Christ Child, but also signified the extension of salvation to non-Jews, or Gentiles. Before leaving for vacation, each boy had drawn the name of a fellow student from a bowl and was asked to bring him a wrapped present worth no more than ten dollars.

The room buzzed with chatter and laughter as classmates shared news of the past two weeks and opened their gifts. At one point, Dan strolled by Father Joe, who was talking with a group of sophomores.

"Aw, did you miss us, Father?" Dan asked.

"Most of you, Mr. Hannigan," he replied with a wink. "Most of you."

Jack, who'd been chatting with Ben, walked over to Brian and Jared to see what presents they'd received.

"Did you hear?" Brian asked.

"Hear what?"

"Riley's not coming back. He quit over vacation."

"WHAT?" Jack exclaimed. "You gotta be kidding! Son of a …."

"Biscuit?" Patrick said as he walked up behind the group. "I take it you just heard the news about Riley."

"I can't believe he left," Jack moaned. "What a huge loss."

"I feel sorry for the guy Riley drew for the gift exchange," Brian said. "He got squat."

"You're a big bananahead, Tron," Jack said. "We lose a top scorer, and you make jokes. Plus Riley was a good guy."

"Boo-hoo," Brian said. "It was his choice to bail. And I'm the bananahead? He never said a word to anybody."

"As a matter of fact, I spoke with Riley yesterday," Patrick said to everyone's surprise. "He wished us the best, and I wished him good luck from all of us, even you Brian. Riley told me it was a tough decision for him, but something he needed to do. At least we don't have to play against him when he starts classes at Blessed Heart in the City."

"Did he sound okay?" Jack asked.

"Yes, excited about his new surroundings and living at home again. He's got regrets too. I told him not to feel like he let anyone down because Saint Paul's will kick butt with or without him."

"It would have been a lot easier with him," Jared said.

"Probably," Patrick said. "Now it's time for you and the rest of us to step up and fill the void Riley leaves. Agreed?"

Jared nodded his head.

"Guess this means Artie will start at wing, huh?" Jack said.

"And Gabriel will see more time on the field too," Patrick predicted. "They both logged minutes while you were sidelined with the bad ankle. They're ready. Even though we'll miss Riley, we have good replacements. Worrying about it won't help."

"That's the big problem I've always had with this place," Jack said with resignation as Patrick and he left the hall to head upstairs. "It's like going to school in quicksand, where friends can disappear in an instant."

"I get it. We all want certainty, which often is impossible to attain. Let's just hope that instability won't ruin us or cause what we're building here as a team to collapse before we've had our moment to shine."

Chapter 18

A cold, unseasonably dry January, during which all students endured three grueling days of final exams to end the first semester, rolled into a warmer, often sunny February. With Jack back in the line-up, the team continued to mow down opponents, logging seven straight wins in the New Year to run its record to 17-1-1.

"Looks like nothing can stop us now," Jimmy proclaimed.

One Friday morning, the food service prepared a special breakfast egg dish covered in red sauce mixed with bits of sliced vegetables. When the platters arrived at the tables, some older boys began to make derogatory jokes about the main entrée's unappetizing appearance.

"Yuck," Dan said. "Time to hit the cereal rack."

The servers soon cleaned out the entire assortment of tiny boxes of Cheerios, Frosted Flakes, Corn Flakes, and Sugar Pops, and delivered them to their hungry customers. As the boxes piled up on each table, the negative comments grew louder. Infuriated by what he heard, Father Webb stood up at the head table and rang the bell loudly. The entire refectory fell silent.

"By damn, this is called Spanish Omelet, and it's good," he shouted while waving both index fingers frantically in the air. "You'll eat it and like it. The next complaint I hear come out of anyone's mouth will be his last at this school."

"Whoops," Patrick whispered to Jack. "At least someone's figured out what the heck this is."

The boys finished breakfast and left the refectory in near silence. When the 8:00 o'clock bell rang to start Latin class, Jimmy sat down at his desk feeling a bit queasy.

"Good morning, boys," Father Joe said. "Please open your books to page one twenty-five, where we'll pick up translating Cicero."

Sweat covered Jimmy's forehead. His guts churned in painful chaos. He felt like vomiting. *"Oh no,"* Jimmy thought. *"I gotta go."* He suddenly jumped up from his desk and ran out of the classroom, not bothering to shut the door. The room watched in hushed surprise.

"I used to feel the same way about Cicero," Father Joe deadpanned without missing a beat. "Seriously, can anyone tell me what's wrong with Mr. Rhodes?"

"Maybe he's just a quick learner, Father," Dan said. Several boys laughed.

"Like you would know, Hannigan," Brian replied.

"Not to complain, but did you see that Spanish Omelet thing at breakfast this morning?" Jack said. "I think Jimmy's going a couple of rounds with it right now in the first-floor jakes."

"Father, Jimmy might have food poisoning," Patrick explained. "He appeared pale in the refectory, and probably needs to see the nurse."

"Not to worry, Father, Jimmy always looks like that," Dan added. "He heard pasty is in this season."

Father Joe waved his hand in the air for silence.

"Mr. Hannigan, since you're so sympathetic to your classmate's condition, go find him and make sure he gets to the infirmary. Better to nip it right away than have a possible stomach bug spread around the school. We all remember the outbreak a few years back that sent everyone home for three days. Once was quite enough."

Dan found Jimmy kneeling over a toilet in a jake across from the refectory. By the time they reached the fourth-floor infirmary, Jimmy was dehydrated and had a fever. As a precaution, the nurse requested that one of the priests drive her only patient to the local hospital in Mountain View.

With his left midfielder out for that afternoon's road game, Coach Shumaker decided to start Chuck Wallis in Jimmy's spot. The junior substitute took advantage of the rare opportunity to crack the lineup by contributing an assist in the Battling Bishops' 4-1 thrashing of Jefferson High, a San Jose public school with a huge population of more than 4,000 students.

*****

The next morning, an overcast, chilly Saturday, Patrick and Jack borrowed Father Joe's personal car – a stylish, white 1972 Chevrolet Chevelle SS coupe with a black fabric roof – and drove to El Camino Hospital to check on Jimmy. They found him sitting up in bed, wearing a light blue hospital gown, watching cartoons on TV. A breakfast tray rested on the moveable table. The food appeared untouched.

"How you doing today, Jimmy?" Patrick asked as he walked over to shake his teammate's hand. "Feeling better?"

"Yeah, Jimmy, you need to get well fast," Jack added. "All the guys missed you yesterday."

"Thanks, I'm doing a lot better, guys. That's the last time I ever eat a Spanish Omelet, no matter how much Spider yells. More like upchuck omelet. As you can see, I still don't feel much like trying the local cuisine here either."

"You must have eaten a bad egg or something because no one else got sick," Jack said.

"Something," Jimmy answered. "I'll be back at school this afternoon. By the way, Danny boy called to check up last night and told me about the win. Good job. He said Chuck played okay too."

"He's not you, but he did just fine," Patrick said.

"Pull over a couple of chairs and fill me in."

The boys talked about the game, laughed about how Jimmy had rocketed out of Father Joe's classroom, and cracked jokes for a half hour before Patrick and Jack stood up to leave.

"How'd you guys get here, by the way?" Jimmy asked.

"Father Joe let us borrow his Chevelle," Jack said.

"Are you kidding me? After what happened last time?" Jimmy displayed a wide grin. "Better make sure Patrick ends up with the keys."

"Thanks for bringing that up," Jack said. "Like I already didn't feel bad enough about popping a priest."

During the fall, Father Joe had lent Jack his car so he could drive a group of seniors to the movies on a Saturday night. The boys grabbed a bite after and returned to campus late, so Jack kept the keys. Around 6:00 am Sunday morning, on his way to say Mass in a local parish, Father Joe stopped by Jack's room hoping to pick up the car keys without disturbing him. Unable to find them, the priest decided to wake Jack, who slept facing the wall. Just as Father Joe leaned down to tap him, Jack sensed a presence in his room and, still half asleep, lashed out with his right arm, striking Father Joe hard in the shoulder.

"Sorry, Father," Jack had said, unsure if he had hit his confessor.

"I need my car keys," Father Joe replied.

"Oh, uh, they're in my pants pocket, that pair hanging over the chair," a groggy Jack said.

Father Joe left the room rubbing his shoulder, while Jack fell back asleep. Wondering if he'd dreamt the whole thing, Jack sought out Father Joe in his suite later that day.

"Father, did you come into my room this morning to get your keys?" Jack had asked.

"Yes, and I came away with a bruised shoulder. You pack quite the punch."

A look of horror seized Jack's face. "So it was real? Father, I'm so sorry. I was asleep and…oh, geez!"

"Don't worry, son," Father Joe had reassured. "From now on, I'll think twice before sneaking up on someone while they're sleeping."

"That's history, guys," Patrick said, looking at the clock on Jimmy's hospital room wall. He moved toward the doorway. "Let's get going, Hazy. See you tonight, Jimmy." Jack smiled and waved his right hand.

“Thanks for coming. It gets pretty boring here.”

The two boys made their way out through the automatic glass doors and into the packed hospital parking lot. Patrick unlocked the car doors and got in. He didn’t start the engine. Jack could see something was bothering him.

“If you don’t mind, I’d like to drop by to see Millie,” Patrick said. “She seemed a little down during my visit last week. The home is just a few blocks from here. Is that okay?”

“Sure. Let’s go cheer her up.”

The drive took only a few minutes. When the boys walked into “Millie’s Place,” as Patrick liked to call it, a young nurse dressed in dark blue slacks and a multi-colored blouse stood at the front reception counter studying a chart. Neither Patrick nor Jack recognized her. “Must be a new hire,” Patrick whispered as they approached.

“Hi, we’re here from Saint Paul’s to see Mildred Johnston,” Patrick said. “We wanted to check on how she’s doing.”

The nurse jerked her head up. Her brown eyes opened wide, like a deer caught in headlights.

“I’m, I’m sorry, but… I mean to say, Millie passed away last night.” The nurse stared down at her hands for a moment and drew a deep breath. “She hadn’t been feeling well the last few days….” She paused. The regular nurse, Agnes, hearing Patrick’s voice, emerged from her office located a few steps to the left of the desk.

“We’re all very sorry, boys,” Agnes said. “Millie died in her sleep. The funeral home picked up the body early this morning. I can give you the address if you’d like to pay your respects.”

Patrick’s face turned ashen gray. His eyes lost their sparkle. Jack stood staring, not believing what he’d heard.

"Okay," Jack murmured. "We'll take the address."

Patrick handed the car keys to Jack on their way out the door without saying a word. As they drove, Jack glanced over and saw Patrick's bottom lip begin to quiver. Unable to fight the pain, Patrick covered his mouth with a clenched left fist, but he couldn't stop the tears from streaming down his cheeks. His body shuddered with emotion. Jack had never seen Patrick cry. He felt tears well in his own eyes. No words would come. He reached over with his right hand and gently squeezed Patrick's shoulder.

Upon reaching St. Paul's front parking lot, Jack pulled in and turned off the car's engine. Patrick sat motionless, staring straight ahead. He took a deep breath and shifted slightly in his seat toward Jack.

"You see, I came to think of Millie as my special grandmother," Patrick said. "The news just hit me real hard."

"I understand. I really do. I barely knew her, but, well, I feel the same way."

"Losing my mother shattered me," Patrick revealed, his voice filled with pain. "Nothing else will ever hit me that hard. I walked around in a trance for more than a year, depressed and numb to the world. I was lost. One day, with my Dad's help, I realized that I could feel nothing for the rest of my life, like a zombie, or feel everything. I chose everything. And that makes some days tougher than others. Especially one like today."

Jack nodded his head.

"A heart can break only so many times," Patrick said in a whisper. "One day. . .one blow too many...I'm not sure if it can recover."

"Hang in there, bud. Today's not that day. We'll get through this one too."

Patrick managed a sad smile.

"'Weeping may last through the night, but joy comes with the morning,'" he sighed. "Even the Psalms ring hollow today. "

"Then let's go with 'this too shall pass,' and wait for time to lessen the blow."

Patrick took a long, deep breath. "Yeah. It better get to it fast."

Millie's passing weighed heavy on Patrick's mind during the coming days. Her death also affected Jack more than he expected. After a third straight night of not sleeping well, Jack trudged into Father Townshend's Russian Literature class at 8:50 on Tuesday morning and slumped into a desk.

"What's wrong?" Patrick asked. "You seemed down all through Latin."

"I had a terrible dream last night, probably because I've been thinking about Millie. I was an old man, maybe late eighties, lying in bed and near death. And I kept asking, 'Where did it go? I was just in school.' I woke up in a sweat and couldn't get back to sleep."

"Sounds creepy. On the bright side, at least you made it into your eighties," Patrick said, trying to lighten the mood.

Jack managed a weak smile. "It spooked me. And now I feel lousy."

"You could toss a pillow on the floor and take a nap during class," Dan suggested. "Maybe old Pete won't notice."

"Not your best idea," Jack replied, too tired to laugh. "Plus I don't want to take your favorite spot."

"Remember, Jack's pushing ninety," Jimmy pointed out. "He'd never to be able to get back up."

"At least he's not a total bananahead, like you two," Patrick said. "Hazy, your dream reminds me of the warning to keep watch because we don't know the time when the Lord is coming."

"Or maybe that we can't stop the runaway time-train that's rolling into eternity," Jack said. "It made me realize we better make the ride special now, so we don't wake up one day wondering where the time went, like in my nightmare. By the way, guys, wake me when Russian Lit is over."

Patrick couldn't stop thinking about Jack's dream and Millie's passing for the rest of the period. He felt worse by the minute. Fed up with the lingering, oppressive sadness, Patrick decided to take out his frustration in Father Volk's religion class.

"Any questions?" the priest asked while walking toward the blackboard.

No hands popped up. The room grew still. Patrick sat back in his chair. His bold voice broke the silence.

"Why all the secrecy, Father?"

Father Volk turned abruptly to face the questioner.

"What do you mean, Mr. Keane?"

"Why reveal our Lord's Resurrection to only a small group of true believers? Why not let everyone see the power of God through an overwhelming display of truth and love?"

Patrick's words reverberated around the classroom with intense passion. They almost sounded accusatory to Jack's ear.

"I mean a real mind-boggling marvel, something to light up the entire sky, with choirs of angels and booming voices," Patrick continued. "Seems to me it would have been an epic opportunity to convert a large portion of the ancient world and reach out to the far ends of the Roman Empire. That's the essential goal, right, to spread the Good News to people everywhere?"

"John wrote, 'Blessed are those who have not seen, and have yet believed,'" Father Volk said, keeping his voice calm but firm. "And remember, it was Christ who sent the Holy Spirit to help reveal His resurrection to all mankind."

"I agree that faith is critical, and I'm certainly not questioning the ways of the Lord. All I'm saying is that an even more dramatic miracle witnessed by thousands of people might have produced the kind of immediate impact that moved human history irreversibly toward a more Christian direction."

Jack had seen Patrick get on this type of roll before and knew his friend was not about to relinquish the floor.

"In other words, why not simply say, 'Here's the truth of resurrection, the most profound event in human history: believe in me as your Savior through the inspiration of the Holy Spirit, try not to mess up too much during your time spent on Earth, and as your reward I will bring you home to the Father, your Creator, who offers a reunion of life eternal beyond anyone's wildest imagination?' Direct, open, and to the point. Even a Roman emperor might have second thoughts when faced with that incredible reality."

"I'm not so sure; that has been the ongoing work of the Church through men like Saint Paul and her priests for two thousand years, yet many people still reject the Word," Father Volk said. "In John 14, Christ tells us 'Because I live, you shall live also.' These are the permanent things that represent the bedrock of our faith: the risen Christ's gift of life and final victory when we enter God's Kingdom. Our mission is to continue to lead all men and women toward that salvation."

"It just seems to me a more dramatic show might have made a huge difference, that's all," Patrick finished, realizing the debate had run its course. "Am I wrong, Father?"

Father Volk placed the thumb and index finger of his left hand against either side of his chin and thought for a few seconds. He started to speak when the bell rang.

"As usual, Mr. Keane has given us much upon which to reflect. While you're contemplating his unique theological perspective, please don't forget to prepare for tomorrow's quiz by reading chapters nine and ten. Class dismissed."

"Saved by the bell," Patrick said as he left the classroom.

"Fang or you?" Jack asked. "You do plan on passing his class, right, so you can, for example, go to college? One can only rock a boat so much until it capsizes."

"Or washes the decks clean?" Patrick said.

"Guess we'll find out when grades come out."

"Father Volk is okay; he gave me an A last semester, so how much worse could it be this time around? In the meantime, let's keep the boat rocking."

CHAPTER 19

"What do you want, more than anything?" Patrick asked Jack one evening at a mahogany table in the otherwise unoccupied library. The boys had chosen the quiet sanctuary to cram for an anticipated tough exam in Father Townshend's Russian Literature class. Old school in nearly every way, Father "Pete" had a well-earned reputation as a stern taskmaster with a "You give me nothing, I give you nothing" attitude toward negligent students who showed up in his class without a solid grasp of the assigned material.

"Victory," Jack said without hesitation, "both on and off the field. Whether winning games, graduating or solving mysteries, you name it. Plain old success, to be the best."

"And knowing what's important so that winning and being the best matters?" Patrick asked.

Jack flashed back to when he'd gotten into trouble for talking during Prayer Period just days before the end of his junior year. Father Webb had singled him out from a group of three boys. When

Jack protested, the Dean made him sit alone in an empty, second-floor room for two hours as punishment.

"All the wrong things are important to you," Father Webb had declared in anger before shutting the door. "Sit here and think about that, and about your future at Saint Paul's."

Jack bristled at the memory. "You sound like Spider."

"No, he overreacted. I'm just checking your compass."

Jack grinned. "Okay. I'll try to keep it pointing in the right direction."

"Look, Hazy, it's great that you want to take things on your shoulders and shoot high. Just remember that none of us need to go it alone and usually can't do it by ourselves. A lot of time we need to ask for help. Even then, sometimes we're going to lose. Teammates and brothers support each other no matter what. That you can count on."

"Got it."

"Now let's go out and kick butt the rest of the season. First, what say we ace old Pete's test."

*****

With only a few games left on its soccer schedule, St. Paul's maintained the top record in the entire Central Coast Section. Coach Shumaker knew victories in the upcoming road matches against San Francisco's Archbishop Hannah High and St. Pius Catholic in Sunnyvale – the team with the second most wins – could decisively tip in his team's favor the argument that the CCS board should add two at-large berths to the 1978 boys soccer playoffs.

St. Paul's notched its 20th win of the season in overpowering fashion, beating the City school 5-0. Five players contributed goals, including Tony Lombardi's first of the year on an overlapping run and give-and-go from Jack that rewarded the fullback with an easy tap-in only six yards outside the goal mouth. One down, one to go.

"Win or tie today, and we cement our case to make the CCS playoffs for the first time," Coach Shumaker said shortly before kickoff against Saint Pius. "Pain, torture, agony. Leave it all out on the field, men. Time to give it our best shot and show everyone we belong."

The game quickly turned into a physical defensive battle with tight marking. Neither team gave ground, and the score remained knotted late in the second half. When an overzealous Jared took down his opponent with a hard slide tackle in the penalty box, the St. Pius shooter stepped up and calmly converted the kick from the 12-yard spot. St. Paul's trailed 1-0 with time running out.

"Press the play, boys," Coach Shumaker shouted from the sidelines. "It's now or never."

After collecting a weak shot by a St. Pius forward, Ben booted a long kick high into the air. Jack challenged for the ball near the center circle, gained control, faked right, and dribbled with speed down the left side at a 45-degree angle toward the corner flag chased by an outside fullback.

Patrick's instincts took over. "Last chance!" he shouted at Jared. "I'm going forward."

Patrick crossed the halfway line at full speed, waving his right arm over his head as he dashed past two St. Pius defenders. The sweeper had moved over to help stalemate Jack, who caught Patrick's rush from the corner of his eye. Feinting to his left, Jack pushed the ball a few yards back toward the center of the field with the outside of his right foot, away from the goal, giving Patrick just enough time to reach the top of the box. The clock showed 15 seconds.

With one fluid motion, Jack crossed the ball hard, using the far right goal post as his target. A good four inches taller than his defender, Patrick jumped with elegant precision, snapping his neck forward with tremendous force. The black and white leather sphere flew off his forehead as if shot from a cannon. The St. Pius goalie sprang hard and high to his right, his gloved hand reaching in desperation to deflect the incoming round. Jack leaped in anticipation, fists raised, ready to celebrate. On the sideline, everyone held their breath, watching the ball sail toward the unguarded left post.

*****

Jack stretched out on his bed, staring at the ceiling. The small Winchester clock he received for Christmas struck nine soft chimes, while a beam of Saturday morning sunlight tried to warm the room. Two days had passed, and he still felt swallowed by a black cloud. Over and over in his mind, Jack watched Patrick's head shot glance off the top edge of the crossbar, bounce high into the air, and fall harmlessly onto the lush green grass. The ball came to rest a few feet behind the goal, oblivious to the great pain it had inflicted on the entire St. Paul's Varsity soccer team.

How could it have missed? Jack asked himself for the hundredth time. *Patrick never misses those shots. How? It's so unfair.*

The sound of shoes pounding hard on the corridor floor jolted Jack out of his daze. Jared burst through the door, excited and out of breath.

"We're in, Jack!" he exclaimed. "Did you hear? The Central Coast Sports Authority decided to expand the post-season to sixteen teams and granted us 'at large' status because of our record. They couldn't ignore the twenty wins. We're in the playoffs!"

"What about the loss against Saint Pius?"

"Coach got word about half hour ago that it didn't matter. The board president told the members he believed Saint Paul's was one of the best teams in the state, and that the CCS shouldn't even hold a playoff if we weren't allowed to play."

"Unbelievable!" Jack shouted, jumping off his bed. "Do the guys know?"

"Not yet. I'm like Paul Revere spreading the news."

"I'll help. I can't wait to tell Patrick."

Of all the Battling Bishops players, Patrick had seemed the least affected by the missed shot. After all, it was simply physics. Too much force on the ball to allow gravity to drag it down under the crossbar and into the net. Or perhaps he'd decided to put on a brave face for everyone.

Jack ran down the hall and opened Patrick's door without knocking.

"We're in the CCS playoffs," he said with utter joy.

Sitting at his desk reading a magazine, Patrick displayed a look of pure astonishment that Jack had rarely seen.

"What?"

"We received a berth as a non-league team. The board couldn't ignore our incredible record, with all the big schools and top teams we beat. We made it."

Patrick gave a small nod of approval.

"That's fair," he said in a calm voice. "They did the right thing. We earned it."

"Darn right," Jack practically shouted. "Score one for the good guys." He lowered his voice. "Although I do wish Riley could have come along for the ride."

"For sure. We got what we wanted. Now the rest is up to us."

*****

The St. Paul's soccer team appeared both nervous and relieved when they took the field for the first CCS playoff contest in school history. Although the match played close, the Battling Bishops managed a lethargic 2-0 win over La Honda High on a warm afternoon. Patrick nailed the game-winner on a 30-yard free kick in the 70th minute, while Artie, playing right wing, scored an insurance goal on a nicely placed through-ball from Dan, beating the opposing keeper with a hard, low shot.

On the bus ride back to school, Coach Shumaker addressed his players.

"That wasn't the prettiest game, but it's a W," he conceded. "We'll need to raise our level of play in the quarterfinals to avoid an early exit."

Everyone sat in silent agreement for a few seconds. Jack spoke up first.

"We stunk," he said, his voice angry above the hum of the bus engine. "It's not enough to win. We need to play Saint Paul's soccer like the newspapers described. Winning ugly doesn't cut it."

Ben, along with a chorus of other players, also expressed disappointment with their lackluster effort.

"We're way better than what we showed today," the goalkeeper said, his voice rising. "Who's willing to work extra to make it happen?"

"No better time than tomorrow morning," Patrick urged. "Can everyone make it?

The answer came quickly. By a show of hands, the entire squad decided to stay at school for the weekend and hold an unscheduled practice.

"Great, guys," Patrick said. "See you on the field after breakfast."

Led by their captain and a boisterous, charged-up Ben in net, the players pushed themselves for three hours, perfecting two-touch passing, shooting from all angles, working three-on-three drills, and running "Superman" conditioning sprints until their leg muscles burned. At the end of the grueling session, the boys huddled up for three booming cheers of "Victory," then headed off for showers followed by lunch, chomping at the bit for their next playoff match.

*****

From the outset of the following Tuesday's quarterfinal against Valley Brook High in Milpitas, the three St. Paul's midfielders made it clear they came to play. Dan tallied first off a sweet pass from Tom, and Mateo Castro followed with a head shot from about eight yards out. Jimmy capped off the scoring with a high, curving corner kick that found its way into the far top corner of the goal. Thanks to their stellar efforts combined with relentless, smothering defensive play by the fullbacks and Ben in goal, the Battling Bishops cruised to an easy 3-0 win.

Coach Shumaker was pleased to see a focused, energized team during Wednesday's light practice. He sensed that many of his players, and especially Jack, burned within to show what St. Pauls' could do against the best when it counted. He also knew playing a large Catholic school in the semifinals would put them to the ultimate test.

"We face a strong Holy Cross squad at home tomorrow," Coach Shumaker explained at the end of practice. "They beat last year's champions four to nothing yesterday, and from the reports I received they looked real good doing it. The Cross is also as close to a Catholic school rivalry as we've got, so P.T.A., men. We've trained hard for almost five months to reach this point. No one can match our conditioning, skill level, or speed when we play our game. Let's leave everything out on the field, and walk away with our heads held high at the end of the game."

CHAPTER 20

Throughout the next morning and even during Mass, the players felt like horses on race day, ready for action. Concentrating in any of their classes proved difficult. Jack constantly fidgeted as he imagined streaking down the field and firing shots past the opposing goalie. Jared left his classroom three different times to visit the jakes. Even the usually calm Patrick seemed distant and distracted.

By the time final period calculus rolled around, the boys, and especially Jack, found it almost unbearable to sit or think. Thankfully, they knew Father Delacroix's gentle, understanding nature would preclude him from disciplining anyone for their nervous preoccupation with the playoff game. This approach stood in sharp contrast to sophomore year when the boys' disciplinarian Geometry teacher, a layman, would routinely fire small pieces of chalk at the heads of inattentive students.

"Why do we study calculus, Mr. Hayes?" the priest asked.

“Because God is the greatest mathematician, Father,” Jack answered in a robotic tone, repeating what his professor had taught him.

“Correct. The deeper science looks, the more brilliance and complexity it finds in how the universe works. The hand of the Lord wrote the divine equations before men such as Newton, Einstein, and Heisenberg discovered them.”

“He could have made it easier to understand,” Dan complained to no one in particular.

“Mr. Hannigan, where is your sense of the hunt?” Father Delacroix said, rising from his desk with a textbook in hand. “After all, God says, ‘I know. You find out.’ You boys must think like explorers or detectives to uncover the grand mystery that awaits you, the challenge of solving the mathematics of Creation.”

“Not even Einstein found all the answers, Father,” Patrick pointed out.

“True, but someone is this classroom may one day contribute to mankind’s deeper understanding of our universe. Look at the young Michael Minovtich, who used math to describe the slingshot effect that is right now allowing the Voyager spacecraft to visit the giant planets in our solar system. Or think about the four forces of gravity, electromagnetism, the weak force, and the strong force, and how their precise balance made life on Earth possible. When we consider who created that perfection, math comes alive and offers evidence of His power and glory. So, when someone asks why you should bother to study calculus, there’s your answer.”

“Who knows, Father, maybe another world or universe like ours exists out there, the kind with semi-intelligent life forms such as Dan,” Jimmy said with a smile.

“Heaven help us, Mr. Rhodes,” Father Delacroix declared. “I’m not sure even the Lord could imagine such a fascinating notion.”

The bell rang ending class. All eight senior soccer players scattered, eager to get to the gym and dress for the game. Patrick, who'd headed up to his room to drop off his books and grab a new pair of black shoelaces, ran into Jack in the hall.

"Ready for action?" Patrick said, soccer cleats in hand.

"Shoot, I left my boots in my closet," Jack said. "Just a minute."

He rushed back, grabbed a pair of freshly buffed Adidas Speeds, and met Patrick outside his room. As Jack closed his door, old Father Oliver appeared around the corner, his hunched figure creeping down the long corridor with the help of a wooden cane.

"Good afternoon, Father," Patrick and Jack said in unison.

"Hello," the crusty, aged priest grumbled, not bothering to raise his head.

"We hope you'll come watch the big game today," Jack continued. "If we win, Saint Paul's plays in the CCS soccer championship for the first time in school history."

Father Oliver stopped and looked up at the boys.

"It changes nothing," he said.

Jack and Patrick stood in frozen silence. They watched the priest continue to inch down the hall toward the elevator.

"What a crabby old fart," Jack finally said in a low voice brimming with disgust. "Unreal."

"Don't listen to him. It doesn't matter. Right now, we better get going."

The boys flew down the stairs, out the double doors, and toward the gym. They reached the locker room, now filled with players, and began changing into their freshly laundered white and gold uniforms.

"He's right, Hazy," Patrick said, as they dressed.

"Who's right?" Jack asked.

"Grumpy old Oliver. Win or lose, life goes on pretty much the same as before."

"He didn't have to say it like that. What a miserable grouch."

"It looks like he got you extra fired up."

"Damn straight," Jack said, burning with anger. "Just get me the ball today."

From the opening kick-off, Jack's intensity swept across the field, making him an unstoppable force. He controlled a chip pass on the run from Jared in the third minute, dribbled at full speed past two defenders, and finished with a powerful, bending shot that bounced off the left post and into the net.

Stunned by the quick goal, the Holy Cross defenders pressed forward to find the equalizer. They also inflicted several ferocious tackles on Jack, Tom, and Artie to combat their speed. The tactic failed; nothing seemed to slow down the Bishops' front line.

Jack jumped high during one play and headed the ball forward toward the wing. His opponent landed a not-so-subtle shove on the way down that sent Jack tumbling to the turf. Sprawled on the ground, he heard the referee's whistle blow. Jack reacted angrily nonetheless, fed up with the over-the-line rough play.

"You dirty son of a …" he began to bark.

Patrick had run up and stood towering only a few feet away.

"Hazy!" he interrupted with force. *"Imago Dei."* Patrick reached down and helped Jack to his feet.

Jack looked hard at Patrick, irritated by the unwanted Latin lesson.

"What are you talking about?" he snapped.

"In God's image. Forget the foul. The best way to get even is put another one in their net."

The black-clad referee jogged over, removed a yellow card from his shirt pocket and thrust it into the air, pointing at the Holy Cross player. He wrote down the jersey number in a small book, placed the ball at the spot of the foul, and whistled the game to continue.

Patrick walked over to take the free kick. "You good?" he asked Jack.

"Yeah, yeah." Jack brushed some dirt off his white and gold jersey.

Patrick looked in Jack's intense eyes. He could see the outcome of the game was no longer in doubt.

"Go get 'em," Patrick said. "Let's do this."

"You can count on it."

Jack once again used his lightning quickness only minutes later to disrupt the defense, turning a dazzling give-and-go sequence with a charging Dan into St. Paul's second goal. Jimmy added a stylish third score just before halftime, chipping a well-placed shot into the net's top right corner, while the defense maintained its clean sheet. During Coach Shumaker's locker room talk about the need to continue to play hard and take nothing for granted, Patrick could see Jack still fuming despite the comfortable lead.

“Keep it going, all-star,” he said as both teams jogged into position for the second-half kick-off. “You’re on fire.”

“We’re not letting them back into this,” Jack promised.

Holy Cross surged in the opening minutes as expected, taking several solid shots on goal that Ben handled flawlessly. Sensing Jack – who moved about the center circle like a hungry tiger waiting to strike – needed to run free, Patrick blasted a long ball down the right wing into acres of space. Jack pounced on the opportunity, sprinting 50 yards like a bullet to outrace the Holy Cross sweeper. A few feet from the end line, he cut the ball back with his right boot, and with one motion slammed a 30-yard, left-footed cross to the six-yard box, which Tom Hardin headed past the goalie. The Battling Bishops’ bench and fans erupted. When the final whistle blew ending the match, St. Paul’s 4-0 whitewash of their top Catholic school rival advanced them to the Saturday night championship game at Santa Clara University’s historic Buck Shaw Stadium.

The St. Paul’s players howled and laughed while they showered in the gym after the game, elated with the big win. Needing something for a blister on his foot, Jack walked into the empty coach’s office, opened the First-Aid kit, and sat down in a chair to apply the dressing. A game summary sheet sitting on the desktop caught his attention. Next to Jack’s name Coach Shumaker had written a short evaluation: “A fantastic team display of strength and silk. Speed, quickness, and skill make Hayes a nightmare to mark. His hustle and endurance provide the steam that drives us and made the difference today. Brilliant effort by everyone.”

The school buzzed with excitement over the next three days. The largest San Jose newspaper published a full page article with photographs in its sports section on St. Paul’s improbable rise to the top, calling the Battling Bishops a “Cinderella team” beneath a headline that read, “St. Paul’s Saga Grows.” The article quoted Patrick, who a reporter had interviewed following the semifinal victory.

"Why do you think such a small school like Saint Paul's has achieved so much success this year?" the journalist had asked the formidable center fullback.

"Good coaching and superb conditioning make us competitive, but our extra edge comes from being a close-knit group, sort of one big family," Patrick had explained. "Having everyone live on campus provides an advantage. There's not a lot to do at a seminary on Friday and Saturday nights, so we routinely play pick-up soccer games in the gym until eleven o'clock when the janitor locks up. It's nothing like a practice, just a chance to kick the ball around, try out new moves, develop ball skills, and create team unity. And by the way, we may be small, but we never consider ourselves underdogs."

With one game left to play, St. Paul's had made a name for itself that surprised even the most experienced observers of South Bay high-school sports. The players knew the final step would prove the most difficult. Patrick called a team meeting in the senior lounge the evening before the championship match. After all 16 players had taken their seats on the couches or the carpeted floor, Patrick stood up facing his teammates.

"We've given ourselves a chance to do something special tomorrow night, something big that most people never thought possible, maybe even some of us in this room," he said. "This is the first time in the fifty-four year history of Saint Paul's that one of its sports teams will play for a championship. I believe, and we all need to believe, that we can finish what we set out to do last October.

"Personally, I'd like to win for ourselves and for every great athlete who played intramural sports here over the decades. All the guys who never had the chance to compete against other schools or show they could hang with the best and finish on top of the pile."

"Let's win the title for everyone who ever went to this school," Ben declared with feeling.

“Good call, Keep,” Patrick said. “If anyone else has something to say, feel free to jump right in.”

“If we play our game and do what we do best, I think we’ve got a real shot,” Tom said.

Several players nodded their heads.

“Tommy’s right,” Dan agreed. “Each one of us needs to step up and get the job done. We’ve trained too long and too hard not to take home the hardware. This is THE year for Saint Paul’s soccer.”

“I don’t want any excuses or regrets,” Jared said. “It’s our time.”

“It’s important that all eleven players on the field work as a team, and none of us try to do too much on our own,” Patrick cautioned. “Well, maybe except for Jack. Hazy, the way you’ve been playing the past couple of weeks, feel free to go any darn place you want and do as much as you can.”

Several players laughed, and Jimmy teased, “Our hero. Go get ‘em, Jackie Jack.”

“By the way, Coach said to expect about eight thousand people in the stands,” Patrick said. “We can’t let that distract us. In fact, I say we give the crowd a great match, something they’ll remember and talk about for years. How about it, boys?”

“You got it, Captain,” Jared said with enthusiasm. “We’re ready to roll.”

“Now everyone get a good night’s sleep. Prepare yourselves to show the world that we’re slingers like David, and not afraid to take on Goliath.”

As the boys filed out of the lounge talking and joking, Tom, Dan, Jimmy, and Ben gave each other the new phenomenon known as “high fives.”

"Everyone's ready," Jack told Patrick. "It's going to be a long day tomorrow waiting for game time. But Tom's right. We've got a real shot if we do simple things well and take advantage of our scoring opportunities."

"I agree. Just remember to bring your slingshot."

CHAPTER 21

Father Joe stood near home plate on the baseball diamond early the next morning holding a golf club. He set up his stance, aimed the clubface toward center field, drew the 9-iron back slowly, and made a smooth pass at the ball. The little white sphere rocketed off, tracing a perfect arc until it landed softly near a clump of cypress trees by the fence, about 130 yards away.

"Nice shot, Padre," Jack said. Only moments earlier, he and Patrick had jogged down from the gym and across the bridge dribbling soccer balls. Both had stopped to watch their mentor hit his shot. "There wasn't much rust on that swing."

Father Joe turned toward his appreciative audience.

"Good morning, boys. If only they all behaved so well."

"That looked easy to me," Jack said.

"Life is a lot like golf," the priest explained. "You never really 'get it,' do you? Sometimes you fall into a groove, a winning zone, and things go well. Unfortunately, it's usually never long before you find yourself hunting for a new rhythm."

"Thanks for the warning, Father," Patrick joked. "I'll stick with soccer and baseball."

"What are you two doing this fine day?"

"We're going to stretch and kick the ball around a bit to get ready for tonight's championship," Jack said.

"I suppose you never can be too prepared for, without a doubt, the biggest sporting event in school history." Father Joe looked toward the outfield. "Tell you what, guys, that last one was a good shot to finish on. If you pick up all the golf balls out there, I'll let you borrow my car one evening to go eat or catch a movie."

"Heck, yeah!" Jack said, grabbing the green plastic basket sitting by Father Joe's golf bag. "A few of us wanted to check out a new burger place that opened in Cupertino. You've got a deal!"

"One thing: please drop my car keys off when you get back. No need for an encore."

"Absolutely," Patrick said. "At least going one round with Jack hasn't affected your swing."

Father Joe smiled. "Good luck tonight, boys. Everyone, including all your teachers, is pulling hard for you. Remember what Saint Paul wrote in Philippians 4:13: 'I can do all things through Christ, who strengthens me.'"

"Thanks," Jack said. "We're ready."

"Yes, thank you, Father," Patrick added. "We'll give it our best shot."

*****

That evening, the St. Paul's team sat in the stadium locker room preparing for the game. Coach Shumaker stood up and motioned with his hand for silence.

"Listen up, men." When the coach saw everyone paying attention, he continued. "I want to tell you a story. Years ago, a young man and his wife were about to have their first child. He was a fireman, a fearless worker and loyal friend known for his kindness and sense of humor. Everyone liked him. One day he made an appointment to see the doctor because he'd been having stomach pain and didn't feel well. It turned out that, at age thirty, the young man had a serious illness. His condition grew worse in the hospital, and the doctors told him and his pregnant wife that he wouldn't live to see the birth of his baby boy. On the verge of death, the fireman spent his last days writing eighteen birthday cards to the son he would never see. Messages the boy could open each year so he'd understand how important he was to his Dad, and how much his Dad wished he could be there celebrating with him.

"On the day before the young man died, his buddies from the firehouse walked into his room and carried him home on a gurney, not wanting their friend to pass in the sterile hospital. Instead, they brought him to the place of love and happiness that meant so much to him. That fireman was my Dad, guys, and the baby boy was me. I'd like to read you the final message my Dad wrote for my eighteenth birthday.

My dearest son,

You became a man in the eyes of the world today. You're probably looking forward to attending college, staying out late at parties, and spreading your wings. But growing up means so much more. I know your beautiful mother has done an incredible job preparing you with the same qualities that made her so special to me. Did you take it to heart when she showered you with patience, kindness, generosity, and unconditional love? Did you see your mom's strength when she rose above her pain and loss to raise you to the man you are today?

In these final hours, my greatest wish is that the Lord will bless you with a sweet girl who will love you as much as your cherished mother loved me. It breaks my heart when I think about what I will miss, never being able to teach you to throw a baseball, buy your first car, share a beer, or one day play grandpa to your children. Even though my hopes for you were cut short, I pray that you will strive to fulfill your tallest dreams no matter how difficult or distant they may seem at times. If you ever falter and need to ask for strength, the Lord will answer.

I will forever love you and be part of you as you make your way in the world. I only wish I could have been there to witness that proud moment when my little boy took his first step as a man. Whenever you feel your heartbeat, or take a deep breath, or gaze into the heavens, know I am there, inseparable and proud, watching over my precious child. Your loving Father

Like many of his teammates, Jack kept his head down. He tried to hide the sting in his eyes, not wanting anyone to see his reaction to the coach's emotional appeal. What Jack knew is that he'd run through a brick wall, and do whatever it took, to make this dream come true for his Coach, his teammates, the entire St. Paul's community, and himself.

"The point is that we never know how much time we have, or when another opportunity will come along, guys. We need to do our best to live our dreams now. What do you say we get this done tonight?"

Jared stood up and yelled, "Let's do this!" and the rest of the team joined in until the deafening din could be heard even outside in the parking lot.

At precisely 7:15 pm, the blue-clad Mount Royal Knights and the St. Paul's Battling Bishops, looking sharp in their white and gold uniforms, lined up less than five yards apart outside the locker rooms waiting to take the field. Their respective captains positioned themselves at the traditional head of the pack, followed by the goalkeepers. Players from both squads stretched and nervously moved as butterflies filled their stomachs. In contrast, Patrick stood motionless.

"This is the hour of our splendor in the grass," he said in a quiet voice, quoting the poet William Wordsworth.

Jack overheard. "Amen," he replied, barely audible.

The late winter temperature at kick-off registered a mild 60 degrees, while the bright stadium lights bathed the lush green playing surface under clear skies, perfect conditions for a championship match. When the whistle blew, St. Paul's looked unsettled for the first ten minutes, missing open players with passes and giving the ball away in the midfield. A poor back pass by Jared to Ben resulted in a steal and dangerous scoring chance for Mount Royal that barely cleared the crossbar. The Battling Bishops ran out of luck in the 16th minute when Brian failed to head the ball out of the penalty box. The Mount Royal striker, a burly, physical player with a booming right foot, charged the bouncing ball and volleyed a powerful shot past Ben and into the back netting, giving his team a 1-0 lead.

The goal seemed to calm the St. Paul's side. Their nervous play vanished. Connecting on strings of passes, the Battling Bishops controlled the ball artfully, using their skill to dictate the game's pace and create several good scoring opportunities. Still down by a goal two minutes before the half, Jared fouled the Knights' striker at the outer edge of the 18-yard box. The referee immediately pointed to the penalty spot. As captain, Patrick protested the dubious call in a firm yet respectful way, knowing the ref could hand out a yellow card caution if he dissented too aggressively. A Mount Royal midfield player converted the 12-yard kick, and St. Paul's headed into halftime trailing by two goals.

Inside the locker room, several players continued to fume over the referee's call. Others urged their teammates to work hard and keep fighting. Calling for silence, Coach Shumaker addressed the team in a calm, confident voice.

“First, your captain told me he has something to say.”

Patrick stood up and looked around the room. “Just one thing. GET OVER IT. The call was lousy, but it’s done. Move on. We’ve got a game to win.”

He sat back down on a wooden bench next to Jack, who nodded approval as he handed Patrick a cool, moist towel to place on the back of his neck.

“Excellent advice, men,” Coach Shumaker said. “Aside from the rocky start, we’ve had the better of the play, and I’d say even dominated the game for most of the first half. Yes, we’ve dug a bit of a hole for ourselves, but with our offensive ability to explode, being two goals down is not the end of this story. There’s no reason for heads to drop. Use your pace to keep pressure on the defense. Keep cracking shots. Play like you’re capable, as a disciplined, attacking team, and we can get right back in this match. Time to show everyone what a Battling Bishop is made of.”

Both teams emerged from their locker rooms eager to restart the game. Patrick tapped Jack on the shoulder just before they reached the field.

“No regrets, Hazy,” he said.

“No regrets,” Jack replied.

St. Paul’s wasted no time slicing the deficit following the second half kick-off. A series of crisp, accurate passes from Patrick to Tony to Dan to Jimmy and across to Artie ended with the ball on Jack’s right foot only 12-feet in front of the net. In total control, he found an opening and slipped the ball past the goalkeeper along the smooth green grass that had grown damp from the cooling night air.

Unfazed, the Knights answered 12 minutes later with a well-struck 20-yard shot from outside the penalty box that glanced off the post and ricocheted into the goal, giving Ben no chance to make a save.

Down two goals with 30 minutes left, Jack placed the game on his shoulders. He told himself that whether St. Paul's won or lost was now in his hands and his responsibility alone.

"I'm going for it," he said to Jimmy and Tom, who stood next to Jack in the center circle waiting for the whistle to blow for the restart. "You both may need to switch off and cover the middle, so don't hesitate."

"You got it," Tom confirmed. "Time to turn on the jets."

Playing with speed and abandon, Jack relentlessly hawked the ball up front, which created open space for Dan, Tom, and Jimmy to run into or send through passes. After receiving the ball with his back to the goal about 25 yards out, Jack knocked a diagonal pass on a line with the right corner flag and rolled hard off his man toward the left post. Artie reached the ball first and sent a pretty, one-touch cross flying through the box, just a bit too far away for the goalkeeper to snag. Jack flung himself out in mid-air with perfect timing and blasted a head shot past the stunned defender and keeper. Many in the crowd of 8,000 spectators jumped to their feet, appreciative of the incredible score that narrowed the gap to 3-2.

A defensive breakdown in the Knights' defense midway through the second half led to the equalizer. Collecting a soft shot attempt, Ben booted a long, arcing ball high into the night sky. The Mount Royal center defender misjudged its flight, and the ball bounced hard about two yards in front of him and flew over his head. Jack pounced like a cheetah at full sprint, touching the ball past the flat-footed sweeper toward the center of the penalty area. The keeper charged in desperation to no avail. Jack once again had time to pick his spot. He floated a shot that landed on the chalk line, bounced once, and sweetly settled into the white mesh side netting. Hat trick. Tie game.

The St. Paul's substitutes rose as one off the bench, jumping with their fists thrust high into the air and whooping in exuberant celebration. Teammates surrounded Jack on the field, patting him on the back and yelling, "great job." Patrick put his arm around Jack's shoulder and proclaimed, "Nice job, Hazy. Keep it up." In a voice dripping with determination, Jack declared, "You can count on it."

In the 80th minute of the 90-minute match, however, the Mount Royal center midfielder pushed a sharp pass through to the right-wing, who lofted a high ball toward the penalty spot. The striker trapped the ball facing away from the goal, faked left like he was going to shoot with his dominant right foot, but spun hard, nailing a left-footed rocket toward the upper "V." Ben reacted to the fake and lurched to his left, leaving him out of position for the save. At the last instant, Patrick appeared seemingly out of nowhere to flick the shot with the very top of his head, sending the ball hard off the crossbar. It bounced high and far outside the penalty area where Jared cleared it into the packed stadium stands.

"Man, close one," Jared said as he trotted by, tapping Patrick's hand in congratulations. "Let's not have any more of those."

The clocked continued to tick down. The teams tangled like two experienced prizefighters, bobbing and weaving, prodding and pushing. The raucous crowd sat on the edge of their bench-style seats, or stood in the aisles, thoroughly entertained by the flowing, back and forth play.

During a short break in the action when a Knights' player cleared the ball far out of bounds, Jack took a breather at midfield. He stood drenched in sweat, his uniform stained with blotches of grass and dirt, scanning the crowd. Jack spotted Father Joe sitting three rows below the press box with several other priests and a group of about 70 seminarians. Listening to shouts from the crowd, he also realized for the first time that many voices were now exuberantly supporting St. Paul's, urging the tiny school Davids to find a way to slay the large school Goliaths. *Wow*, Jack thought. *That's amazing.*

Exhausted, all 22 warriors fought with every fiber in their battered bodies, stalemating the opposition's efforts to break free. With less than a minute remaining in regulation, Patrick's hard slide tackle won the ball from a Mount Royal attacker. He popped up quickly with the 15-ounce, black-and-white orb at his feet, and pushed forward as he peered downfield.

Reading the opportunity, Jack took off from inside the center circle directly toward the right sideline. Patrick finessed a nice chip pass over two midfielders' heads that connected with Jack's downfield run. The Knights' outside back came up to cut off his line of attack. Dribbling with the outside of his foot, Jack rushed directly at him, touching the ball to his opponent's right as he sprinted past him on the left. The nifty move freed Jack into space leaving one man to beat. As the last line of defense, the Mount Royal sweeper hesitated, bracing for a game-saving tackle. Jack saw an opening through the player's feet. He pushed the ball between them for a perfect "nutmeg," and found himself alone on goal.

The Knights' keeper, a tall, lanky senior, rushed off his line well and dove bravely at Jack hoping to smother the ball. An instant before the lunging goalie could stop him, Jack fired off a clean shot and was immediately knocked hard to the turf when a desperate Knights' defender crashed into him at full speed from the left.

The rising ball rocketed off the top of the post and careened into the air, looping out high above the pile of bodies lying in front of the net. Tom, who had trailed the play from his left wing position, rushed in unmarked. With perfect timing, he slammed a full volley with his right foot at the open goal. The leather sphere skimmed metal as it barely dipped under the crossbar and tore into the netting.

Sprawled on the ground, Jack heard the referee's whistle blow. He immediately looked up at the electronic scoreboard. The glowing, bright red numbers showed eight seconds left on the clock.

Bedlam followed. Jack jumped up and raced at a full sprint toward Tom with both arms in the air, screaming "Yeeeeeeeeesssssssss!

Thousands of fans were on their feet, clapping wildly and cheering at the top of their lungs. Many gave each other emphatic high fives. The entire St. Paul's bench bolted onto the field and joined their teammates, mobbing Tom and Jack, and creating a scrum of happy, ecstatic players.

"Unbelievable," Artie yelled, grabbing his head with both hands in disbelief.

"Taahhhmmee!" Jimmy shouted as he jumped up and down, his arm wrapped around the back of his teammate's neck. "You're puuuuurfect!"

After about 30 seconds of raucous celebration, the referee came over to restore order, get the subs off the field, line up the teams, and restart the game.

With no time to waste, the Mount Royal striker ripped the ball as hard and as far as he could toward the St. Paul's goal, which sat 55 yards away. Seeing the shot attempt would fall short, Ben dashed off his line and grabbed the ball out of the air before it could bounce, then pulled it tight against his Kelly-green clad chest. Game over. Bishops win.

The crowd continued to cheer. A chant rose from the stands behind the north goal and swept over the entire stadium: "Saint Paul's, Saint Paul's, Saint Paul's!" The priests and students joined the chorus, standing on their seats with arms raised in triumph. Father Joe lifted his eyes toward the heavens and nodded in thanks, a mix of relief and joy radiating from his face.

On the field, Jack and Patrick ran toward each other and hugged.

"I knew you'd make it happen, Hazy," Patrick said with complete jubilation. "The Lord provides."

"And so did you! Great pass. And what a finish by Tom. We did it, Patrick, we all did it!"

Jumping and yelling, Jared, Dan, Artie, and Jimmy soon surrounded them both. Coach Shumaker also joined in the celebration, still emotional from the realization of an unlikely dream.

"Unreal, boys," he said, eyes glistening, as player after player shook his hand. "Simply unreal. I couldn't be prouder of you."

Players, coaches, students, family members, and soccer fans milled about the field, giving the stadium a party-like atmosphere. At one point the Mount Royal striker walked by hand-in-hand with a pretty brunette cheerleader, who wore his blue and gold Letterman's jacket.

"Hey, buddy, great game," the striker said to Jack, stopping for a second. "That was real tough for us to lose, but you played incredibly." He looked over at Patrick. "You too, man. I can't believe you guys want to be priests."

"We're hoping it's just a phase," Jack joked, taken off-guard by the compliment. "You played a great game too."

The couple moved on and disappeared into the crowd as hundreds of fans continued to file out toward the parking lots.

"If we get kicked out of the seminary in the next couple months, we'll know which school to enroll in," Patrick told Jack. He looked around, first in one direction, then another, until it seemed he spotted what he was looking for, and smiled broadly. "Let's wander over here for a minute, okay?"

Both boys walked over to Tom, who was excitedly recounting some of the game's highlights with Ben. Patrick stepped between the two boys, grabbing Tom's complete attention.

"Great game, Patrick," Tom enthused. "We did it."

Patrick smiled for a few moments, looking Tom in the eye the entire time.

"You are my sunshine, my only sunshine," Patrick sang softly, then turned his head to the right.

Confused, Tom followed Patrick's gaze. Then he saw her. The initial wave of recognition nearly made his knees buckle. Tom's eyes opened wide as he stared in disbelief. His heart jumped, grasping the miracle before him. Tom's birth mother, the woman he had not seen in 15 years, stood near the stands about 100 feet away, filled with apprehension and hope.

"Oh, my God," Tom exclaimed. "Is that, is that really her?"

"She's waiting," Patrick said. "I think you've both been apart long enough."

Tom's eyes filled with tears, He practically leaped forward, giving Patrick a big, heartfelt hug.

"Wow," Tom said, stepping back. "I, I don't know what to say. I mean, how, how did you do it?"

Patrick responded with a warm smile. "As we like to mention now and then, the Lord provides."

Tom shook his head in amazement. "Thank you for this. Just thank you. This is incredible. Guess I owe you one, brother."

Jack and Patrick watched Tom run over and embrace his mother, who appeared overwhelmed at their long-awaited reunion.

"Is that …?" Jack asked

"Yes, it is," Patrick interrupted in a matter-of-fact tone.

"Amazing. How did you ever find her?"

"Through Millie's old contacts at the social services agency where she'd worked. Millie made all this happen. Even at the end, she was helping other people."

"What a gem, that Millie," Jack said, shaking his head. "Let's hope this fairy tale has one heckuva happy ending." He watched Tom and his mother walk across the field arm-in-arm under the bright stadium lights toward Coach Shumaker. "Looks like it's off to a great start."

"Well?" Patrick said.

Jack looked puzzled. An astute grin slowly took its place.

"Aren't you going to tell me how it feels being a genuine champion, something no one can ever take away?" Patrick finished, his voice escalating to a crescendo.

"The best. Maybe even better, which is impossible. But I doubt as good as what it feels like being the greatest friend Tom could ever wish for. Only you would know that."

"I bet you say that to all the guys who reunite sons with their long-lost birth mothers."

"All I know is this has been a day to remember," Jack said with satisfaction, "and it's not over. I heard talk that Father Joe is hosting a party for the team and coaches at a friend's home in Saratoga. Some of the priests will give us rides after we shower up."

"Now that sounds like a plan," Patrick said. "Tom and his mom will probably want to be alone, although it would be great if they stopped by later so everyone could meet her. And by the way, no choir boys tonight. With Father Joe's blessing, you and I are going to tip a beer or two and hold a celebration that we'll still talk about even at forty."

"Sounds great. We'll make it one for the ages."

The next morning, two bold headlines in the Sunday sports sections of the largest local newspapers told the story to the entire South Bay:

CHECKMATE! Bishops Top Knights To Win CCS Soccer Title

Tiny St. Paul's Claims Soccer Championship With Miracle Finish

In honor of the unprecedented achievement, Father King canceled Monday's classes and arranged for the entire school to go ice skating at a rink in San Jose, followed by an afternoon movie in the gym, and special celebration dinner.

Ben summed up the fun, relaxing day by declaring, "If the faculty treats us this well just for doing simple things well like Coach always says, we should try doing them more often."

*****

Several seniors decided to extend their CCS title celebration into the next weekend by covertly bringing beer and hard liquor back to school from home. On Saturday night, Dan, Jared, Jimmy, and Jack carried the hidden cans and bottles up the Grinder, where they sat drinking, laughing, shouting, and reliving their victory for hours.

Jimmy jumped up at one point holding a bottle of forbidden Irish whiskey and started doing a war dance, which somehow evolved into an Elvis Presley impression, followed by a series of howls that a lonely wolf would make.

Exhausted, he finally fell back on the damp grass and placed his palm over his forehead.

"I'm not very impressed with my behavior right now, guys," he said in a sloppy voice. "And my head is starting to hurt."

"Talk about self-incriminating," Jack shouted. "If only Mrs. Rhodes could see what has become of her little boy."

"Forget about taking the Fifth, Jimmy," Dan added. "We have too many witnesses to whatever that was, plus it sounds more like you drank a fifth."

It was after midnight by the time the boys stumbled down the hill and back to the fourth floor. Jack still felt no pain when he walked by Father Joe's suite. The door was open and, not thinking clearly, Jack entered and plopped down in a chair.

"Hi, Father. How's it going?"

Father Joe sat at his desk working on some papers. He looked up with a smile.

"Just fine, Mr. Hayes. It's late. What were you up to this evening?"

"I went for a hike up the Grinder with some of the guys. That stupid hill is hard enough to climb during the day, much less in the dark. What were we thinking?"

"Sounds like you weren't. I'd say a movie or a night in the gym might have been a better choice."

"Or translating Virgil – that's always a hoot," Jack replied, laughing at his joke. "Father, do you like teaching a language that almost no one can speak or read? We might as well learn Martian, which at least would come in handy if they ever decide to attack our planet."

Father Joe's face shifted into a puzzled look. "I'm not sure we need to worry about a Martian invasion, do you?"

"Maybe not, but it's always some damn thing, isn't it?" Jack said without inhibition.

"Yes, I suppose at times, it can be," Father Joe agreed, trying his best to follow the conversation.

"I recall a story Jared told me about some guy who had just finished building an expensive new home, and when he opened the front door the entire place fell into a sinkhole and was swallowed up…now that's what I call a bad day, Father. When you think about it, all we have to do is translate a few paragraphs in Latin. It's not so awful."

After hanging out in Father Joe's room talking silliness and laughing for almost 15 minutes, Jack suddenly began to feel queasy. A few seconds later, his stomach wrenched like it was ready to explode.

"Father, I've got something to tell you. I'm drunk." He grabbed his stomach with both hands. "And I think I'm about to get sick."

Father Joe looked at him with complete surprise. "What? Really?" He jumped up from behind his desk and rushed over toward Jack. "In that case, get into my bathroom quick before you throw up all over my carpet."

Jack barely had lifted the toilet lid when a flood of vomit gushed into the bowl, followed by two more productive heaves. After the intense urge passed, Jack lay down and fell asleep on the cold, white tile floor. He awoke an hour later, tired and with a horrible taste in his mouth. Jack stood up on wobbly legs and walked slowly through the bedroom. He stopped and leaned against the doorway to the office, where Father Joe still sat at his desk reading.

"Doing better?" the priest asked. He held up a glass half-filled with brown liquid. "How about a drink?"

"Oooh," Jack moaned, feeling his stomach start to churn from the suggestion. "No thanks, Father. It's the last time I ever try scotch. That stuff is brutal."

Father Joe laughed. "Welcome to the school of hard knocks. Maybe next time you'll think twice before going overboard."

"Couldn't you tell I'd been drinking?" Jack asked.

"Not at all. You hid it well. And I've been around a lot of men who like to tip the bottle. Now you need to get to bed. If you have a headache in the morning, stop by, and I'll give you something to help get rid of your first hangover."

"Thanks, Father," Jack said as he stepped out into the corridor. "Never again. Please lock me up if I even think about it."

CHAPTER 22

With winter's chill on the wane, replaced by the warm, cloudless days of approaching spring, baseball season moved into full swing. Jack and Patrick relished their time on the diamond, especially the enticing smells of freshly mowed grass mixed with oiled leather gloves. Although Jack wondered about Father Martin from time to time, Patrick remained deeply troubled by the unsolved puzzle the old priest had brought them.

"I went back into the tower last Saturday," Patrick said while the two boys warmed up by themselves in right field before practice. "I figured you weren't interested, so I didn't ask."

"Did you try to get into the belfry?"

"No, I just checked the storage room again. Everything seemed the same."

"Is that finally the end of it? No more playing detective?"

"Hardly. There's an answer out there. My vow is to find it."

While Patrick continued searching, Jack and his senior classmates immersed themselves in other priorities. Back-to-back evening performances of *Inherit the Wind* – including one attended by the public – during the second weekend of March enjoyed critical success, with Tom and Dan receiving standing ovations for their excellent portrayals.

"I never knew playing a shallow, opinionated cynic like Hornbook could be so much fun," Dan said after. "Maybe I'd make a better newspaper columnist than a priest."

By late March, the entire community's focus had turned to the greatest highlight of St. Paul's calendar year: the celebration of Easter following six weeks of Lent. Classes ended on Spy Wednesday of Holy Week, and about half the student body left campus that same day to begin their ten-day break. Boys who stayed, however, participated in a display of solemnity, pomp, and ceremony during Holy Thursday, Good Friday, and Easter Midnight Mass services that exceeded even those held in their home parishes.

The Easter vigil began at 11:30 on a brisk Holy Saturday night with the solemn Service of Light in the middle of St. Paul's darkened courtyard, attended by students and Catholics from nearby communities. Jack and Patrick watched captivated while the priest who served as the main celebrant kindled the Easter fire. Despite being engulfed by hundreds of warmly dressed worshippers, Jack could only hear the crackling sounds of flame on wood in the hushed outdoor setting. The celebrant's deep, resounding voice finally broke the exquisite quiet as he blessed and lit the large Paschal candle.

Holding small, unlit candles, members of the congregation formed a long procession behind the priest, who carried the burning Paschal flame through the courtyard toward the college chapel. Jack felt himself swept forward, becoming one with the current of the crowd. The celebrant stopped three times along the way and dramatically chanted, "Light of Christ," to which the assembly responded, "Thanks be to God." At each pause, groups of worshippers lit their candles from the Paschal flame, until the Light of Christ had spread throughout the entire gathering.

Inside the dark chapel, Jack and Patrick entered a pew near the back. They waited in sacred silence, watching the priest place the Paschal candle on its stand in the sanctuary and the crowd fill row after row. Jack stood mesmerized, savoring how the hundreds of tiny, flickering flames added to the vibrant holiness of the scene.

The lights came on, and the worshippers extinguished their flames. Ten Sulpician Fathers dressed in bright white vestments surrounded the altar, accompanied by the intense smell of incense that filled the air. One priest stepped to the lectern to read aloud a series of passages from the Old Testament known as the Liturgy of the Word. When he finished, another Sulpician followed with the recitation of the Renewal of Baptismal Vows.

Throughout the Eucharist honoring the Resurrection of Jesus Christ, Father Delacroix played the massive pipe organ while the congregation sang hymns of praise. The grand ceremony culminated with Holy Communion; the newly baptized Catholics received the host first, followed by long lines of the faithful fulfilling their "Easter duty." When the service ended at around 1:30 am, Jack and Patrick headed upstairs, too tired to sample the coffee and cake served by the school in the refectory.

"That service was something to see, even though it took two hours," a sleepy Jack told Patrick. "Saint Paul's does Easter right."

"I agree. I always went home to help out in my parish. Now I kind of wish I'd stuck around before to experience what an impressive show the Sulps put on here."

*****

The week after Easter vacation, Jack sat in Patrick's room on a warm April evening studying for midterm exams. The door suddenly swept open after a quick knock. Father Joe stood menacingly in the corridor, his eyes shooting daggers in their direction.

"Gentleman, I need to see you in my room. Now!"

The three walked down the long, wide hall, with Jack and Patrick trailing, all the while giving each other anxious glances. Jack tried to calm himself with a deep breath but felt his front teeth bite down on his lower lip as their pace quickened. Once they sat down in his office, Father Joe looked both boys in the eye, first Patrick, then Jack, and said in a firm tone, "I received a note that you've been seen sneaking up into the bell tower. Any truth to this?"

All the color rushed from Jack's face. He sat still in his chair, unable to move or speak.

"Yes, I've been inside several times," Patrick admitted straightaway.

"And you, Mr. Hayes?" Father Joe questioned.

"Yes, I've been inside too."

"I asked Jack to come along and help explore, Father," Patrick said. "It was my idea."

Father Joe sat back in his chair. "First, it's against the rules, which you both know very well, and, second, it can be dangerous, which is why we keep it locked. This building is old and in need of retrofitting, especially the tower. It's not safe."

"We only went into the bell room once to check out the view," Jack said. "Getting to see that beautiful mosaic of Saint Paul's conversion on the road to Damascus was amazing."

A baffled expression crossed Father Joe's face. "How did you get into the belfry to see the mosaic, or even find out it was there? The entrance has been nailed shut for years, ever since a building inspector determined it wasn't stable enough to go into anymore. Father King made it impossible to reach the top."

"Father Martin let us...." Jack stopped, realizing his breach of confidence.

"Father Martin?" Father Joe said with incredulity. "What are you talking about? Who's Father Martin?"

Both boys hesitated, unsure what to say.

"It's true," Patrick finally disclosed, seeing no way to put the cat back into the bag. "Father Martin McGrath, the older Sulp who lives near the tower. He asked us not to say anything because of the restrictions the Vicar put on his contact with students. Father took us up to see the view one time and showed us the mosaic. We never went without him. We've even been to his room. Have you seen his incredible baseball card collection and those great old games he keeps?"

Father Joe's face glowed a slight tinge of red. "If this is a joke, I'm not laughing, guys. I'm aware of Father Martin McGrath's history at this school." He leaned forward once again in is chair. "It might interest you to know he died last year at a retirement home back East. So who or what in the Lord's name are you talking about?"

Jack's jaw dropped, while Patrick's eyes widened in pure astonishment.

"But, Father, we saw him a few months ago, you know, before he was reassigned," Jack pleaded, his voice rising. "He looked fine. We're not making it up. Come with us to his room. I remember him saying he'd see Patrick again. Maybe he left some of his stuff behind."

"Really? That's your story?" Father Joe paused. His face froze in a stern glare. "I have no idea what you two are up to, but I'm in no mood for nonsense." He grew silent again, considering what to do next. “Okay, have it your way. Let’s go see this room and meet your remarkable Father Martin.”

The trio hurried down the hall. Tom heard the footsteps and came out of his room to see who was still awake.

“What’s up?” he asked.

“Nothing, Mr. Hardin,” Father Joe replied without breaking stride. “Go to bed.”

When they reached the room next to the tower, Father Joe took out his keys, unlocked the engraved wood door, and pushed it open. The three stepped inside. Jack and Patrick stood in shocked silence, their disbelieving eyes moving methodically around the room. Nothing looked familiar. In fact, it appeared that no one had lived in the suite for years. The empty bookshelves that lined the far wall held only dust. Even the soft, welcoming leather chairs had disappeared, replaced by two beat up desks stacked top-to-top, the upper one’s scratched and scuffed legs sticking straight up toward the cold ceiling. The stifling air smelled fetid and musty, as if no one had bothered to throw open a window for decades.

“What is this place?” Jack started to implore. “This can’t be his room. It was totally different….”

Patrick interrupted. “Sorry, Father. Jack and I messed up on this one. We have no explanation for any of this.”

“Were you boys drinking up in the tower?” Father Joe demanded. “Is that why you invented this Father Martin charade?”

“No way!” Jack declared.

“We may like to explore, but Jack’s telling you the absolute truth. At this point, it would be dumb to bring alcohol on campus. Aside from Jack’s one little slip that you saw up close and personal, the only time I recall drinking was in your room last fall when you let us try a sip or two of that Hendricks gin you prefer. And, of course, at the soccer party."

The harsh scowl faded from Father Joe's face, replaced by an embryonic smile. He thought back to Jack's rough encounter with scotch and how he had sworn off alcohol.

"You got me there, Mr. Keane." He looked around. "I'm not sure why you made up this crazy story. And it is crazy." He looked each of them in the eye. "Maybe we can chalk up this whole thing to a bad case of senioritis. Understand this, guys: I'm furious right now, and you both need to promise me two things – no more unsupervised excursions into the tower, and no more using the keys to unlock places you're not supposed to go. Ever! End of story. Are we clear?"

"Yes, Father," Patrick said. Jack only nodded his head in agreement, still stunned and confused by the inexplicable state of Father Martin's room.

"Now get to bed. I've got some things to look into, but this is not over. You two really are something else."

The boys went to their respective rooms, while Father Joe reached his suite and closed the door behind him. After a few minutes, Jack tiptoed down the hall and slipped into Patrick's room, who sat at his desk staring at the wall.

"What the frick was that, Patrick? Are we going insane? You can't tell me we didn't sit in that very room talking with Father Martin."

"Take it easy, Hazy. No one's insane, although we have to admit there's been a strange shift in the plot. Something's at work that we never figured on. Something we can't explain."

"You mean bizarre, mind-boggling stuff like a dead priest walking around here at night, and store rooms turning into furnished suites? Kind of like a scene out of that weird Stephen King book, *The Shining*?"

"No, my gut feeling tells me that it's a good thing," Patrick said. "We just need to trust and let the answer come to us."

"What kind of answer are you expecting after all this time?"

"Look, we know Father Martin wanted to uncover a secret or help someone. Why he chose us is another story."

"Well, one thing's for sure – having a ghost for our new best friend is way too spooky for me. And I'm not going back up into that tower ever again. Never!"

"In a way, we go into it practically every day. After all, our senior lounge is inside the tower."

"I'm talking about the actual tower above the roofline that no one can access without the key." Jack paused. He felt more agitated by the second. "You know what, I don't care anymore. This whole thing is too creepy. I'm done."

"Don't you see? Father Martin was on our side. And he appeared here for a reason. It can't just be by chance or some crazy *Twilight Zone* time warp anomaly. He came to see you and me. And we need to stay the course and find out why. You with me, bud?"

Jack let out a heavy sigh. "This is nuts, even for this place. You get that, right?"

"Oh yeah. Looney fringe nuts. White jacket stuff. And a once-in-a-lifetime challenge too. We still need to keep quiet about it, or I'm guessing we'll find ourselves sharing a padded room at the local funny farm."

"And miss graduation too. As desperate as the Church is for vocations, it won't allow total nutcases to stick around long."

"I agree, but only if you don't count half the faculty."

Jack smiled. "This isn't funny. I don't mind saying I'm freaked out." He moved toward the door to leave. "And by the way, I'd like to know who finked on us. I wouldn't put it past Tron, the big jerk. Well, good luck sleeping tonight."

"See you in the morning, Hazy. We've got more searching to do."

In the days that followed, Patrick twice checked Father Martin's unlocked room. Nothing about its neglected appearance had changed since the night Jack and he entered with Father Joe. For his part, left hanging with no explanation, Jack wanted to feel normal again. Nonetheless, thoughts of the old priest haunted him, and he struggled to fall back into his routine.

"He's gone," Jack finally told Patrick during a walk around campus one evening after dinner. "And it looks like for good. I say we forget about it, play ball, and get ready for graduation."

Patrick refused to let the riddle lay unsettled. Having finished his homework early, he walked into Jack's room later that night carrying an open Bible.

"I'm thinking John 18:38 might provide a clue to our little problem," Patrick said. "Take a look."

Jack took the book from Patrick and read the passage out loud: "Pilate said to him, 'What is truth?' After he had said this, he went back outside to the Jews and told them, 'I find no guilt in him.'" Jack looked up at Patrick. "How does this apply to Father Martin?"

"If Father Martin was innocent of the charges against him, then those who falsely brought them are guilty, right? I think he chose us as his champions to rectify an injustice."

Jack sighed. "I suppose it's possible. I don't know what to believe, or why it even matters now that he passed away. Can't we just let this whole thing go?"

"No. Remember what Father quoted from the Sermon on the Mount – 'Seek, and you shall find.' It's up to us to answer the call."

"I'd rather just ignore it," Jack protested.

"And another thing," Patrick continued undeterred. "What is reality? Was Father Martin part of our reality? Do you believe he was real?"

"He sure seemed real to me."

"In fact, more real than a lot of things you and I take for granted every day, like the existence of far-off galaxies we can't even see. Or a divine Creator."

"Geez," Jack said, throwing up his hands. "What are you suggesting we do now?"

Patrick chuckled. "Don't sound so enthusiastic. I know how you feel, but we can do this."

"Do what?"

"Get to the bottom of it."

"What bottom, Patrick? All I see are questions with no answers. More like a bottomless pit. At a certain point, we're just chasing our tails."

"I have faith it will come. I can feel that the answer is near if we trust enough.

*****

Jared walked to the elegantly carved wooden pulpit at the south end of the great refectory hall. Patrick rarely paid close attention to these brief, pre-dinner Biblical readings. Tonight, the fact that his good friend had adorned a sports coat and tie made him take notice.

He watched Jared climb the three steps, then raise the Bible with both hands above his head for a moment before setting it on the lectern. Jared next took hold of the long red ribbon that marked the passage he'd selected, swung the page open, and broke the dining hall's silence with his powerful voice:

"Tonight's reading is from Hebrews. 'Do not forget to show hospitality to strangers, for by so doing some people have shown hospitality to angels without knowing it.' This is the Word of the Lord."

Jared closed the book and descended the steps. Before he reached his seat, activity buzzed throughout the refectory, as the servers hurried to bring out aluminum platters heaped with thick slices of a meat dish and large, cream-colored ceramic bowls filled with potatoes and vegetables from the kitchen.

Oblivious to the bustle around him, Patrick sat staring at the empty podium, lost in thought. *Could it be that simple?* He churned Jared's words over in his mind. *Was that the key?*

Jack had just finished sliding a juicy piece of what looked like meatloaf onto his plate when he finally noticed Patrick's intense gaze.

"Hey," he said, breaking his friend's trance. "Where did you go right then?"

Patrick, once again aware of his surroundings, relaxed and drew a big breath.

"Just reflecting on the reading. Jared did a nice job, don't you think?"

"What? I dunno. Sounded kind of routine to me. And short, which is never a bad thing when you're hungry. Why? What caught your ear?"

"The part about showing hospitality to angels. Or do you think that's a little too on the nose?"

"Oh," Jack said, understanding the reference. He glanced around the table to make sure none of the other boys was listening. "Well, I didn't see any wings," he joked in a quiet voice. "I suppose it's as good an explanation as any. At least if you're serious."

Patrick shrugged his shoulders and took the platter from Jack.

"As I said before, the answer is waiting for us. For right now, I need to figure out exactly what the heck they're serving tonight. Where are those wonderful nuns when you need them?"

CHAPTER 23

Daily Mass in the high school chapel often offered a welcome sanctuary from classes and the bustle of seminary life. In fact, Patrick had entered the chapel 15 minutes early for three straight days to pray over whether Father Martin's angelic presence had been a warning. The time alone had helped ease his mind. Today's service felt different, wracked with tension. As the Mass proceeded, Patrick grew acutely aware of some strange vibe in the air.

Everyone sat down when the time arrived for the sermon. Father Webb, the principal celebrant, walked over to the side of the altar. Without saying a word, he slipped off the green outer vestment – a chasuble – and placed it neatly on an empty chair, as if he needed extra time to prepare his thoughts. Surprised by this unusual act, the student body watched the priest's every move, waiting for him to get on with it. Father Webb stepped up to the lectern and placed his hands on either side of its wood frame. He glared out over the congregation of students with tense eyes. Once the room fell completely silent, he launched into his sermon.

"Some things I've seen and heard lately make me wonder who we are, and what we are all about here at Saint Paul's," Father Webb said sharply.

The entire congregation, including the three concelebrant priests who had taken seats behind the altar, sat upright in rapt attention. Patrick and Jack glanced at each other in the back row. They knew this was not the usual fare even for Sulpicians who spoke their minds freely.

"As Christians, are we not called to set the example for others to follow? Isn't it supposed to be a better place inside here than out there?" His face flushed red with anger and his tone intensified. "And if we're no better than the rest of the world, why are we here? Ask yourself, 'Is God missing from the way I treat others?'

"I've witnessed student behavior that has no business in our home," he continued. "And this IS your seminary home and family. Each of you has committed to studying for the priesthood and doing your best to follow God's teachings. We all fail at times, but intentionally demeaning classmates, calling them terrible names or cursing has no place at Saint Paul's. None. Let me be clear – there will be no shits, damns, fags, or derogatory language of any kind at this school."

Jack looked over at Patrick and mouthed the word, "Whoa." Patrick frowned, doing his best to grasp every word.

"Not everyone has been blessed with the same gifts, strengths, or families," Father Webb declared. "In God's eyes, we are equal and equally loved. Before you tear someone else down, look in the mirror and see the imperfections and tainted person staring back.

"Let me repeat: if such a shameful lack of understanding and compassion is pervasive at this sacred sanctuary that we call home, our seminary where we're supposed to follow Christ's example and care for one another, what are the chances it's not one hundred times worse out in the world? If we cannot lead by example, how can we expect others to follow? If we are so quick to judge or criticize, how can we expect others to overlook the log in our eye? Let him without sin cast the first stone."

Most of the boys sat in confusion, embarrassed and taken aback by Father Webb's shocking outburst. Some asked themselves, *Is he talking about me? Did I do or say something wrong? What's his problem?"* Others tried to recall if they'd mistreated someone, or at least dished out worse than the usual give and take with their friends.

Father Webb walked over and pulled the chasuble back over his head. "Please stand for the Apostle's Creed," he ordered.

While reciting the lengthy prayer, Jack saw Brian standing rigid with his head bowed, his lips not moving. He wondered if Tron's typical derisive comments had inspired the brief but hard-hitting sermon.

Patrick saw the outburst through a different lens. Father Webb's words brought a passage from Matthew to mind: "He who has ears, let him hear." What Patrick heard made him uneasy. Unlike those around him, including Jack, he felt he might know too well what the priest was saying, and why. Patrick prayed he was wrong.

During lunch, the refectory pulsated with speculation about what had ignited Father Webb, who did not appear at the head table. Jimmy concluded that the entire faculty had approved the sermon as a warning shot at underclassmen caught swearing or breaking some rule, and who were about to get the ax. Others remained skeptical.

"What the heck was Spider talking about?" Jared asked while a group of senior boys sat in the physics classroom following the noon meal, waiting for their teacher, Mr. Jones, to arrive. "Someone really must have messed up bad, or the guy is plain nuts."

"Maybe he's fed up with babysitting some of the ignorant clowns at this place who don't belong here and never did," Brian spoke up.

"Look at the dweebs around here. You've got to concede the school has admitted some real winners in the past couple of years."

"Speak for yourself, Tron," Jimmy said. "What's wrong with you? Our team won the soccer championship, we graduate in two months, and even the vanilla cupcakes were great at lunch today."

"Why are you so angry, Brian?" Patrick asked in a calm voice while holding eye contact.

"Because, well, because, uh, Webb is right. People are quick to judge or criticize others, without understanding the reasons for... well, all I know is he's right."

"You mean like you criticize others?" Jack said in a sarcastic tone. "Not everyone is a dweeb just because you say so. Maybe admission standards should have been higher three years ago."

"Up yours, Hayes," Brian said.

"Now, now, Tron, we must not use bad language. Remember what Spider said."

Mr. Jones walked in, ending the discussion.

For the next 45 minutes, Patrick tuned out the class and agonized in his thoughts. He ruminated on the terrible things he now suspected, and how best to confirm his sad suspicions. The puzzle of Father Martin's visit had become clear. Patrick knew what he had to do, and resolved to take action as soon as the abhorrent circumstances permitted.

*****

When the Angelus bell rang that evening, and a mob of hungry students flocked into the refectory, Patrick was not among them. Instead, he stood outside Father Webb's suite listening for any sounds of movement. Patrick knew entering a priest's room without permission would mean certain expulsion. He was willing to take the risk.

Convinced Father Webb had gone to dinner, Patrick turned the door handle slowly. It was unlocked. He pushed in and called out softly, "Dean Webb?" When no answer came, he moved to the middle of the room, his sharp eyes scanning every nook and cranny. What Patrick hoped to find was evidence.

Seeing nothing unusual, he walked into Father Webb's bedroom. Simply entering the space made him uncomfortable. Patrick suppressed the feeling and looked for any sign that Brian had been there. He opened the nightstand drawer. Tucked inside a book, he found two letters and began to read. As the words sunk in, Patrick reflexively made a fist with his left hand and covered his mouth.

"Oh, no," he thought. *"It's true. This is terrible."*

Patrick folded the letters and placed them in his back pocket. Just as he closed the drawer to leave, Patrick heard the main suite door open, followed by footsteps.

Patrick froze. He listened as the person dialed a phone number and began to speak. It was Father Webb's voice.

"Hello, Jim. It's Lawrence. I'd like to meet with you next week to discuss the Society's plans for Saint Paul's administration next fall."

Patrick composed himself during the call and planned out what to do next. He decided not to hide when Webb came into the bedroom. Instead, he would confront him, and even prepare for a scuffle. Confident of his mission to help Brian, Patrick took a deep breath and steadied himself for the worst. He listened as Father Webb hung up the phone. Patrick waited. His heart pumped furiously. His senses grew extra sharp. Patrick clenched his fists and felt his jaw tighten. Time stood still.

But the priest did not come in. To his great relief, Patrick heard the suite door open and shut. He waited for about a minute to make sure the coast was clear, then swiftly left without being seen. Patrick headed downstairs to the refectory, hoping an appearance – even a late one – would save him from an interrogation by Jack and other classmates, or discipline from a keen-eyed faculty member who'd noticed his absence.

"Care for a walk around the grounds?" Jack asked when Father Delacroix rang the bell ending dinner.

"Not tonight, Hazy," Patrick said. Jack heard an unfamiliar worry in his voice. "Too much going on right now. Thanks for the invite. I'll catch you next time."

Chapter 24

Early May felt like a magical time to Jack. With lingering sunlight easing the warm days into dusk, and the calendar advancing unhindered toward the brink of June – his favorite month of the year – Jack found the soft twilight beauty mesmerizing. He also loved listening to the San Francisco Giants or Oakland A's night games play in the background on his clock-radio while he studied, making it even harder to concentrate.

Despite the welcome distractions, Jack sat at his desk on this quiet evening reviewing class notes for Classical Music Appreciation. An elective course, it turned out he enjoyed learning about the great composers and their works far more than he ever thought possible.

Patrick shattered the serenity without warning when he bolted into Jack's room and closed the door behind him.

"Something's going on, Johnny," he said sternly. "And it's bad."

"Geez, Patrick,' Jack said, startled by the abrupt entry. "What do you mean? What's going on?"

"Something that involves Brian."

"Involves him how?"

"In a horrible situation."

"What are you talking about?" Jack said with growing concern. "Did he get booted?"

"No, nothing like that. Maybe it would be better in this case."

"Patrick, tell me what's up," Jack demanded. "NOW!"

"I've been sneaking out more lately to stargaze and think about Father Martin, especially when I can't sleep. I've seen Brian walking the halls late at night a lot. It became almost like a routine for him. I made sure Brian never saw me because if he said anything, the Warden or another prof might hear us. I'd duck into an empty room or a jake when I heard footsteps, and wait. Once Brian passed by so close, I could smell alcohol on him."

"He's drinking? Are you sure it's Tron?"

"Yes, although that's not the biggest problem. I came to know Brian's pattern and realized he always walked down the same corridor at around the same time."

"So what?"

"Don't you see? Brian came from the far end of the old freshman corridor, then climbed two flights of steps to get back to his room. The second floor's empty except for Bucky up front and Webb's room at the rear, away from everything."

"And?" Jack asked, still confused.

"Don't you get it, Hazy? It's what Father Martin wanted us to uncover. Webb must be sexually abusing Brian."

Jack jumped up from his chair, shocked, trying to comprehend the charge.

"What? You've got be kidding. That's crazy. No way, Patrick. No frickin' way."

"Then tell me, what's Brian doing coming out of Spider's room at two in the morning, smelling like booze? Spiritual counseling?"

"Webb's his confessor. Maybe they're just talking. I mean, you're the one who told me Tron's home life had been pretty messed up. And even Father Joe let us try his gin once."

"Johnny, look at me. That's not what this is. I even snuck into Webb's suite during dinner the other night to look for evidence that would confirm my suspicions. I found it. Read this."

Patrick handed Jack a piece of paper. He unfolded it and read.

"Oh, geez," Jack said.

"We need to do something. Brian needs our help."

Jack paused and shook his head slowly back and forth as if gripped by a tremor. He looked his friend in the eye. "I don't know, Patrick. What if he doesn't want help? What if this is…well, as bad as it seems, mutual? Tron is seventeen. Almost eighteen."

"And that somehow makes it acceptable? Anyone who ignores something this appalling has no business attending a seminary. What if it's been going on for years?"

The blood drained from Jack's face. He found the possibility too ugly to contemplate. Jack dropped back into his chair, placed both elbows on the edge of the desk and sunk his forehead into the palms of his hands.

Patrick touched Jack's left shoulder. "We need to do the right thing, no matter how difficult," he said in a softer tone. "Brian may be a jerk sometimes, but the guy's part of the family."

Jack lifted his head. "The whole thing just seems so unreal. And I swear, if it's true, I'm going to kick the crap out of both of them."

"No, you're not. And we're not turning our backs on a friend. You're better than that."

"Actually, no, in this case, I'm not."

Patrick's face took on a stern look. "Listen, I feel we should talk to Brian first. Like an intervention. And then we'll tell Father Joe once we know more. I don't care that he'll find out about my Grinder excursions. Agreed?"

"Here I was studying music, minding my own business, and you drop this on me. Man, Patrick. It's always some damn thing."

"Sorry, bud. You needed to know."

"Should we tell any of the guys?"

Patrick contemplated the suggestion for only a few seconds. "How about talking to Jared? Think that's a good idea?"

Jack nodded his head. "Yes. I'd like another opinion about what to do."

Patrick and Jack made a beeline down the corridor. Jared sat fully immersed in a Pushkin novel for Russian Literature class when the two entered his room.

"Got a minute?" Patrick asked.

"Sure. I've had enough of Eugene Onegin for tonight." Jared closed the book. "What's up?"

"You're going to think what we have to say is crazy," Patrick said. "We believe Brian's in trouble and needs help."

"What kind of trouble?"

"The worst kind – we think Spider's abusing him," Jack said. "You know, sexually."

"What? Is this a joke?"

"Anything but," Patrick said.

"You're both off the deep end."

"At least hear what Patrick has to say," Jack urged.

Jared leaned forward in his chair. "Okay. Spill it."

Patrick laid out his case while Jared listened, more in shock than disbelief.

"Unreal. That idiot. Looks like he's got an A sewed up in at least one class."

"Not funny, Bones," Patrick said. "This is serious. We've got to do something."

"What if you're wrong, Patrick?" Jared challenged. "Aside from the note, where's the stone-cold proof? They'll kick all three of us out for making wild accusations. We've got a lot to lose here too. I think you need to confront Tron about what's going on before making another move."

Patrick considered Jared's objections, then nodded in agreement. "Yeah, that's got to be our plan. Jack and I will handle things. I'll set it up. Until we find out more, none of us can say a word to anyone. Got it?"

"Got it."

*****

A few minutes before 3:00 the next afternoon, Patrick, Jack, and Brian met in the senior lounge.

"What's so important that you had to see me before baseball practice?" Brian asked, sounding annoyed.

"It's about Webb," Patrick said. He drew a deep breath. "We know what he's doing to you."

Brian threw his hands hard on his hips and took a defiant posture. "You think you know *what?*"

"That he's messing with you, sexually," Patrick said. "I've seen you coming from his room late at night."

Brian's face and neck reddened until they resembled the color of a ripe tomato. "You idiots have no idea what you're talking about."

"We just want to help you, Tron," Jack said. "To stop him."

"There's nothing to stop unless you're talking about your adventures into the tower or midnight trips up the Grinder. You think you're so special and have us all fooled. I've seen what you guys have been doing. And I don't need your pathetic help."

"Then understand we're going to take this to Father Joe and the Warden," Patrick said in a no-nonsense voice. "Webb is hurting you, taking advantage. I found a note in his room. It's beyond despicable."

Brian's entire body grew tense. "Is that what you two geniuses think?" He practically spit the words. "You've got it all figured out, huh, like a couple of real Sherlocks, so damn sure you know better than everyone else. Well, you don't. And now you want to ruin everything."

"Ruin what?" Patrick demanded harshly.

"Tell me, rich boy, when have you ever had to fend for yourself or struggle just to survive? Webb was the first man who ever treated me decently and gave a damn. He cared enough to get me into this school so I could have an education. When did you have absolutely nothing, not even hope? And another thing, clown – it's me, not Webb. Me. I've been in control the whole time, not him. Me! I call the shots."

"The whole time?" Jack questioned, stunned at the admission. "What does that mean? How long has this been going on?"

Brian turned to Jack, his eyes fired with rage.

"And you, Hayes, Mr. Perfect with your immaculate GPA and superficial friend to all," he hissed. "You pretend it's all so easy, like we're living in Oz. Well, you don't know jack, Jack."

Brian took two quick steps and shoved Jack hard through the half-open lounge door and out into the corridor. Taken off guard, and unable to maintain his balance, Jack reeled backward and crashed to the unyielding floor, landing squarely on his right shoulder.

"Stop!" Patrick shouted. He grabbed Brian's arm and spun him around. Patrick's face flushed in anger. "What the hell's wrong with you? We're on your side!"

"Get your hands off me, Keane." Brian lunged at Patrick's waist, and the two boys tumbled to the carpet. Stunned, yet consumed by fury, Jack scrambled to his feet in the corridor. His upper arm hurt but he ignored the pain. All Jack could see, and all that mattered, was Brian and Patrick brawling inside the lounge. He started to charge toward the room.

In an instant, the world changed.

The first jolt froze Jack in his tracks. His body filled with frightened recognition. *Earthquake!* Jack's heart pounded. Adrenaline saturated his cells. *This is big.* The second shock knocked him off his feet. As Jack fell, his head took a glancing blow off the stairway's wooden top rail. The floor beneath him rolled like a wave, and the old building seemed to groan in agony as it rocked and shook. A long crack appeared above the lounge door. Each second passed like an hour while the loud, tortured rumble rose to a crescendo. Jack watched in complete horror, dazed by the head blow and paralyzed by fear. The bell tower was collapsing before his eyes.

Through the open doorway, Jack saw Patrick clinging with one hand to the far windowsill as he tried to pull himself up and regain his footing. Brian kneeled on the carpet, in shock and bleeding, howling like a wounded beast. A bookcase had fallen forward, striking Brian's temple and crumpling him into a pained heap. Jack knew their only escape, their only hope, was to crawl out of the lounge and into the corridor.

"Get out," Jack screamed. "You've gotta get outta there."

His gaze locked with Patrick's. Through his terror, Jack was surprised to see no panic in his best friend's eyes. Instead, Patrick's face took on a look of peaceful surrender, and a familiar, knowing, half-smile crossed his lips as if to say goodbye. The words "His will be done" popped into Jack's head.

In the next moment, the room vanished.

"Patrick! No, please, God, nooooo...."

Standing along the shaking walkway in front of the refectory, Father Joe and three students had watched the top of the tower sway back and forth, first in slow motion, and then more violently. With a sudden final jerk, the 110-foot tall edifice ripped in half and dove toward the courtyard. It hit with a deafening roar, like an exploding bomb. Pieces of wood, stucco, tile, and concrete sprayed in every direction. A large dust cloud rose above the trees, blocking the sunlight.

The tremor subsided. Within seconds, voices began calling out from windows. Dozens of students appeared in the courtyard, staring with disbelief at the tower's destruction. Many covered their noses and mouths with handkerchiefs or shirtsleeves to stop from choking on the thick dust.

"Get out of the building to the front lawn," a voice bellowed. It was the Warden, taking control. "Get to the front NOW!"

Father Joe looked up and, through the opening in the wall where the tower had stood, saw Jack crawling toward the splintered edge, pointing and yelling as loud as possible.

"They're inside the pile!" Jack screamed. "Patrick and Brian were in the lounge. Help them. We've got to help them."

Father Joe sprang into action. He instructed one boy to call 911 for an ambulance, then, ignoring his personal safety, rushed to the sacristy and grabbed a wooden box that contained the tools needed for administration of Last Rites. Returning quickly, the priest sprinted toward the huge heap of rubble, followed by a group of students.

"Patrick!" everyone yelled. "Brian!"

"Look toward the steps, closer to the building," Jack shouted down, with desperation in his voice. "Where the tower split."

Huge sections of the tower walls covered the ground. Several looked precarious. Father Joe warned the boys to step cautiously while they searched. Some began tossing smaller fragments to the side, hoping for any sign of Patrick and Brian.

Inside the building, Jack carefully made his way down to the first floor, surprised by the lack of damage to the marble and wood of the main staircase. Reaching the foyer, he found his path to the courtyard partially blocked where a shattered piece of the tower had collapsed near the large doorway. Undeterred, he opened a window, crawled out and, holding the ledge, dropped several feet to the ground. Jack ran toward where Father Joe and two students were lifting a large piece of concrete.

"Did you find them?" Jack asked breathlessly.

"Yes," said Father Joe, sweat streaming down his face. "We can see a shoe. Are you injured, son?"

"No," Jack said.

"Thank God for that. Can you give us a hand here?"

Strength filled Jack's body. He tossed aside massive chunks like they were weightless. Jack spotted navy slacks and a hand at the end of a white shirtsleeve. With a superhuman surge, he shoved a small slab of concrete away along with the remains of a wooden door, revealing Patrick's entire body.

"It's Patrick," Jack cried out.

Father Joe leaned over to see if he could hear the bloodied and unconscious boy breathing. Patrick's clothes were torn, and dust and sweat crusted his distorted face. His left arm appeared mangled. Seeing no signs of life, Father Joe immediately began to administer Last Rites.

Sirens blaring, a fire truck and an ambulance arrived at St. Paul's front steps. Four paramedics and three firefighters rushed into the building, ran across the foyer, forced their way through the damaged double doors, and zigzagged down the littered steps into the courtyard. Father Joe, Jack, and Jared attended to Patrick. At the same time, a growing crowd of about 20 students and priests worked feverishly to rescue Brian from the rubble.

"Over here," Father Joe directed. "We've got two seriously injured boys."

One first responder checked Patrick's vital signs, and another prepared an oxygen mask. They detected a weak pulse.

"Get him on the gurney," the first instructed. "He needs to get to the hospital fast."

Jack followed close behind as the rescue squad carried Patrick through the building and out the front steps. Jack stopped on the landing, watching in helpless silence while they prepared to load his friend into the waiting ambulance. He searched for any signs of life. Patrick remained still.

Just as Jack felt all hope drain from his weary body, the scene transformed in the blink of an eye. Patrick lifted his right hand, the palm facing sideways, almost like a wave. Jack was about to call out when he saw the true reason. Standing next to the gurney in his black robe, Father Martin had grasped Patrick's hand warmly, cupping it between two brilliant orbs of bluish light. Jack stood stunned, not believing his eyes. The medics continued their frantic work, oblivious to the priest's presence.

"I've come to take you to your mother, Patrick," Father Martin whispered. "That's a good lad. It's time to go home."

Jack heard each word clearly through the chaotic clamor. Father Martin looked over at him and gave a slight nod. The priest appeared decades younger to Jack, his face bathed in radiance, more angelic than human.

"Carry on, Johnny," Father Martin said with a sweet, comforting softness. "Carry on."

To Jack's surprise, a feeling of intense love engulfed him, and his pain and sadness faded. He understood. Patrick had found peace.

As quickly as Father Martin had come forth, he vanished from view. The paramedics finished loading the body, and the ambulance sped down the seminary driveway toward El Camino Hospital. Jack knew Patrick was not inside, but his friend had begun a different journey filled with joy. He sat down on the brick steps and thought of Patrick holding his mother in his arms – the same priceless gift his friend had given Tom Hardin only weeks earlier. Tears flowed down his cheeks. Jack knew he had been allowed to see, to share a joyous moment of light with Patrick at the end, and witness the new beginning. He felt blessed.

Jack closed his eyes to pray. He asked God for strength to face the sad days ahead and thanked Him for taking Patrick home into His Kingdom. When he opened his eyes again, Jack saw Jared standing a few feet away, staring into the distance.

"At least Patrick's at the hospital," Jared said.

"No, he's not," Jack said, rising to his feet. "He's not at the hospital."

Both boys stood dazed, not knowing what to say or do.

Jared finally spoke.

"They found Brian," he muttered without emotion. "Let's go see how we can help."

Before Jack could grab the big brass handle on the front door, Father Joe pushed it open from the other side. He looked exhausted, and his face was the color of snow.

"Father," Jared said. "Any news?"

"The paramedics told me they believe Brian died instantly when the tower fell," the priest said with great sadness. "The hospital called…" His voice wavered and cracked with emotion. "Patrick didn't make it."

"I know, Father," Jack said. "I know."

The three stood without speaking as the paramedics carried Brian's body past them on a stretcher, placed it into the second rescue vehicle, and drove away.

"I need to call the families," Father Joe finally said. "Please help make sure everyone's out of the building."

Boys, priests, and office personnel continued to gather on the front lawn. Some students cried. Others watched in silent dismay, left speechless by the shocking damage. Once the faculty could account for all 156 students, Father King addressed them in a grim voice.

"It's been a tragic day for our entire community. Two sacred lives have been lost. Please bow your heads and pray for our dear brothers, Patrick Keane and Brian Weaver."

Everyone lowered their heads and closed their eyes, some with tears still streaming down their cheeks. Father King prayed aloud, asking for God's mercy and blessing on the souls of the fallen boys.

"...this we pray, in the name of the Father, and of the Son, and of the Holy Spirit. Amen," he concluded.

"Amen," the students said as one, lifting their heads.

"Gentlemen, we don't know the extent of the damage to the building, or if it's safe to go up to your rooms," Father King said. "As many of you witnessed, the earthquake destroyed the top half of the tower. We just don't have enough information at this time to take risks because an aftershock might cause further destruction. Sadly, I must close Saint Paul's immediately and send you home until further notice. Once we have the facility inspected thoroughly, we'll contact each of you. The faculty is calling your families right now to explain the situation and assure them that you're safe. God bless you all. You'll hear from us once we know more."

CHAPTER 25

Jack lived in a tortured daze, drowning in sorrow, for the next ten days. Questions swirled through his mind: Had he seen Father Martin at Patrick's side, or just imagined it? And why had God let this happen to two of his children with so much promise, especially Patrick, the son arguably best suited of any St. Paul's student to become the kind of inspirational priest the Church so badly needed? Nothing made sense.

When Jack picked up the phone on a Friday evening, he heard Father Joe's somber voice at the other end of the line.

"Hello, Jack. How are you?"

"Terrible, Father. These have been the roughest days of my life. My mom and dad have been great. Despite all the hours we've talked, nothing seems real to me. I keep thinking about what Patrick used to say, 'It's always some damn thing,' and 'it never ends.' That's what this nightmare feels like."

"It's been tragic for everyone, son. Brian's family held a small private funeral service today that his mother asked me to attend. It was terribly sad. And even though we'll all gather for Patrick's funeral Mass tomorrow morning in San Francisco, I wanted you to be the first to hear a little good news for a change."

"I could use some," Jack said.

"The engineers conducted a detailed structural evaluation of the building and found the damage mainly limited to the portion of the bell tower that collapsed. It's a miracle the foundation and walls withstood the blow, aside from minor cracks. The haulers finished removing the debris in the courtyard today. We're confident the inspectors will declare Saint Paul's safe to reoccupy once the contractor finishes repairing the wall where the tower tore away.

"Father King sat down with the faculty and decided classes will resume a week from Monday for the final weeks of the school year," Father Joe continued. "Your graduation ceremonies will take place in the college chapel as scheduled on Saturday, June seventeenth."

"That's good," Jack replied without emotion. "I guess life, such as it is, moves forward. Not to change the subject, Father, but I need to talk to you about something."

"Can it wait until you return to school?" the priest inquired.

"Well …," Jack contemplated for a few seconds. "No, I don't think it can. It's that important."

"Okay. Let's sit down after the service," Father Joe said. "We can find a quiet spot in the cathedral's rectory. I'll see you tomorrow morning. God bless you, Jack."

Jack awoke that night from a dream in a cold sweat. He'd been sitting alone at the top of the Grinder when Father Martin appeared.

"Father, what are you doing here?" Jack had asked. "I thought you left us."

"Listen, my son: you don't need to worry."

"About Patrick? Where is he?"

"Patrick is where he should be. God is everywhere. Move toward the Light, where Patrick now lives. Move past the sadness and lift up your heart to the Lord. Be brave and authentic, Jack. Live with purpose."

"How, Father? How do I find the Light? I feel lost."

"Look to what you already know. Your pain will fade in time. You must fight all doubt. Believe the secret in your heart."

"I've been miserable, Father."

"Carry on, son, and make a difference. For all of us."

Father Martin disappeared. Jack was left sitting alone again on the hilltop. Just as he started to call out, he woke up.

That was weird, Jack thought. The dream troubled him. He struggled to fall asleep again for more than an hour until fatigue finally caused him to drift off.

When Jack awoke the next morning, much of the dream had faded from his memory. A single phrase stuck in his head while he dressed for Patrick's funeral Mass: "Look to what you already know."

What did Father mean? Jack wondered. *What do I already know?*

*****

The final notes of organ music resonated throughout the great San Francisco cathedral, ending Mass. A large gathering of mourners, including Patrick's grieving father, made their way to the nearby meeting hall for the reception. Father Joe and Jack spoke with many of the extended family members, as well as St. Paul's students, for about 30 minutes before they slipped away to a small conference room in the parish rectory.

"The ceremony was nice, Father," Jack said as he took a seat. "I just can't believe Patrick is gone."

Father Joe shook his head in remorse. "Such bad timing that he and Brian were in the lounge when the tower fell. If only they could have gotten out."

The final moments of the tower's collapse flashed through Jack's mind. "Yes, if only. You need to know the reason we went to the lounge, Father. That's what I wanted to talk to you about."

"You were in the tower too? Thank God you made it out safely. How did that happen?"

Father Joe sat in complete silence listening to Jack tell the story of Patrick's suspicions and Brian's angry, violent reaction. When Jack finished, the priest rose from his chair and paced the carpeted floor, back and forth, clearly agitated at what he'd heard. Father Joe stopped and stared out a window that overlooked several densely packed blocks of city buildings, seething and shaking his head.

"I should have paid more attention," he said. Jack detected deep regret mixed with fury in his voice. "I should have known."

"How could you? No one really knew anything. If Patrick hadn't seen Brian out late at night so often and made it a point to find out why, no one would have suspected a thing."

"That's not exactly true. I occasionally can't sleep and walk the halls. Once, I saw Brian coming back to his room well past midnight. I meant to say something to him. It just always slipped my mind."

Father Joe sat back down in his chair. "Before he left the seminary, Riley also complained to me that Father Webb had said and done things that made him feel uncomfortable. I spoke with Webb about it in private. He convinced me it was nothing." The priest leaned back and placed both palms on top of his head. "Lord help me, I should have connected the dots. I should have done more."

"Brian made it sound almost like it was his idea," Jack said.

Father Joe's face turned red with anger. "I don't buy it! Webb is the adult and mentor who holds all the power. Brian was his student. Webb broke a sacred trust."

"What are you going to do, Father?"

"What's right, and what I should have done months ago." He paused, and let out a deep, anguished sigh. "I'm sorry, Jack, for everything. I failed you boys."

"Patrick wouldn't see it that way, and neither do I. Please just don't let Webb get away with it. I mean, what if he's targeted other guys?"

"I guarantee this will all stop now." Father Joe jabbed his index finger into the tabletop to emphasize the point. "I have to ask one more thing, Jack: do you have any idea why Patrick pursued this for so long or even suspected what was going on?"

"Partly because of an article he read. You wouldn't believe me if I told you all the reasons. I suppose it's best to say Patrick had an extra sense about things and claimed he sometimes received signals."

"Well, somehow that doesn't surprise me. Patrick was a unique, gifted young man." Father Joe stood up from his chair. "I saw Riley Moody at the reception and would like to speak with him before he leaves. Would you mind?"

"I'll head back with you."

"I promise that I'll personally deal with Father Webb as soon as possible."

"Thank you, Father. I know you will."

"You're a good man, son. Now it's my turn."

Back at the reception hall, Father Joe found Riley sitting at a round table with Ben, Dan, Jared, and two other boys eating platefuls of macaroni salad and sandwiches.

"Hi, Father," Dan said. "Look who's here."

"Yes, I see. In fact, I was just looking for you, Mr. Moody. Do you have a few minutes to spend with one of your old professors? I thought we could go for a walk in the cathedral gardens to get some air."

"Sure, Father," Riley said as he rose from the table. "See you guys in a bit. And don't mess with my plate, Dan!"

Out in the courtyard, Father Joe and Riley meandered among well-manicured rose bushes, Japanese maple trees, and a colorful array of lavender and lantana. They spoke about the funeral and tragic earthquake before Father Joe broached his main topic.

"I hear from your new teachers that you've been doing well at Blessed Heart," Father Joe said.

"Yes, I like it there and living at home again too. I still miss a lot of things about Saint Paul's, especially the guys."

"It's wonderful to hear your new school is a good fit. But I have something important to ask you, son, and it's directly related to your time at the seminary. It's about Father Webb."

Riley flinched a little and looked directly at Father Joe.

"What about him?"

"You once told me that Father Webb had made you uncomfortable. Can you tell me exactly what happened? It's important because we have evidence he may have been inappropriate with Brian Weaver and perhaps other boys at school."

"Whoa!" Riley said. "Others, huh? It's a little tough to talk about, Father. The guy creeped me out."

"Please do your best. It's important that I know if Webb did anything improper to you."

Riley hesitated, He took a deep breath, trying to calm his nerves.

"Well, nothing too serious I guess. A couple of times Father Webb made weird comments, saying what a handsome boy I was. He also invited me into his room for help with a homework problem from his class, and after I sat down, he stood behind me and started to rub my shoulders. Webb also put his arm around me before I left his room and told me I was his favorite. I knew it was over the line; that's why I brought it up. I didn't think much of it at the time, but Brian made a comment that I should be nicer to Webb because I was special and could go far. I just thought he was talking about getting a good grade." Riley stopped and sighed. "So, Webb might have been doing stuff to Brian?"

"That's what I'm trying to determine, and thank you for being candid," Father Joe said. "Was that the full extent of his inappropriate behavior?"

"Yeah, pretty much. Webb tried to put his arm around me another time, but I slipped out of it. That's everything. After what happened, I avoided him as much as possible."

"I'm thankful it ended there. And you were right to stay away from Father and tell me your concerns. I did speak to him about it. He claimed it was a simple misunderstanding. He obviously fooled me. So I owe you an apology for not digging deeper. Please know that what you've told me today will help ensure Father Webb won't harm students ever again."

"What will happen?"

"Father Webb will be held accountable. I'll do my best to see to it. In the meantime, could you please keep our conversation private."

"That's the easy part. It's not something I care to tell any of my friends. To be blunt, Webb is a total jackass who needs his butt kicked."

"I understand how you feel. One final question, son – did Father Webb's actions cause you to leave?"

"To be honest, not entirely," Riley assured. "I had other reasons too, the ones we'd discussed before I made my decision. As much as I miss the seminary some days, I have no regrets."

"Thank you again for speaking with me. It's helped immensely. Now get back inside and spend time with your old friends. They miss you."

Later that day, upon returning to St. Paul's, Father Joe met with Father King to alert him about the allegations against Webb. The two men spent nearly 45 minutes discussing how best to uncover the truth and handle the looming confrontation. Despite his initial objection, the rector agreed to allow Father Joe to face Webb alone, hoping a man-to-man talk might limit any fallout from the scandal.

"I need to speak to you right away, Lawrence," Father Joe said when he called Webb early in the evening.

"I'm busy right now," Father Webb protested.

"I insist that you see me, Father. I'll be down to your room in five minutes."

After he'd arrived and both men took a seat, Father Joe wasted no time.

"I'll get right to the point," he said, trying to control his anger. "We have evidence indicating that you engaged in a highly improper relationship with Brian Weaver. Brian admitted it to both Patrick Keane and Jack Hayes in the senior lounge right before the earthquake hit. In fact, Patrick and Jack had asked Brian to meet them there to help stop what they believed was molestation."

As Father Joe anticipated, the cornered priest reacted badly.

"How dare you, coming here with these accusations!" Father Webb jumped up from his chair. "This is an outrage!"

"Sit down, Father, and listen, unless you want to end up in prison." Father Joe glared with disgust. Webb sat back down. "The welfare of all our students and the school *is* my business, as it should have been yours. I also spoke with Riley Moody. He told me about your unwanted advances, and how you touched him. Unless you admit the truth to me right here, right now, Father King and I are prepared to go to the Archbishop, the Sulpician Vicar in Baltimore, and the police to have them investigate further. I guarantee it won't end well for you."

"You can't do that. The scandal could destroy Saint Paul's. What about the school?"

"If that's what you want to avoid, do the right thing: resign today – and I mean immediately – and accept your punishment. Either way, you're done, Lawrence; your despicable, hypocritical behavior ends here. You broke your Sulpician vows, especially our Order's eleventh commandment not to abuse children, and trampled on our sacred trust to watch over and protect these boys. And make no mistake. I will take this to the Vatican if necessary to find justice for Brian and Patrick. And any other boy you harmed!"

"I meant no harm," Father Webb pleaded. "It was done out of love. I didn't mean for anyone to get hurt or…."

Father Joe raised his hand abruptly, halting Webb in mid-sentence. "I won't listen to your pathetic excuses. You've heard our terms. Make a decision."

Trapped in a tangled web of his making, the Spider saw no way out.

"Can we do this quietly?" His voice had lost its crusty edge. "With the least amount of turmoil as possible?"

"That depends on what you do next, and what Father King decides to do. But there will be pain."

That same evening, Father King accepted Father Webb's resignation "for medical reasons," and referred the issue to Society headquarters in Baltimore. Similar to Father Martin's case more than a decade earlier, Father Webb was sent back East to contemplate his sins and seek forgiveness.

*****

Jack returned to school eight days later and walked into his room on the senior floor at 2:00 in the afternoon. No other classmates had arrived yet. He could see someone had checked the room for damage because his clock-radio, several books, and a pile of athletic gear had been set neatly on the bed. He found nothing broken or damaged. After putting everything back in its proper place, Jack walked down the corridor to Father Joe's suite.

"Hi, Father," he said through the open doorway.

"Mr. Hayes, I'm happy to see you." Father Joe stood up from his desk, walked over and gave Jack a gentle hug. "I understand how difficult it is coming back here today, knowing Patrick and Brian won't be with us. I feel the same way. Unfortunately, nature never seems to play favorites when it comes to tragedies."

"Any news about Webb?"

"The situation has been handled. Father Webb is no longer at Sant Paul's."

Jack nodded his head. "That's good. I just wanted to tell you I'm back. I'll stop by later."

Jack returned to his room and flung himself onto the bed. He felt lost and depressed without Patrick, like a rudderless vessel adrift with no destination. He stared at the ceiling, struggling to subdue his despair, and thought of his friend. Minute by minute, Jack gained strength. He vowed to see the year out through graduation, the way Patrick would have done. *I can do this. I need to do this.*

Jack got up, walked down to Patrick's room and opened the door. It felt strange not seeing his iconoclastic friend there. He envisioned Patrick half-sitting on the edge of the desk smiling, and heard his voice say, "Never feel sorry for yourself, Hazy, or let the bananaheads get you down. And when you do get blue, just think of the kids in Africa, China, and non-Catholic schools."

Jack began to cry. He left quickly and headed back to his room, where he stood for a long time staring out the window.

"I know what I saw, Patrick," he whispered softly, trying to convince himself. "I know what I saw."

CHAPTER 26

Three weeks later on a perfect June day, St. Paul's High School held a somber graduation Mass in the college chapel. No one quite knew whether or not the group of 28 seniors would be the school's last Rhet class, or if the seminary could rise from its ashes and failings in the fall.

As co-valedictorian, Jack had been selected to speak to the gathering of families and friends who filled the pews. The entire day felt surreal to him. Fighting the feeling, Jack vowed to stand firm for his classmates, for himself, for Brian, and most of all for Patrick. He pushed the single page of notes aside near the end of his short talk and gazed over the congregation.

Guide me, Holy Spirit, Jack requested silently and walked in front of the podium.

"Some graduates here today will continue their journey as college seminarians in the fall, while others will move out into the world, taking jobs or attending other schools. We wish them all well. For the brothers we knew and loved, and who God now holds in His special and sweet embrace, this world no longer has claims on their souls. They live free to soar, and in their perfect freedom, show us the heights, the depth, and the power of God's love for all of us."

Jack's voice wavered, choked by emotion. His eyes began to sting. He took a deep breath to compose himself.

"We'll miss them deeply, these sons and brothers, classmates and teammates, beloved children of the Most High, and we pray for the intense pain in our hearts to ease one day. And Patrick, I'll never forget your wit and wisdom, your style and grace on and off the field, your strength and counsel, and showing us the meaning, in its deepest sense possible, of genuine friendship. You were the glue that bound our family together, like pages secured in a book. Without that bond, the book falls apart, and the sheets scatter to the wind. "

Jack returned to the podium.

"The English poet William Wordsworth wrote, 'For him, a Youth to whom was given, So much of earth – so much of Heaven.' That was Patrick, the best friend I'll ever have in this life. Today, in heaven the bells are ringing, because Patrick now lives with Christ, the Good Shepherd, who promises to bring each in his flock home one day to His Kingdom of eternal peace and love. So, we rejoice that what once was lost, now is found. And to that promise, we say Amen."

*****

By evening the next day, most seniors said their goodbyes and headed home to begin summer vacation. Jack had stuck around and now stood in the front parking lot behind the open trunk of the blue coupe his Dad loaned him for the weekend. After loading two suitcases, several boxes of books, and other personal belongings, Jack closed the trunk lid and headed back upstairs. He poked his head in through Father Joe's open door. The priest sat in a stuffed chair, reading.

"I wanted to say goodbye before I take off, Father."

Father Joe immediately put the book down and rose from his chair.

"I'll walk you down."

"Before we go, Father, I need to tell you something: I've decided to leave the seminary."

A pained expression passed over Father Joe's face. He looked down at the carpet, thinking, before raising his head.

"I understand, Jack, although it saddens me. I can't say I'm surprised, after everything that's happened. Have you decided on a college? I'd be happy to write a recommendation for you."

"I've applied to two Catholic schools, St. Mary's College and Santa Clara University, plus Stanford. And, yes, I'd appreciate a recommendation from you very much."

"You might also want to ask if they can offer you an academic or soccer scholarship."

"I contacted the coaches about fall tryouts, and they expressed interest. All three attended the CCS championship game. So maybe I have a shot."

"More than a shot, Jack. You'll do very well at any of those schools."

Jack and Father Joe descended the main staircase side-by-side, walking in silence through the Grand Foyer, down the portico's brick steps, and into the dusk. Several outdoor lamps that rimmed the front lawn lit the parking lot in a muted amber glow. The building appeared gloomier than usual to Jack as the last glimpses of sunlight faded, an impression he knew was unfairly colored by his sullen mood.

"Well, Father, I guess this is it. I can't thank you enough for all you've done for me." He paused. "Patrick would feel the same."

"An old mentor of mine once told me that a teacher must render himself gracefully superfluous in the end. I can't say I've always been graceful. I wish you the best, Jack."

The men shook hands and hugged.

"You did your job, Father, better than you know. In fact, I want to believe more than ever in one thing: resurrection. Life after death. And that we don't need to wait to discover if it's true. It's already part of who we are, right here, right now."

"That's wonderful to hear, son. It's the key to faith."

Jack unlocked the driver's side door. He began to open it but stopped and turned back to face his confessor.

"My parish pastor told me before I arrived here that on average only about four percent of seminarians who start on the road to priesthood reach ordination. Only four out of one hundred." Jack shook his head slowly. "I thought I'd be one of the chosen few who made it."

"You are chosen, Jack. God just has a different plan for you now. I'm certain one day the time you spent at Saint Paul's will play a positive role in your most important life decisions, whatever path you find. God bless you."

Jack smiled, slid into his car seat, and turned the key. With a wistful wave, he headed down the long driveway, maneuvered through a busy neighborhood, and turned north onto Highway 280.

Jack could think only of Patrick as the miles passed. Maybe such an incomprehensible death had been nothing more than bad timing. Or perhaps God had chosen Patrick in a different, mysterious way like Father Joe said. Or was it random Nature, a grotesque geological outburst without reason, yet one that revealed the elusive Father Martin as a beautiful Phoenix and death as nothing more than an illusion. Jack wanted so much to believe, without a doubt, that all he had witnessed was as it seemed. Regardless of whichever force oversaw the brutal events that destroyed so much, he knew he could never see the world in the same way, as if the disaster had lifted a veil and revealed the truth.

"His will be done, not ours," he whispered.

Jack fixed his eyes ahead. Driving into the night, the words of the best friend he'd ever have played over and over in his mind.

"Life is a vale of tears. Understanding that often painful reality makes it vital to seek and find, if you can, the joy, the little miracles, and especially the love for those you hold close every single day Heaven gives you. Nothing comes easy because it's always some damn thing. Do your best to keep the faith, live without regrets, and remember this above all, Hazy – the Lord provides."

CHAPTER 27

Spring 2000

A truckload of broken stucco and concrete roared past, bringing Father Joe and Jack back into the moment. With the demolition of St. Paul's complete, the crane operator turned off his machine's noisy engine, leaving the wrecking ball hanging lifeless from its long steel cable with nothing more to do.

"So, Father..." Jack hesitated, uncertain how the priest would react to his next question. "I need to ask something. Whatever happened to Webb?" He hoped his voice had not betrayed undue harshness.

"Mr. Webb left the Church shortly after your graduation." Father Joe paused while another truck rolled by filled with rubble. "No charges were ever filed. He moved to San Francisco. Last I heard, he died some years later of pneumonia."

Jack quickly did the math. Webb couldn't have been much more than 50 years old at the time. Someone who died at such a young age during the 1980s from a lung infection, especially in the City, often meant one thing.

"Oh," Jack replied. It was all he could muster.

Both men stood motionless, taking in the sounds around them. Father Joe drew in a deep breath and exhaled, like an athlete preparing himself before a momentous event.

The priest reached into his jacket pocket. "I need to show you something, Jack. Something important. It's about Father Martin. What I'm about to tell you may sound strange, but I believe it's the reason we're both here today."

He took out a small white envelope and handed it to Jack.

"I was looking through some boxes that the workmen found in a storeroom when they cleaned out the building to prepare it for destruction. One of the boxes contained hundreds of photos taken at the school decades ago. I've been carrying two around with me for days, praying and considering what to do."

Jack opened the envelope and removed a pair of old color photos. One showed a wide angle view of a priest's suite, centered on a man in his mid-60s sitting at a large oak desk, surrounded by shelves filled with board games, baseball cards displayed in glass, and two overstuffed chairs. The other showed a youthful Patrick and Jack superimposed over the tower mosaic of St. Paul. Jack studied the photos briefly until recognition flooded his entire body.

"This is Father Martin's room that Patrick and I saw," Jack said, his voice alive with excitement. "I can't believe it." He stared again at the second picture. "And, this one, Father…I mean, it makes no sense. Somehow this one shows the mosaic of Saint Paul with Patrick and me in front of it." He felt breathless and could barely get his words out. "I remember the night Father Martin took this photo in the tower."

"I know, I couldn't believe these photos either. That first one was taken in 1965 when Father Martin served as Financial Director. The room looks exactly as you boys described it. The other is dated 1977."

The priest placed his left hand on Jack's shoulder. "I've thought about both these photos for hours and hours, and I believe Father Martin deliberately left them for us to find all these years later. If we were lawyers, Jack, I'd say what we have here is called indisputable evidence."

Tears filled Jack's eyes. His throat tightened, preventing him from speaking. The revelation overwhelmed his spirit. Plagued by tormenting memories of Patrick's terrible death for more than two decades, and never certain if what he'd seen was real, Jack now held in his hands the freedom he'd prayed for, freedom from doubt. Father Joe had brought him a priceless gift, one that confirmed Jack's greatest hope: that the Creator of all things had bestowed upon him the glorious, unimaginable privilege to witness the resurrection of Patrick, made possible through the sacrifice of the Lord and Savior Jesus Christ. Jack knew with certainty his beloved friend had reunited with his mother in Paradise, and that one day he, too, would see him again.

Filled with joy – and relieved of the burden that had weighed so heavy – Jack reached out and embraced Father Joe in a hug of intense gratitude, breaking down in his former mentor's arms.

"In more ways than we can know, this was a blessed place" Father Joe whispered through his emotion as he held Jack close. "The Lord truly does provide."

"Thank you, Father." Jack stepped back and took a long, full, calming breath that filled him with the lightness of blissful peace. "This means everything to me. I've waited so long for this, to know this greatest truth. I can never thank you enough."

Jack looked to the heavens, thrust both fists into the air and let out a resounding cry of pure elation. Two workmen in hard hats lifted their heads and gazed over from where they sat eating lunch on the sideboard of the crane, wondering what had sparked such a commotion.

"He sure sounds happy," one said. "Must have heard some good news."

Father Joe wiped the tears from his eyes.

"All is possible with God, Jack. To quote one of my favorite Psalms, 'This is the day the Lord has made, let us rejoice and be glad.'"

"I couldn't say it any better, Father. Today has made all the difference, more than anyone could ever dream." Jack looked down at his watch. "I'd like to head over to see Patrick before it gets too late. Again, thank you for the gift of a lifetime. It's been an incredible day of days, and I hope we can get together real soon."

"You're welcome, Jack. I can't begin to tell you how wonderful it was to see you." Father Joe words were bathed in warmth. "It's been far too long. Let's promise to do better keeping in touch."

"You once told me that promises are always easier to make than keep; I intend to honor this one," Jack assured with a huge smile. "You can count on it."

Jack gave Father Joe a final hug. He walked to his car, started the engine, and drove down the sloping driveway, much like he'd done 22 years earlier. This time, however, his heart pulsated with happiness, his soul rejoiced in a promise fulfilled, and the brilliance of a fresh world surrounded him, renewed in God's love.

The End

Made in the USA
San Bernardino, CA
28 April 2018